DEADLY
DECEPTION

To John —

Hope you enjoy the new novel. My best wishes —

always,

Darrell

2011

DEADLY DECEPTION

A NOVEL

CARROLL MULTZ

Tate Publishing & Enterprises

Published by Tate Publishing & Enterprises, LLC
127 E. Trade Center Terrace | Mustang, Oklahoma 73064 USA
1.888.361.9473 | www.tatepublishing.com

Tate Publishing is committed to excellence in the publishing industry. The company reflects the philosophy established by the founders, based on Psalm 68:11,
"The Lord gave the word and great was the company of those who published it."

Book design copyright © 2011 by Tate Publishing, LLC. All rights reserved.
Cover design by Amber Gulilat
Interior design by Joel Uber

Published in the United States of America

ISBN: 978-1-61777-767-7
1. Fiction; Suspense
2. Fiction: Legal
11.05.25

Dedication

This book is dedicated to the loving memory of my wife, Rhonda, who fought valiantly in her quest to conquer cancer and who has gone to be with the Lord.

Also by Carroll Multz
Justice Denied

To err is human, to forgive, divine.
—Alexander Pope

Table of Contents

Author's Note

Midway through *Deadly Deception* my wife, Rhonda, was diagnosed with stage IV cancer. This novel was put on hold for the four months of her treatment and for two months following her death. On her last night, she elicited a number of promises. One was for me to continue my college teaching, and another was to finish this novel.

I had barely finished writing *Justice Denied* when Rhonda entreated me to write *Deadly Deception*. Since Rhonda had typed and helped edit the previous manuscript, I was surprised she wanted to take on another project especially so quickly. She knew the plot for this novel had been conceived a number of years before and put on hold to write *Justice Denied*—a plot involving a bank embezzlement frame-up, and with Rhonda being a banker, it was an easy decision for me as to which novel would be written first.

Rhonda was an avid reader and loved mystery novels, particularly those involving intriguing courtroom drama. I shared her passion. After reading one such novel, Rhonda remarked that the glamour and glitz of trial lawyers as depicted in the literature made it appear that the lawyers should be paying for the honor instead of the other way around. I assured her all is not what it appears; all that the public views is the tip of the iceberg glimmering in the sun.

I explained that boxing great Mohamed Ali, for example, did not become a legend when he defeated heavyweight champion Sonny Liston in the ring. He became a legend when he studied, practiced, and became embroiled in the art. The time spent in the ring was the tip of the iceberg. It represented very little of what it took to become the heavyweight champion. I explained that the same was true of the trial lawyer. The trial lawyer's life in court involves little actual time in the courtroom and the rest preparing for that brief moment in the sun.

Wouldn't it be refreshing, fascinating, and informative, Rhonda mentioned to me, in light of my aforesaid revelation, if the main focus of *Deadly Deception* was devoted as much to what goes on behind the scenes of a criminal jury trial as to what actually occurs in the courtroom. I agreed and hence the impetus for my deviation from tradition.

Deadly Deception is an insider's view of how legal factories, law firm sweatshops, and the legal machine itself actually function. The machinations and intricacies of trial strategy and trial secrets will be revealed to show the legal profession as it really is—a profession of competent, devoted, creative, and vigilant advocates committed to the advancement of the ideals of our whole system of justice.

Special thanks to Sherri Davis for taking over where Rhonda left off. But for her patience and technical savvy, *Deadly Deception* would have remained an unfinished novel. Thanks also to Kelly Matthew, Juli Jacobson, Judy Blevins and my daughter, Lisa Knudsen, for their handiwork in preparing the manuscript. And to Rhonda: you continue to be my beacon, my bright light, and my shining star. To be loved by you is a dream come true. I will always love you too!

The editing process in preparing the final product was performed by an editor of which authors only dream. As with the previous novel, I would be a ship adrift without a rudder had it not been for Hannah Tranberg and the extraordinary staff at Tate Publishing. To them I will always be deeply indebted.

Disclaimer

The occurrence of the great nightmare and the aftermath described in this novel as well as its cast of characters is pure fiction. The incident never occurred, and the people never existed. Any resemblance to real people and events is purely coincidental.

The case of *People of the State of Colorado v. Roberta Kay Young* is a real case, and Dr. Lenore E. Walker is a real person. However, any supposed connection to *Deadly Deception* by the aforementioned case or Dr. Walker is *rhetorical hyperbole* and not meant to be taken seriously.

The Day the Earth Stood Still

Friday, September 12, at four p.m., he was supposed to be preparing for a two-week criminal jury trial starting that next Monday. Instead, he was standing over the lifeless figure of a woman in her early forties, an artist whose talents would be lost forever. He hadn't meant to push her back so hard, causing her to hit the jutting moss rock on the two-story double fireplace that was the centerpiece of this minichalet.

If only she hadn't grabbed him by the front of the blue flannel shirt he had borrowed from the house when they went on their walk, tearing the pocket and popping the buttons. He had never seen her in such a rage, screaming the war cry of her Comanche ancestry. She was uncontrollable. When he finally was honest and said he couldn't leave his wife and children, that was the start of the end.

Drew Michael Quinlin grew up in Colorado Springs, Colorado, and graduated from Palmer High School in 1981 at the age of eighteen. He graduated from the University of Colorado in Boulder, Colorado, and Harvard Law School in Cambridge, Massachusetts. He took, passed, and was admitted to the Colorado Bar in 1988. He was a third-generation attorney and had been admitted as a partner in the firm started by his grandfather,

Franklin E. Quinlin, after he left the El Paso County District Attorney's Office in 1992.

As a chief trial deputy under Terrence Rangland, Drew was tabbed as the "golden boy." He prosecuted everything from DUIs to first-degree murder cases and had a win-loss record Warren Spawn would have coveted. His area of specialty listed in *Martindale Hubbell* was criminal defense. His sixteen years of criminal defense resulted in the well-known mantra "When in trouble, hire Drew Quinlin." Now *he* was in trouble, but then "he who represents himself has a fool for a client."

Drew had had a number of high-profile cases both as a prosecutor and as a defense attorney. He was well known throughout the state having been a special prosecutor in a number of other jurisdictions and defended major criminal cases literally the full breadth of Colorado. If word got out that he was having a two-and-a-half-year affair with a local artist that would be bad enough. But to be involved in her death, that would be total disaster.

Missy's face came on the screen of the theatre of his mind, radiant and smiling, pearl-white teeth blinding, warm dark eyes piercing, and long auburn hair flowing. This was the face he had known since his college years at CU. She had been everything he had wanted and more. Loving, tender, and true, she never suspected her husband had been cheating on her. How could he have deceived her for so long without her having a clue?

Molly, age fourteen; Karen, age seventeen; and Kevin, age twenty-four, popped up on the screen. He had always been their hero. Now he would be known as the deceiver, the great impostor, and the traitor. It would be tough on all the children, especially the two youngest. Molly was in the eighth grade; Karen was a high school senior. Drew did an instant replay of his formidable years when he witnessed firsthand the cruelty of fellow classmates when one had accidently shot and killed his father while cleaning his gun after a hunting trip. He did not want to wish that on his children.

Drew watched on television, one after another, the wives of public officials and politicians stand next to their husbands while the latter confessed to acts of indiscretion. He watched the likes of a former first lady who stood courageously and maybe foolishly beside her man, despite his sexual indiscretions. Drew was not going to let Missy share in his public disgrace. He, despite appearances, loved her too much to put her through all that.

Reality was setting in. Unlike a former United States senator, he stayed at the scene and did everything within his power to revive Joy. "Joy" was her nickname. Her given married name was Joyce Carol Dawson. Her husband was an orthopedic surgeon, Dr. Rolland J. Dawson. They had no children. On the day she went to reside in the still of her drawings, Dr. Dawson was home with the flu.

The Dawson summer retreat was an impressive lodge-like structure with all the amenities of home and more situated in the majestic Black Forest. It was built in the late nineties and had logs imported from Montana. It was magnificent in its location with views on all sides. It was surrounded by towering ponderosa pines, groves of aspens with leaves that changed colors with the passing of the seasons from deep greens to reds and oranges and then its patented gold, and the lush alfalfa meadow with its own chameleon-like characteristic that was its backyard.

Black Forest is located on the north end of Colorado Springs less than fifteen minutes from the city. The Dawson Chalet, as Drew learned to describe it, was hidden from the view of the county road as the private drive meandered through the maze of thick pines and aspens. It was the perfect hideaway or getaway. The western exposure allowed a clear view of the rocket-like arches of the chapel (more like cathedral) at the United States Air Force Academy.

———————

Joy had never worried about her husband paying a surprise visit. She spent many an hour sketching and painting the landscapes for which she had gained notoriety. He always called first, which gave Drew a head start. Drew always wondered what Dr. Dawson thought as he went to the summer hideaway and always passed the same white BMW driving in the opposite direction at about the same place. Joy sometimes, before giving Drew the green light, would check at the clinic to make sure her husband was in surgery or otherwise engaged.

Two and a half years back, Drew and several fellow members of the Fine Arts Center Board of Trustees had stopped on their way from a meeting and while passing the most contemporary local artists exhibit spotted a landscape of a mountain lioness in a grove of aspens with her cub. It obviously was captured during the autumn because of the yellows, reds, golds, and oranges. The eyes of the mountain lioness were piercing and caught his attention.

While admiring the painting, he heard a soft, sexy voice ask, "Do you like it?" Turning around, he stared into the penetrating turquoise eyes of a most attractive, slim, athletic-looking woman with a tanned face and broad, bright smile.

"Those eyes intrigue me," Drew said, "both sets."

Upon learning that she was the artist, Drew confessed to always having had an interest in art.

"You should try it," she said. "You might like it."

"I would like to try it," Drew said, knowing he would like it.

Both knew he wasn't talking about art. A few coffees, then a few toddies, and before they knew it, Drew was trying it and both were liking it.

That vivacious, vibrant, engaging specimen of perfect assembly line engineering was now nothing more than a memory and would never be anything more. All the "would ofs," "could ofs," and "should ofs" were not going to bring her back. To report the dark, nasty things would not only tarnish her memory but bring public scorn and ridicule to the living. The less Joy's husband and Drew's wife and family knew, the better.

Drew thought about staging a burglary gone wrong but thought better of it. It was an accident and would be perceived as such. Other than his clandestine sexual affair the past two and a half years, he was not otherwise deceptive. He didn't like to deceive, nor did he like to be deceived. Discretion, however, was the better part of valor, and for now he would just sneak away in the still of the shadows of late afternoon and hope no one would be the wiser.

Illicit Interludes

For Drew and Joy, their affair was somewhat of an aberration. Neither had had an affair; neither had ever cheated on their spouses before. Affairs were foreign to both of them. Theirs was not just some nasty animal lust or the kind of thing of which cheap romance novels were made. Theirs had a spiritual and philosophical flavor all its own.

When Drew awoke at 5:30 a.m., the morning after the great nightmare, he was not sure it had really happened, and at 7:30 a.m., when the morning newspaper was delivered and no story appeared, he was even more unsure. He only knew he was indeed the great impostor who had fooled a lot of people for an awfully long time.

As Missy snuggled beside him in her usual comfortable place, Drew speculated what she would do if the whole charade was exposed. Had he chanced too much for too little? Was it worth risking all the chips on one roll of the dice? He decided it wasn't.

Affairs are the most ideal arrangements in the world, he thought. The two lovers rendezvous for an illicit frivolous interlude, shutting out the world without care or concern from the massive and pervasive problems of humankind. Lost in each other, they are a universe unto their own. The clever nature of their deception

CARROLL MULTZ

spurns their boldness and contributes to the participants' feeling of invincibility. There is the burglar-like rush that all risk-takers experience. There are the odds that stack up that make the next romp maybe the one too many.

Drew had never told Joy he would marry her. Maybe their intimacy was construed as an implied promise on the part of each of them. Maybe under the legal doctrine of estoppel he was estopped or precluded from denying the existence of an enforceable agreement. Was it a unilateral contract, an act in exchange for a promise: her submission to intimacy for his promise to marry? Did she submit in reasonable detrimental reliance? Was he unjustly enriched? All these mental legal musings were playing havoc with his head and were accomplishing nothing.

When Missy awakened next to him, blinked sleep from her eyes, and purred like a kitten, he asked himself the same question he had been asking himself the last two and a half years. How would he feel if Missy was the one having the affair? How would that affect his perception of her, not to mention his trust, love, and respect? He couldn't bear to think about that. That would hurt too much.

If he was to carry off the great escape, what would he do the next time his eyes were impaled into the deep blue turquoise reflections of the soul attached to another fine face and sleek-figured super specimen of femininity? Would the two ships pass in the fog, or would it result in another long wild fling?

He had been selfish and cared only for his own temporal thrill. He had never really thought about what consequences his actions would have on others and what lasting effect his willful and wanton disregard for their feelings would generate. It was not a matter *if* he would be punished but *how much*. If he could fast forward, he would probably wave the white flag of surrender right now and not wait for emotional annihilation.

A Twist of Fate

Drew had slept little since the great nightmare. When he arose early on that brisk September Colorado Springs Sunday, he immediately retrieved the newspaper. There it was emblazed in the headline on the front page: "Local Artist Found Dead." On the way back to the house, his heart racing and emotions wrenched, he began reading about Dr. Dawson's discovery of his wife's body.

According to the news report, "Dr. Rolland J. Dawson, prominent local orthopedic surgeon, was concerned when his wife had not returned home for dinner at 6:40 p.m. on Friday, September 12. She was at their summer home in Black Forest finishing one of her landscapes for which she was famous. At 7:00 p.m., when she had not called and he was unable to reach her by telephone, he drove to their property and discovered her lying face-up on the parlor floor. When he felt for a pulse and heartbeat, there were none. He called 911. No further information is available at this time."

Drew could not dispel the image of that lifeless body and the sorrowful look that had been frozen on her face and those accusing turquoise eyes looking straight through him. That once vivacious and vital human being who had brought him so much joy was gone. "What's in a name?" Shakespeare once wrote. Joy brought him joy, joy that would never be again. Not for him, not for anyone except through her paintings, which were the only tangibles that still survived.

On Monday morning, the front page of the morning newspaper bore the following headline: "Death of Local Artist Under Investigation." Along with a brief story detailing the headline was a photograph of Joy holding a pallet in one hand and a brush in the other posing with one of her blue ribbon landscapes.

Drew was leaving for the office earlier than usual. He was to meet with his client at 8:00 a.m., meet with the district attorney and his chief trial deputy with the judge in chambers at 8:30 a.m., and start selecting a jury at 9:00 a.m. The murder prosecution was scheduled for two weeks.

As by a twist of fate, the case involved a wife who shot her husband and was charged with first-degree murder, a capital offense. Drew would be asserting the battered-wife syndrome defense. Even though it didn't rise to the level of self-defense, Drew would be arguing and attempting to prove it was justifiable homicide. The facts were very similar to a 1982 case in Colorado, *People of the State of Colorado v. Roberta Kay Young*, featured in the April 1984 edition of *Redbook* magazine. It was reputedly the first case in the United States wherein the assertion of the battered-wife syndrome defense resulted in a complete acquittal.

Drew would be calling as his expert witness Lenore E. Walker, the same expert as in the Young case. Dr. Walker had been the executive director of the Domestic Violence Institute, adjunct professor of psychology at the University of Denver, and president of the psychology of women division of the American Psychological Association. She was the author of *Terrifying Love—Why Battered Women Kill and How Society Responds*. The book devoted several chapters to the Young case, and that was how Drew first learned of Dr. Walker.

In the Young case, Drew learned, Roberta, while being strangled by her husband, feigned helplessness and slumped to the floor. Her husband then went back to watching television, and while he was distracted, Roberta crawled into her son's room, grabbed a .22 caliber rifle, and, returning, fired a shot that hit Jay in his open mouth. Jay then dialed 911 and made a garbled plea for help. He collapsed, and the live phone fell beside him. Everything that transpired thereafter was recorded on the 911 tape and, of course, was the main prosecutorial evidence in the homicide prosecution. On the tape was Roberta's voice shouting, "Die, you son a bitch, die!" as well as "If you die, I'll never forgive you." Interspersed throughout were "I love you," which never appeared in the transcript but were clearly audible when the tape was played.

Even though Dr. Walker, an advocate for the battered woman, had been tabbed to testify in behalf of O. J. Simpson in his murder case, at least as it was reported, Drew still felt she was their best chance in his case. If she could win an acquittal in the Young case where the defendant had said, "Die, you son of a bitch, die," she could certainly do the same in his case.

Dr. Walker's book exposed "the widespread abuse of women in intimate relationships and the devastating impact of the cycle of violence and the battered-woman syndrome on women's lives." He could certainly qualify as an expert in the field on his own merits. His involvement in the great nightmare would provide him with all the credentials he would ever need.

On Wednesday, the third day of his trial, he only caught the headline of the morning paper: "Artist's Death Suspicious." At the noon break, he read the account in the copy at his office.

It detailed the police investigation at the scene. The detectives found hair and blood on a moss rock that jutted from the two-story two-sided fireplace in the Dawson summer home.

The detectives had found evidence of a scuffle in the parlor apparently finding a large recliner out of place and a ruffled throw rug. Of particular note was the discovery of three loose buttons on the floor near where the body was discovered traced to a blue flannel shirt with a torn pocket that had been slung on the back of a chair near the rear exit. Apparently, fragments traced to the shirt were found clutched in decedent's hand.

The official report from the El Paso County Sheriff's Office was that the "case was still under investigation" and "the reporting agency was awaiting the report from the county coroner's office."

On Thursday, the fourth day of trial, the newspaper headline read: "Coroner's Report Issued in Death of Artist." The story quoted county coroner/medical examiner, Dr. Francisco Mendoza, as saying the cause of death "was massive hemorrhaging of the brain due to blunt trauma." The report related that it was "highly unlikely that the trauma resulted from an accidental fall and the injury was more consistent with trauma caused by extreme physical force." That translated into first-degree murder if it was done with deliberation or premeditation or criminally negligent homicide if it was caused recklessly. Both were felonies although first-degree murder carried with it the possible penalty of life imprisonment or death.

The case had now been turned over to the district attorney's office along with the investigative and coroner's reports.

On Friday, the fifth day of trial, the newspaper headline read: "Autopsy Ordered by DA in Death of Artist." In a press release issued by the district attorney's office, it was hinted that there might be a suspect and a coroner's inquest called.

Drew's defense of the abuser killer was still in the prosecution phase, and the defense witnesses were scheduled to start testifying late Monday or early Tuesday. The prosecution was presenting a strong case with the most damaging evidence being the numerous opportunities his client had to leave, her never having reported the abuse to the authorities and never having sought medical attention resulting from the so-called incidents.

The weekend came and went, and Drew was facing wars on three major fronts. In addition to the first-degree murder case and the investigation into Joy's death, Drew was fighting a war within himself. He had the missing piece in the death of the artist, and he was withholding it. *If it goes away, no harm, no foul. But what if it doesn't? Then what?*

There was nothing in the morning paper regarding the saga of Joy's death this September Monday. That was good. Drew could concentrate on his defense of a woman charged in the death of her husband and the father of their children, a case that would turn not on self-defense but upon an expansive definition of provocation. It was every bit as newsworthy as the death of the artist investigation and a matter of grave public interest and concern, but in Drew's mind it was insignificant in comparison. He hadn't read even one of the news accounts of the trial.

On Tuesday, Drew was in for the shock of his life. As if there could be a jolt as large as or larger than the great nightmare. The front page headline read: "Pathologist Report: Dead Artist Was Pregnant." The headline was an apt description of what followed. The autopsy revealed the death of a three-month old fetus. No wonder Joy had been acting differently the last several weeks. No wonder she was pressing the divorce/marriage issue. No wonder she was so temperamental. No wonder, no wonder, and no wonder!

Joy had told Drew the reason she and her doctor husband couldn't have babies was because of her. They had always wanted a family. That was the void in their marriage. Now Drew found out the reason, and it wasn't that she was the problem—it was her husband. Drew was more likely than not the daddy-to-be. *If they do a DNA test, they will know the daddy-to-be wasn't the good doctor,* he thought. And he worried that it would only be a matter of days before that was confirmed.

That hefty push that jettisoned Joy into the moss rock of eternity not only took the Joy out of his life but prematurely aborted the life of his unborn child as well. How could God forgive him? He remembered a passage from the Bible: "The heart is deceitful above all things and beyond cure. Who can understand it?" He knew one thing: he couldn't understand anything, especially himself.

In the wife-battering case, now in its seventh day, Drew put the defendant on the stand who testified as if she was in a trance, as though she was a spectator watching a drama unfold with all the inflections, cries, and groans providing the soundtrack. She testified to all the marital miseries of those troubled twelve years marred by cycles of violence and marked by learned helplessness. Her husband had threatened that if she ever left him, he would find her. She couldn't hide forever. There was no escape. She had finally been pushed to the edge of desperation and was determined to cheat her fate. And that she attempted to do the day she shot and killed her husband.

On Wednesday, the eighth day of trial, Drew called the witness he had been waiting for as the finale. He started with a strong witness, and now he was concluding with the defense's strongest witness, the aforementioned Dr. Lenore E. Walker. She explained how women become trapped in abusive relationships, when love turns to terror, learned helplessness, the cycle of violence, and how the battered "cheat their destinies." Dr. Walker concluded by explaining Drew's client's "out-of-body" experience on the stand. Dr. Walker testified: "It's something we call *selective psychogenic amnesia*, which occurs during a *dissociative state*. It's similar to being in a state of mild hypnosis."

Thursday, the ninth day of trial, the jury was read the jury instructions, and the prosecuting attorney and Drew made their final arguments and pleas to the jury. The jury was out less than forty-five minutes, barely enough time to select a foreman, and was back in court announcing their "not guilty" verdict.

One down; two to go, Drew said to himself. His preoccupation had not been on the murder prosecution, but on the great nightmare.

That mild early autumn September morning produced two headlines that were shared on the front page of the newspaper. The first captioned a case about the murder case concluded. The headline read: "Wife Acquitted in Shooting Death of Husband." The second heralded in a new dawn on a murder case newly filed. That headline read: "Husband Charged in Death of Artist Wife."

Just reading the second headline made Drew shudder and feel as though he had just been shot between the eyes at point blank range. His own worst fears had been realized. The only thing worse would have been a headline announcing "Lawyer Paramour Charged in Death of Artist." Then, again, maybe he wasn't so sure.

It was traumatic enough having had an affair with a married woman, but having been responsible for her death and the death of her and, in all likelihood, his unborn child was an unpardonable sin. If he could never forgive himself, how could the Judge of the universe?

Drew had been brought up by ultraconservative parents. With his paternal grandfather having been an appellate judge and his maternal grandfather and great-grandfather both having been Baptist ministers, Drew was more than familiar with the Ten Commandants decrying the coveting of thy neighbor's wife, bearing false witness against thy neighbor, and the killing of a fellow human being. He was also familiar with the mandate that required husbands to love their wives and all that was implicit in that directive. And, needless to say, he was no stranger to the criminal statutes of the state.

It was not until his college years that Drew strayed somewhat from his faith. Away from the influence and prodding of his parents, he became lax in his church attendance. That having been said, he had not abandoned his personal devotion nor had he lost his faith. Becoming a husband and later a father rejuvenated his religious concomitance. And, being in the constant company of one or both of his parents upon graduation from law school and his return to Colorado Springs was of no little influence either.

He was now heading into the parking garage of the building where his office was located. Sleeping in was an unusual occurrence. This morning was different in other respects from what it had been since meeting Joy. Things had become tense between Missy and him the past several years. She had become accusatory, and he had become defensive and distant. All that was now changing, and Drew was perplexed by the quandary of whether it was Joy's absence that spawned the rejuvenated interest in Missy or whether it was really for more noble reasons. He prayed it was the latter.

When Drew arrived at the main entrance of the law offices of Quinlin, Devlin & Cummins, at ten o'clock that morning, he was greeted by his father Stephen R. Quinlin and his father's longtime law partners, Bernard R. Devlin and Edward E. Cummins. Lunch would be catered, and in two hours the office would be closed to celebrate the "big win."

It was strange Drew thought. When he completed his stint at the district attorney's office, neither the partners nor the associates were excited about him coming aboard and "diluting the firm" with criminal cases. The firm had mainly business clients and represented the largest bank in town, the largest hospital, and was on retainer for a number of the larger development and construction companies.

The only times the names of the partners or associates hit the newspapers was when one was elected to a local or state bar association office, selected to chair a bar committee, or head up some community fundraising project. With Drew's reputation and high profile cases, his name appeared with regularity not just in the articles but in the headlines as well.

It was not much more than a year before Drew had become the top producer in the firm. He was the "rainmaker." He also became the highest paid. On days like this, he shook his head when he thought how close he came to being "black balled" in his own father's and grandfather's law firm. "Now they're treating me like the Messiah!" he said to himself, still shaking his head more in disgust than disbelief.

His secretary, Nicole Collins, brought in a telephone message from a Dr. Rolland Dawson. "He wants you to call him back. He has been arrested, and because he's charged with a capital case, he does not fit the bond schedule and must go before the judge to get a bond set. He wants you to represent him. See what happens when you're famous?"

Drew's heart skipped more than a few beats. In fact, it stopped for a few fleeting moments. This truly was a twist of fate. He couldn't think. The computer, the calculator, the mind machine—nothing was working. His vision seemed to tilt. When Nicole asked him if he was "okay," it didn't register; he just soared into nothingness. When Nicole kiddingly waved her open hands in front of his eyes, he mumbled something incoherent and shuffled into his office somewhat in a trance.

Back in his office with the door closed and looking heavenward, he said aloud, knowing *she* was listening, "No matter where I am or no matter what I'm doing, I can never be free because every time I close my eyes, it's you I see. It's you I see."

Representing the Innocent

It was after the office victory luncheon that Drew went to the jail to visit Dr. Rolland Dawson. He agonized over whether he could or should represent Dr. Dawson. How could he face the good doctor knowing that he had been romping in the sack with the doctor's wife and was, in all likelihood, responsible for the pregnancy? He was the cause of the doctor's wife's death, and if it had not been for him, the good doctor wouldn't be minus a wife and in jail facing the trial of his life.

The ethical implications were almost as perplexing. Drew clearly had a conflict of interest. Drew would benefit if Dr. Dawson were convicted because then the case would be closed and the authorities wouldn't be searching for alternate suspects. Drew knew that an attorney was required to make full disclosure of all conflicts and potential conflicts prior to any representation. For obvious reasons, Drew could not do this. There was a litany of other ethical considerations that would militate against Drew's representing Dr. Dawson.

Since Dr. Dawson would not be in jail if it had not been for Drew, Drew would never forgive himself if he did not at least get this innocent man released on bond.

Drew didn't feel as uncomfortable as he thought he would when he was allowed into the prisoner's cell. Not uncomfortable being locked up with the prisoner but being uncomfortable about being the great deceiver. The two men shook hands, one not realizing that they shared something in common—the intimacy with the now deceased artist. The once proud doctor was in emotional shambles. Within two weeks, his world had been turned upside down.

Drew explained the bail process and the Colorado rule of no bail in a capital case where "the proof is evident and the presumption great." He said he thought that because of the circumstances, as he read about them in the newspaper, it was likely the doctor would be allowed to post bail. Because the doctor had surgeries scheduled the coming week, Dr. Dawson said he wanted the most expeditious method, not necessarily the least expensive.

Drew used his cell phone and called the district attorney, Norman Dayton, the man whom he had just opposed in the battered-wife syndrome case. Surprisingly, not only did Dayton agree to a bond but, after a little haggling, agreed to recommend bond in the amount of $100,000. Dayton said he would arrange to find an available county judge to set the bond and would call the jailer and have Dr. Dawson brought into court ASAP, since it was late Friday and no judge would be available during the weekend. Drew was to meet him at the district attorney's office.

Dr. Dawson was taken before County Judge Bernard Rigsby. Drew entered a special appearance, i.e., for the bond hearing only. Dayton requested a $100,000 cash, property or surety bond. The request was not opposed by Drew. The court entered an order to that effect and set the bond return date for Friday, October 3 at 9:30 a.m. before the same county judge. That would be the date set for the formal filing of charges and Dr. Dawson's first appearance date.

After Drew had spoken with Dayton, he had called S&B Bail Bonds. Ron Simmons, the bail bondsman, was already at the courthouse and, after meeting with Dr. Dawson, processed the necessary paperwork, which would cost Dr. Dawson $10,000, representing 10 percent of the $100,000 bond that was posted. Dr. Dawson would also have to provide some security to S&B Bail Bonds because of the risk the bondsman had on the $100,000 bond. At least for now, Dr. Dawson was a free man. He wouldn't have to spend the weekend in jail. He could perform his surgeries scheduled for the following week—assuming, of course, his patients hadn't been frightened off. Everything would be back to normal—for everyone that is except for Drew and Dr. Dawson. That bond was later replaced by a cash bond posted by Dr. Dawson's father. All but $1,000 of the bond premium would be returned to Dr. Dawson.

Drew advised Dr. Dawson that he had things stacked in "heaps" at the office because of the two-week trial and extensive trial preparation. He wasn't sure if he could take on the doctor's case. Dr. Dawson pleaded with him to take on his representation, that it didn't matter what the cost. Dr. Dawson's personal and professional life was at stake and both knew it. Drew agreed to sleep on it, and Dr. Dawson was to meet Drew at Drew's office on the following Monday at 8:30 a.m.

The headline of the evening edition read: "Doctor Free on Bond in Death of Wife."

That weekend, Drew whisked Missy and two of their three children, Karen and Molly, to Denver, where they stayed at a hotel with a large swimming pool, workout room, sauna, and restaurant options. Missy sampled the shops while Drew splurged on a massage. They found a theater close by, and there they watched the latest Harry Potter movie, which Karen and Molly had wanted to see; ate popcorn and candy bars; and drank Cokes. Drew watched the screen, but no matter what his eyes captured, his mind captured something else. He could not get *her* out of his mind and could not accept the reality of the great nightmare.

When they returned to Colorado Springs on Sunday, Drew stopped by the office and sorted through the pile of mail and lawyer work that Nicole had organized for him. He was fortunate to have such a competent and devoted legal secretary he thought. He still had not made up his mind whether he would represent Dr. Dawson. He had one more night to sleep on it.

Sunday night, the children all snuggled in bed, Drew and Missy retired to the quiet of their master bedroom suite. There Drew had his home desk; Missy had her computer. Reclining on an old leather couch with feet propped on an oversized coffee table facing a fireplace heralding the early signs of autumn, Drew and Missy settled in for their nightly book reading session and some chatter.

It was Missy who brought up the death of the artist. Drew told her about Dr. Dawson calling to engage his services. Missy asked if the doctor was innocent, and without thinking, he said yes.

"How do you know the doctor or any of your clients are telling you the truth?"

Drew responded, "You never know who is telling the truth. I just know this one is."

Whether he would take the case was another thing. Right now he was much too busy.

That night, Drew woke up in a sweat. Joy had appeared in a dream holding a baby in her arms. Smiling and even more radiant than ever, she assured him she was doing fine. She pleaded with him to represent her husband, who she said was "as innocent as the wind-driven snow." She said Drew was the only one on earth who knew that and who could help and said even if he didn't do it for her husband's sake, "Do it for me."

Lately, no matter what path Drew took or what direction he went, all roads seemed to lead to Joy. No matter where he looked, it was her he saw. And even when he closed his eyes, it was Joy he saw.

The next morning, bright and early, Drew was at work. He had Nicole draft a fee agreement and release authorization forms to obtain information. They would be provided to Bobby Dean, "Bodean" (pronounced Bow-Dean) as he was called, a semi-retired but highly experienced private investigator, who had moved some years before from Steamboat Springs. "From one Springs to another," Bodean liked to boast. Bodean would need the forms to obtain information and documents relative to Dr. Dawson's case.

Promptly at 8:00 a.m., Dr. Dawson filled out the client intake form and was ushered into Drew's office. He signed the fee agreement and a form acknowledging receipt of a document entitled "client advisement form." Nicole then came in while Dr. Dawson signed the duplicate authorization forms, notarized them and made copies. When Bodean came in, the originals would be given to him. Nicole agreed not to deposit the $50,000 retainer check until Dr. Dawson had time to transfer funds from savings.

At Nicole's urging, Dr. Dawson made himself comfortable in one of the two red leather upholstered arm chairs facing Drew's ornate mahogany desk. It was then that Dr. Dawson noticed the canvas landscape of autumn aspen with a lioness and her cub that hung on one of the sidewalls of Drew's office. Inspecting the painting, Dr. Dawson recognized it as one of Joy's.

It was at that moment the door opened and Drew entered.

"You must be Mr. Quinlin," Dr. Dawson said. "I recognize you from your photograph in the newspaper."

"And you must be Dr. Dawson," Drew said, extending his right hand. "I recognize you from your photograph in the same edition." The two men then shook hands for the second time.

"My photograph doesn't do me justice considering it depicts me handcuffed and surrounded by deputy sheriffs. By the way, you can just call me Rolland. Whenever people call me 'Dr. Dawson,' I think they are talking about my father, who was a physician for many years in the Boston area."

"The photograph to which you have reference doesn't do you justice in many ways but mainly because of its negative implications. And I urge you to just call me 'Drew.'"

From that point henceforth the two were on a first-name basis. Mr. Quinlin was thereafter referred to as Drew and Dr. Dawson as Rolland.

As Drew reviewed the client intake form, Rolland's stare at Joy's painting was noticed. *Why didn't I think to remove that?* Drew thought. *How stupid of me!* Both exchanged quizzical looks.

Before Rolland could speak, Drew said, "I thought you might recognize that. I bought that several years ago from an art gallery. It is my favorite painting."

With a frown, Rolland shook his head and with his eyes still focused on the painting said: "That was one painting Joy vowed she would never sell. That's strange that I didn't realize it was missing from her collection."

"Quite a coincidence," Drew said, not knowing what else to say. He was still upset with himself for not having removed the painting prior to Rolland's visit. He knew there was room for few slip-ups.

In a case such as this, it was important for an attorney to know everything he could about his client. Rolland started by describing his background.

Rolland said he was born and raised in Boston; went to college at Ohio State University and Medical School at the Ohio State University College of Medicine in Columbus, Ohio; did his residency at Truman Medical Center, Orthopedic Surgery in Kansas City, Missouri, and Avera McKennan Hospital in Sioux Falls, North Dakota. He was certified in his medical specialty by the American Board of Medical Specialties (ABMS). His age on the intake form was listed as forty-nine. He had marked in the blank next to marital status "separated."

Before Drew could even ask Rolland any questions about the case, Rolland asked, "Well, aren't you going to ask if I did it?"

Drew answered, "No. I know you didn't do it, or you wouldn't be here asking me to defend you."

"How do you know?" Rolland asked and then said, "With your reputation being what it is and with Houdini being dead, it would be more probable than not that I was guilty."

Drew, thinking the better of it for obvious reasons, stated, "Okay, why don't you tell me whether you did it or not? Just for the record."

"No, of course I didn't. Joy and I were married almost twenty-five years, and up to about two and a half years ago had a 'fairy tale' marriage."

Drew sat as still as a pillar of granite. He didn't breathe until Rolland asked him if he was okay. And then Drew took quick short gasps and used the excuse he had not slept well the night before and was a little woozy from not having had breakfast.

About that moment Drew was buzzed on the intercom. *Saved by the bell*, Drew said to himself. "Send him back," he told Nicole. In walked Bodean, boots clicking and a stride that belied his advancing years but with a discernable limp that was a souvenir of his rodeo days. Bodean and Rolland shook hands, exchanged small talk, and Bodean was welcomed aboard.

"Before we start," Rolland said to Drew, "what made you decide to take on my case with your schedule being what it is and all?"

"A voice from above said I should do it. That's all I can tell you. When I receive a message like that, I have to follow it. I just hope we receive help from that someone above as well!"

"We will need it, I'm sure."

Bodean, addressing Rolland, said, "I seem to remember a case you were involved in a year or two ago. Wasn't that your clinic that was sued by a nurse for sexual harassment?"

"Yes," Rolland replied. "Both the clinic and myself were sued. After a three-day trial, the jury ruled in our favor. It was a contrived case. On appeal to the Colorado Court of Appeals, it was affirmed. The case didn't seem to hurt our business any, but looking back, that was the start of the decline in my marriage."

Drew asked Rolland when that occurred, and Rolland answered in May of 2006. Drew recalled that it was on St. Patrick's Day, March 17, 2006, when Drew first looked in greenish-blue eyes that matched the artist's greenish-blue sweater and found what he thought was his lucky four-leaf clover.

After leaving the district attorney's office, Drew was often asked if it was difficult to defend the guilty. His pat answer would be that guilt was in the eyes of the beholder. In the Young case and his latest case, where battered wives shot and killed their husbands in broad daylight, were they *guilty*? They were *guilty* of having shot their husbands, but they were *not guilty* of criminal homicide. "I'm still on the same side as I was as a prosecuting attorney," Drew would say, "the side of justice."

The major difference in the Dawson case from the others was that Drew didn't just *think* the defendant was guilty or not guilty; he *knew* the defendant was *innocent*. Obtaining an acquittal for a guilty client was not as compelling as obtaining an acquittal for an innocent one. There was a lot at stake in his newest defense, and not all of the stakeholders were of this planet. If he lost, the repercussions would be felt all the way to the big court in the sky.

The Sexual Harassment Suit

After Rolland left the office, Drew pulled the Colorado appellate case of *Carla Z. Delajure v. Rolland J. Dawson et ux.* The Court of Appeals affirmed the decision of the trial court, which had held in Rolland's favor.

The plaintiff, Carla Delajure, had claimed that she worked for the defendant clinic as a nurse for one year; that she was assigned to assist codefendant, Dr. Rolland J. Dawson shortly after her being hired; that shortly before she resigned, Dr. Dawson began to engage in sexually offensive conduct by making suggestive and sexist remarks, indecent proposals, and showing her a picture of his bikini-clad wife, which he kept on his desk; that he created a hostile environment; that she found it offensive; that he persisted even though she protested; that she had tripped and fallen while exiting the clinic and fractured her ankle; that while she was in the hospital he came and visited and made unwelcomed advances; and she never came back to work because "the workplace was permeated with discriminatory intimidation that was sufficiently severe and pervasive as to alter the conditions of her employment and created an abusive working environment."

Rolland had filed an answer admitting to some allegations and denying others. He then went on to state by way of an affirmative defense that he had had an affair with Carla several months prior to her being hired; that their relationship was the reason she was hired; that they continued their intimate relationship to and including the period of her hospitalization for the ankle injury; and that she protested his so-called "unwelcomed advances" only after her husband walked in the hospital room interrupting his theretofore "welcomed advances."

What a strange case, Drew thought. Not only did the alleged perpetrator admit to innocuous behavior but to sexually explicit conduct. It was obvious he was asserting "consent" as an affirmative defense. But to admit to a *mortal* sin when he was only being accused of a *venial* sin was incomprehensible. Not too many married men would want to make a mountain out of a molehill when it came to sexual indiscretion.

Apparently, the plaintiff's attorney felt that Carla had a right to change her mind even if she was having an affair—"which she wasn't"—and that the judge erred in not instructing the jury to that effect. When the point was argued at the trial level, the judge ruled that she couldn't very well change her mind if there had been no affair according to her own testimony. The appellate court agreed, and even though other error was alleged, none was found.

When Drew called the attorney who had represented Rolland in the so-called sexual harassment case to find out more about the case and his new client, the strange case got even stranger. Rolland's previous attorney told Drew that he had speculated that it wasn't Carla but her husband, Pierre Delajure, who pushed the suit.

He speculated that Pierre was convinced that Carla *was* having an affair with Rolland. When she denied the affair, Pierre figured that by her "taking the oath" and denying the affair, in open court, he would be satisfied she was telling the truth. The only way to have her take the oath was to go to trial. And, even though the insurance company wanted to settle, even bidding against itself, Carla, the pawn of Pierre, stood firm.

Rolland would make a good witness, Drew was told. He convinced the jury that he was having an affair with Carla before and during her time of employment and that she was in *pari delicto* or complicity with him, and therefore, he was not a sexual harasser and in fact it could have been construed the other way around.

"Sounds to me like he won the battle but lost the war," Drew murmured, thinking of Joy.

Start of the Journey

Friday, October 3, was not the typical autumn day that the natives had come to expect. It was overcast and cold. Moisture was waiting for the starting gun to fire before its inevitable release from the heavens.

Drew had been diverted by an emergency juvenile hearing in another court. It seemed as though one of the firm's business client's teenage son had spiked the punch bowl the night before at a birthday party with some kind of drug that resulted in the hospitalization of the birthday girl. The detention hearing was scheduled at the same time as Rolland's bond return and presumably formal filing of charges.

Linnard O. Blankenship, nicknamed "Lino," one of Drew's partners, was scheduled to appear with Rolland in Drew's absence. At 9:30 a.m. sharp, the Honorable Bernard Rigsby, county judge in and for the County of El Paso, State of Colorado, called the case of *People of the State of Colorado v. Rolland J. Dawson*. Both Norman Dayton, the district attorney, as well as his chief deputy, Edward Terrell, were present.

Dayton filed the felony criminal complaint charging Rolland with murder in the first degree, a class-one felony, carrying a possible penalty of life imprisonment or death. Rolland was charged with deliberately causing the death of his wife. He was not charged in the death of the fetus. The reason given by Dayton was that the killing of a "person" did not cover a fetus. "Person" was defined by Colorado statute as "a human being who *had been born and was alive* at the time of the homicidal act."

Lino, who had been a fellow prosecutor with Drew and was now a partner in the law firm of Quinlin, Devlin & Cummins, acknowledged receipt of a copy of the complaint accompanied by an endorsed list of witnesses. Rolland was advised of his constitutional rights (i.e., the right not make a statement, any statement he made could be used against him, the right to be represented by an attorney, if he couldn't afford one an attorney would be appointed for him, the right to a jury of his peers, the right to a speedy and public trial, and the right to request a preliminary hearing).

Judge Rigsby then asked if Lino would be filing a written motion for a preliminary hearing, and Lino answered in the affirmative. Lino advised that the firm would be filing the motion that afternoon even though they had ten days to do so. The preliminary hearing was scheduled for Monday, October 27 at 8:00 a.m. Rolland's bond would be continued to that date.

That afternoon, the original written demand for a preliminary hearing was filed along with a request for partial discovery. Copies were delivered to the district attorney's office. While that was being done, Rolland was interviewed by Bodean. The defense was preparing for the marathon.

The headline in the evening edition of the *Colorado Springs Star* read: "Doctor Charged with Capital Murder." The morning edition of the *Colorado Springs Times Herald* the next day read: "Doctor Could Receive Death Penalty in Death of Wife."

Actually, El Paso County was one of two counties that comprised the Fourth Judicial District. Colorado Springs, of course, was the county seat. The other county was Teller County, and its county seat was Cripple Creek.

Rolland had quizzed Lino about why the felony criminal complaint had been filed in County Court and would Rigsby be the trial judge. Lino explained that only district courts had exclusive jurisdiction over felonies and that as a result of local rules and the crowded district court dockets the county courts had concurrent jurisdiction over felonies up to and including preliminary hearings. In other words, he explained, if Judge Rigsby finds probable cause or reasonable grounds to believe that a crime was committed and that Rolland committed it, the case would be bound over or transferred to district court and a district judge, usually on some sort of rotation basis, would be assigned to the case. Technically, the charging document in county court was called a *complaint*, and the charging document in district court was called an *information*. When Rolland asked what an *indictment* was, he was told that that was the charging document issued by a grand jury and that because a grand jury determined probable cause no preliminary hearing was held on an *indictment*.

Rolland was advised that Drew wanted to schedule an appointment for sometime in the upcoming week and Rolland agreed to call Nicole and schedule an appointment.

Wednesday, October 8 was the earliest Rolland could meet with Drew. It was a typical Colorado Springs day though a hint of cool autumn at 8:00 a.m. Drew and Bodean were awaiting Rolland's arrival in one of the firm's conference rooms. Drew was in the process of reviewing Bodean's interview of Rolland. It was much as anticipated; no surprises. Nicole ushered Rolland into the conference room just as Drew concluded the read.

"Come in, Rolland," Drew said, standing and extending his right hand.

"We've got to quit meeting like this," Rolland chided. Spotting Bodean, he said, "Where did you learn your interrogation techniques? I have never been quizzed like that."

"In my other life I was a cop. Besides, you handled yourself pretty well."

The three then analyzed Bodean's interview of Rolland. His summary read:

> On Thursday, September 11, Rolland left work early because he had flulike symptoms and Joy insisted that he rest. That was about 4:00 p.m. He slept until 8:15 p.m. or so, and Joy fed him some chicken noodle soup, saltine crackers, and hot tea. He felt somewhat better the next morning and kept his morning appointments and rounds at the hospital. By noon, his symptoms returned, and he cancelled his afternoon appointments, leaving the clinic at approximately 12:45 p.m. and arriving home at approximately 1:15 p.m. When Joy had called midmorning, he assured her he was on the mend and to go ahead to Black Forest and finish her landscape.
>
> When he called her on her cell phone at approximately 2:30 p.m., he discouraged her from returning early and told her he would call if he needed her. Otherwise, she would be home at her usual time 6:30 p.m. When she didn't arrive at 6:40 p.m., he tried to reach her cell phone. Unable to do so, he assumed she had stopped for grocery items at the Rustic Hills Shopping Center and had left her cell phone in the car.

At 7:00 p.m., when he couldn't reach her and she hadn't called, he became concerned. He drove out to their summer place, arriving at approximately 7:15 p.m. The easel with the partially painted canvas stood on the front deck where she usually painted. On a glass-top table close by was a pallet with various oils in their wells, several brushes, and a white rag. He called for her and, receiving no answer, went inside. There in front of the moss rock fireplace, she lay face-up with her head on the low hearth. She must have gained consciousness at some point because there was blood in two spots, one where her head lay and the other several feet away. There was no pulse or heartbeat, and it was apparent she had breathed her last.

It was approximately 7:30 p.m. when he called 911 and reported Joy's death. By 8:00 p.m., two El Paso County Sheriff's Deputies, Roger Milligan and Kevin Stanton, arrived. Within the hour, a lab technician arrived and was in the midst of processing the scene when the county coroner/medical examiner arrived. The county coroner/medical examiner confirmed their fears and called an ambulance to transport Joy's body to the morgue.

Rolland watched as photographs were being taken and items collected from the Dawson's summer place. Draped over a chair in the kitchen was a blue flannel shirt. The deputies asked if he knew who the shirt belonged to, and he said it looked like one of his. He pointed out, however, that the last time he saw it, it was hanging in a hall closet and wasn't in a damaged condition. He told them he hadn't worn it in years and that it was kept for guests.

One of the deputies made a telephone call he presumed to be to the deputy's commanding officer in his presence and, after hanging up, announced that they would need to seal off the premises until their lab people had time to process the scene. It was shortly thereafter that Henry Fisk had arrived.

Rolland said they never became accusatory. After the discussion about the shirt, they only asked him if he knew anyone who might want to hurt his wife. They never asked if he was involved. Initially, they had asked him if he was there when his wife was injured, and, of course, he told them no. He was never interrogated even after his arrest. Part of the reason was that after he was taken to the scene by the deputies, he received a telephone call from his sister, Margaret, and when he told her about Joy's death and being at the summer place with deputy sheriffs, she had him speak to her husband, his brother-in-law, Troy Campbell, who was an attorney in Brighton. Troy told him not to make any other statements, even though he was innocent, until after he talked to an attorney "because they can take innocuous statements out of context and twist them." He said he'd followed Troy's advice and advised the deputies he would answer no further questions.

Rolland then went on to relate that after his arrest, he second-guessed himself for following Troy's advice because he thought his refusal to answer questions might have been construed as an indication of some sort of guilt and the reason for the arrest.

"Joy's accident all of a sudden evolved into a murder, and I was the only suspect," Rolland said.

Bodean told Rolland he could be right. "Unless there is a clear-cut case of foul play by an outside source, law enforcement always zeros in on a family member. Take the Ramsey case in Boulder for example."

The issue of a polygraph came up in the discussion. Rolland said he had no problem taking one. Drew said at some point the prosecution would be asking him if his client was willing to take one. It always came up during negotiations.

"Is Conrad Jenkins still administering polygraphs?" Drew asked Bodean.

"The last I spoke to him, he was on the verge of retirement but had not yet retired. Even if he has he would still accommodate us. Besides, he owes me!"

"We won't ask you 'for what,'" Lino jibbed.

"I wouldn't tell you anyway," Bodean responded. Turning to Rolland, Bodean said, "Conrad is a well-known and respected polygrapher. He was formerly employed by the Colorado Bureau of Investigation, but went on his own and made a mint doing pre-employment polygraphs for various private businesses."

"Too bad we didn't know him before we hired Carla Delajure," Rolland said mournfully.

"Might have made a difference," Drew said wistfully.

"Should I go ahead and schedule a polygraph with Conrad?" Bodean asked Drew.

"If Rolland has no objection," Drew responded and, turning to Rolland, stated, "You realize you will have to travel to Denver to do so?"

"I assume one of you will accompany me and prepare me for the polygraph. I assume they are accurate."

"Absolutely," Drew said reassuringly. "You will be well prepared before the time comes."

"All you have to do is tell the truth, and you will have no trouble," Bodean said. "And we all know you will pass."

In his heart, Drew knew Rolland would pass. Only Drew and Rolland knew for certain.

The discovery from the prosecution, consisting of the investigative reports of the various law enforcement agencies, autopsy and pathologist's reports, photographs of the scene, witnesses' statements, test results, and so forth, would not be ready until Friday according to the DA's office. As soon as they were received, Drew, Bodean and/or Lino would want to review them with Rolland. They scheduled an appointment to do just that for Friday, October 10 at 2:30 p.m.

When the discovery was picked up by Bodean Friday morning, he reviewed it before delivering it to Drew. There were two major surprises. The first was the inclusion of a copy of a restraining order issued by District Judge William Forrester on May 22, 2006, prohibiting Rolland from harassing, annoying, or otherwise contacting Joy or entering the family residence "until further order of the court."

The second surprise was statements from Carla and Pierre Delajure. Carla had said that when Rolland was "hitting" on her, he said he "had a foolproof way" of getting rid of his wife. That would have been in April of 2006. Pierre said he had been listening in on his wife's telephone conversations suspecting that she was having an affair with Dr. Dawson and overheard the same conversation. Pierre said the reason he and his wife were coming forward with this information at this time was because they had read in the newspapers that Dr. Dawson's wife had died under suspicious circumstances and that back in 2006 Dr. Dawson had said his wife's death "would be perceived by the authorities as an *accident*." Bodean noted that the Delajure report was dated Wednesday, September 17, the date the investigation took the criminal turn.

When they met at 2:30 p.m. that afternoon, Drew and Bodean had a lot of questions for Rolland. Bodean especially seemed upset by the discovery. When Rolland walked into the conference room, he could feel the chill, and it wasn't from the north.

Rolland said he had forgotten about the restraining order. He and Joy had separated for about two weeks following his service of the summons in the Delajure sexual harassment suit. Joy, understandably, was very upset and threatened a divorce but never filed. Joy had not been receptive to an explanation and showed an explosive side of her that he had never witnessed in all their years of marriage. All he wanted was for her to at least listen. He admitted to being persistent and maybe too persistent. His mistake was not giving her the "space" she needed. He and Joy ultimately reconciled, and the court dismissed the restraining order.

About the statements attributed to him by Carla and Pierre Delajure: "Pure unadulterated horse puckey." He never said it, never hinted at it, and never thought it. *It's nothing more than retaliation for having lost their civil suit.* He said all that could be asked on the polygraph "so as to dispel that myth as well as the others."

Bodean was more than satisfied with Rolland's explanations and would be even more convinced if the answer to these questions and the ultimate question—"Did you kill your wife?"—were answered in the negative without showing deception. Drew, on the other hand, was convinced beyond a shadow of a doubt that Rolland was telling the truth, the whole truth, and nothing but the truth.

There was that portion of the autopsy report referring to Joy's pregnancy that bothered Bodean. She and Rolland had been married all those years and had no children, and three months into her pregnancy, she was found dead. That might establish motive especially if Rolland didn't want children. Or maybe she was the one who didn't want the child and Rolland did, and they argued over it and words turned to push and push turned to shove.

Rolland actually broke down, and his eyes poured buckets. He sobbed uncontrollably when asked about his wife's pregnancy. Neither Drew nor Bodean had seen a grown man cry the long, agonizing tears of desperation as this man. It was a question that needed to be asked but not maybe at this time. The great nightmare resulted in the loss of two souls, and now watching the excruciating pain and sorrow of this lost soul—all because of him—was almost more than Drew could bear. Wasn't it time to give up the charade and set the captive free? Drew excused himself and went into his office to pray for forgiveness and guidance, something he had not done in many a year.

By the time Drew returned, Rolland had regained his composure to some extent. With a heavy heart, Rolland lamented the fact that he and Joy had no children. Both of them came from relatively large families, and both were family oriented. Although neither was religious, they prayed for a child. Joy thought she was barren, but it turned out she wasn't. That was the closest thing to a smile Rolland would come during this phase of the discussion. Death had cheated him out of being a husband and now a father. It really didn't matter what happened to him now. His world had been turned upside down.

When asked about the blue flannel shirt with the torn pocket and missing buttons, Rolland said that was kept in the downstairs hall closet and used more as a light jacket than a shirt. It was used by unprepared guests when the weather cooled, and he didn't know who might have used it last but he knew he hadn't. It was not in that condition when he last wore it. Sometimes Joy would wear it when her jacket was not handy. He was surprised when the discovery indicated the missing buttons were found on the floor near the fireplace. Also, that was the first he knew cloth fragments were found in one of Joy's hands matching the torn shirt.

Bodean had scheduled Rolland's polygraph examination for Thursday, October 16 at 10:00 a.m. Bodean would be sending the polygrapher, Conrad Jenkins, copies of the charge form and the discovery documents. Conrad and Drew or Lino, depending on which one was available, would be coordinating the questions that would be asked. Rolland had already been advised he would be restricted to "yes" or "no" answers. Bodean outlined the process and instructed him to take a deep breath before answering even the control questions. Rolland understood and said he had read an article on the technical aspects of polygraphs, and since he would be telling the truth, he was not at all apprehensive about the results.

Drew and Lino discussed the areas of inquiry and phraseology of the questions to be asked by the polygrapher, knowing Conrad had his own *modus operandi*. It was decided that Lino would accompany Rolland and would drive the firm's SUV. At the last minute, Bodean decided to go so he would have time with both Rolland and Lino to discuss the direction his investigation was taking. Conrad's office was in the Denver industrial park area on the south side of the city, and the trio arrived early enough to have coffee and pastries before meeting Conrad.

Conrad was a powerfully built man standing six feet three inches tall and militarily erect despite his age, which Lino estimated to be sixty-two or sixty-three. He had thinning gray hair and a thick white mustache. With a broad smile and vice grip handshake he greeted each with inviting warmth. He had known Bodean in years gone by, so there was the usual "remember whens."

Conrad had formulated a series of questions that would be asked of Rolland. He said it was his practice to conduct three separate tests and mix the questions, not always asking the same ones. The only question that Lino had a problem with was "Were you responsible for your wife's death?"

Lino explained that Rolland felt responsible for a number of reasons: Roland had cheated on his wife several years before; their marriage had not been the same since that time; she had found a way to be away from home more; prior to the affair he would have been at their summer place Friday afternoons with her; and the Friday of her death he was home with the flu and delayed seeking her out after she was incommunicado. Conrad agreed that that could result in a false read and that he would change the wording.

Conrad had a series of questions that he would have Rolland deliberately answer falsely to establish a "lie pattern." He would also ask him mundane questions that he was to truthfully answer to establish a truth pattern such as: Do you live in Colorado? Are you an orthopedic surgeon? Did you go to medical school? Were you born in Boston?

Conrad, out of the presence of Lino and Bodean, visited with Rolland discussing his background, his relationship with Joy, his discovery of her body, and other matters connected with the case. He modified and supplemented his pre-drafted questions including the one Lino had objected to. He explained how the polygraph functioned, the process he would be following, and gave Rolland instructions such as be as still as possible, look straight ahead, answer only "yes" or "no," and not to elaborate or say anything else. Rolland said he understood.

With the revisions and additions, Conrad had Lino and Bodean review the questions. They nodded their approval and waited patiently in the reception area while the polygraph examination was conducted. With some polygraph examinations, Lino and Bodean had waited in a room behind a two-way mirror to observe and listen through a sound system while the polygraph was being conducted. But no such arrangement here. They would just have to wait for the results and hope all went well. Rolland was hooked up to all the wires and gadgets that simulated some he made his patients endure.

With a preprogrammed computer, the examination proceeded. Unlike the old machines, with which Bodean was acquainted, Conrad made all marks, symbols, and notations by manipulation of a specially designed keyboard. When it was over, Conrad would be able to interpret the waves and if there was a lie pattern, or what he called deception, determine to which question it applied.

The questions without their numerical equivalents and not necessarily in order of presentment as well as Rolland's answers were as follows:

Q.Did you kill your wife?
A.No.

Q.Do you know who, if anyone, caused your wife's death?
A.No.

Q.Did you strike your wife on September 12, 2008?
A.No.

Q.Did you push or shove your wife on September 12, 2008?
A.No.

Q.Had you had an argument with your wife on September 12, 2008?
A.No.

Q.Is there any reason you would want your wife dead?
A.No.

Q.When you arrived at the summer home at 7:15 p.m. on September 12, 2008, was that the first time you had been there that day?
A.Yes.

Q.Was the blue flannel shirt with the torn pocket and missing buttons found at the scene yours?
A.Yes.

Q.Do you know how the shirt got torn or was missing buttons?
A.No.

Q. Had you been wearing that shirt at all on September 12, 2008?
A. No.

Q. Did you ever tell Carla Delajure or anyone else that you "had a foolproof way of getting rid of your wife"?
A. No.

Q. Did you ever tell Carla Delajure or anyone else that your wife's death "would be perceived by the authorities as an accident"?
A. No.

Q. Have you told me the complete truth?
A. Yes.

Conrad didn't ask all the questions in any one of the three exams conducted with the exception of the first and last questions.

Rolland was unhooked and allowed to join Lino and Bodean while Conrad reviewed, analyzed, and deciphered hieroglyphics. It was approximately twenty minutes when Conrad emerged with glasses perched on the end of his nose and dark, wise eyes peering over the frames and graphs in hand. He announced the results. "Polygraph showed no deception. Dr. Dawson passed the polygraph."

"Whoopee," Bodean said as all took their turn in congratulating the doctor.

As soon as Conrad prepared the report, a copy would be faxed to Quinlin, Devlin & Cummins followed by mailing of the original signed report and, of course, Conrad's billing for services rendered.

The passing of the polygraph was cause for celebration. Lino and Bodean wanted to take Rolland to lunch at his "place of choice." His place of choice was his and Joy's usual place of choice, Ellyington's in the Brown Palace Hotel. Even though it was located in downtown Denver and they would have to fight the noon traffic, Ellyington's it was.

Drew, of course, knew what the results of the polygraph would be. He was still pleased, because the report would be a useful and perhaps a persuasive tool in the plea bargaining process. He didn't want Rolland to be convicted even if that generated an alternate suspect theory. It wasn't only because of the reoccurring dreams but because he had a compulsion to extricate Rolland from the stranglehold of the looming unprovoked prosecution.

Drew had some news of his own. Preston Evans, the attorney who represented Rolland in the Delajure case, had called back as a follow-up to Drew's call to him some weeks before. Preston said that he was on the opposite end of a case with Darren Wheaton, a local attorney, and the two talked about Dr. Dawson and his current case. The discussion then focused on Preston's defense of Dr. Dawson in the Delajure case. Wheaton told him that approximately six months ago he had represented a local businessman who had hired Carla Delajure as a sales representative. Apparently, she had given up her nursing career. The two had sponsored some kind of promotional luncheon that received high reviews and resulted in new clients. It was held at the Antler's Hotel, and afterwards Carla and Wheaton's client went into the lounge and while toasting congratulatory bubbly their lips met.

The next day, Carla didn't show up for work. About 10:00 a.m., her husband, Pierre, called and said she wasn't coming back to work and was contemplating contacting the Civil Rights Commission and an attorney about the sexual harassment "predicament." About 1:30 p.m., Carla called Wheaton's client and said she wished she hadn't told her husband about the lounge incident and said she could persuade him to drop the whole thing for $10,000.

Wheaton's client was married, had several children, was a very successful businessman, and couldn't afford the adverse publicity especially in the category of sexual harassment. Wheaton confirmed that the "lips touching" incident happened but stated it was an aberration, that Carla had only worked for him several days, and that that was the first and only such occurrence.

Wheaton had done some checking and found when he spoke to Carla's previous employer, whose name and telephone number was listed on her employment application, that something similar had happened. Although he didn't want to become involved and would deny he even mentioned it, the previous employer went on to relate the following: He was a one-man firm having semiretired three years before. Carla Delajure had answered an ad for a part-time secretary. She was vivacious and appeared competent and anxious to work for him.

He was in his sixties and was flattered by Carla's thoughtfulness and attentiveness. She brought pastries every morning and greeted him with a "nice" kiss and said good-bye the same way. When she left at noon on Friday at the end of her first week, while saying her good-bye, he patted her once "on the tush." The following Monday, the one-man firm received a call from Carla's husband, Pierre, saying Carla would not be returning to work because of his sexual advances. He made it go away with a $2,500 payment.

Drew asked about the outcome in Wheaton's case. Preston said Wheaton "fired" his client when his client, against Wheaton's advice, offered the Delajures $5,000. Wheaton didn't know whether it was accepted or not. He said he had bailed because he didn't want to be an "enabler to an extortion plot."

The day after Rolland's successful completion of the polygraph examination, Drew received the official report. The same was delivered by pre-arranged appointment to Chief Trial Deputy Edward Terrell. Terrell announced he would be handling the preliminary hearing as his boss, Norman Dayton, was scheduled to be out of state.

The two met in Terrell's office. Drew asked Terrell if the DA's office still gave credence to Conrad Jenkins's polygraph results. Terrell said they did but applying the Frye test (*Frye v. United States*) polygraphs were still considered by the DA's office and the courts as novel scientific evidence and, therefore, not given much weight. He said polygraphs had not received general acceptance in the relevant scientific community because of their unproven underlying theory or principle. Drew then asked why the CBI, of which Conrad had been a part, and the law enforcement community in general were administering them. Terrell said they provided some indication of innocence or guilt but weren't dispositive. He said he would bring the results to Dayton's attention and discuss the matter with him.

Drew then asked if the polygraph results might have some bearing on a plea disposition in the case and maybe result in a dismissal. Terrell told Drew not to get his hopes up as Dayton had a husband and wife team come in and "raise hell" about him not opposing bail after Dr. Dawson was arrested.

"Their names wouldn't be Carla and Pierre Delajure, would they by chance?"

"How did you know?'

"There, of course, is the 2006 case of *Carla Z. Delajure v. Rolland J. Dawson et ux* where the jury determined that Carla's sexual harassment case was bogus and the judgment was affirmed on appeal. And then today, I learned from Dr. Dawson's attorney in that case, Preston Evans, that there were two more 'shake downs' by Carla since that date involving two other prominent members of the community. You need to talk to Preston and Darren Wheaton for the details."

"The Delajures seem pretty convincing, and your client telling Carla that he could stage his wife's death to look like an accident seems to be the 'smoking gun' along with the torn blue flannel shirt."

"If Dr. Dawson had said what the Delajures told the sheriff's deputy, why wasn't that brought out in the civil case? Maybe they'd have won their case if they had fabricated the story back then."

"They said their memories were 'jarred' by the appearance of an accident in Dr. Dawson's wife's death."

"Oh, come on! They are still feeling the sting of the defeat in their suit against the doctor and have found a way to even the score. After you talk to Preston and Darren, you'll feel differently about the Delajures."

"What about the torn shirt?"

"Come take a look at my work shirts. Dr. Dawson spent a lot of time wrestling with the fallen trees and tangled branches on his property. Don't tell me you don't have any shirts like that. Anyway, from what we can determine, he hadn't worn the shirt in years. Besides, if he was guilty, he had more than ample time to remove the shirt from the scene before the deputies arrived and didn't."

"Drew, some years ago you had my job, and from what I can tell, you did it well. Don't tell me the whole thing wouldn't make you a little skeptical if you were sitting where I am. You want to know what I think?"

"Tell me."

"You have a client who cheated on his wife. He was used to living a life of lies and apparently was pretty good at it. He fooled his wife for over a year. The only way his wife found out about the affair was when Carla filed the civil suit."

"Wait a minute. Are you suggesting that men who have affairs are wife killers?"

"Let me finish. I'm saying Dr. Dawson was living a 'foot-loose and fancy free' lifestyle. When he found out his wife was pregnant, he knew his life would change. He felt threatened and deceived by her pregnancy. He became enraged and shoved his wife harder than he intended. The back of her head hit the moss rock protruding from the fireplace, causing her death."

"If that's the way the DA's office surmised it, then why wasn't Dr. Dawson charged with manslaughter, which is reck-lessly causing the death of another, instead of murder in the first degree, which is the deliberate and intentional killing of another? There's quite a difference in the penalty, you know."

"The investigation wasn't complete at the time of the fil-ing of charges and still isn't complete. As you know, once you charge you can't go up, but you can always come down. Besides, I just gave you my opinion. I don't speak for Norman or the rest of the office."

"I appreciate your candor and hope we can continue to have an open discussion on this case."

There was a buzz on the intercom. Terrell had an important appointment waiting. Drew agreed he would call Terrell the first of the week to discuss the preliminary hearing and whether the defense would be waiving it. Drew knew a dismissal or the low-ering of charges was pie in the sky.

The Litmus Test

The purpose of the preliminary hearing, or PH as it is sometimes called, was to determine whether probable cause or reasonable grounds existed to support the prosecution's charge that the accused committed a specific crime.

A PH provides the accused with an opportunity to challenge the sufficiency of the prosecution's evidence at an early stage. It has been described as a screening device designed to weed out unsupported charges and spare the accused the expense and embarrassment of a frivolous trial.

Colorado cases have ruled that hearsay evidence and evidence that would be otherwise inadmissible at trial could be "the bulk of evidence at a preliminary hearing." If the court finds probable cause, it will bind the case over to district court. If it finds there is no probable cause, the case will be dismissed.

Drew was particularly interested in the chief trial deputy's comments, because at a PH the county court judge has the power to bind a defendant over on a "lesser included charge." In the Dawson case, since manslaughter is a lesser included charge of murder in the first and second degree, it would be a moral victory if Rolland were bound over on the manslaughter charge instead of one of the murder charges. Murder in the first degree carries a possible penalty of life in prison or death. Manslaughter, on the other hand, carries a minimum of two years and a maximum of six years imprisonment. Quite a difference in penalties. Then there was criminally negligent homicide, a lesser included charge of manslaughter.

That Monday, October 20, was an ideal day for golf. However, Drew was to meet with the rest of the defense team at 8:00 a.m. at his office. Nicole had stopped by the bakery and had fresh pastries, hot coffee, and an assortment of juices at their disposal.

Rolland was walking a little straighter this day and appeared to smile. The polygraph results no doubt brought him renewed hope. He wasn't sure how it would be used, but at least it validated his proclaimed innocence.

Drew briefed everyone on his discussions with Terrell as well as the calls on the Delajure connection. Rolland didn't say anything, just shook his head when he learned of the existence of at least two other "victims" in the Delajure connection. Bodean speculated that that was only the tip of the iceberg. "How many more are there out there who are victims of this nefarious scheme?"

It was premature to make a decision on whether to have a PH or waive it. They needed to discuss the possibilities and likelihood of getting the charges lowered at this point.

Lino hypothecated on what evidence would be presented by the prosecution. It was his slant that they would call the two sheriff's deputies involved in the case: Roger Milligan and Kevin Stanton. They would testify as to their "crime scene" investigation; Rolland's statements including when he arrived at the scene; his discovery of his wife's body; identification of the blue flannel shirt; their finding the three buttons; the coroner's report; the autopsy report; their conversations with the Delajures; their conversations with Rolland's neighbors; and their conversation with the receptionist/secretary/bookkeeper at Rolland's clinic.

The statements from the Delajures would prove the *deliberation* and *intent* necessary to supply the probable cause for murder in the first degree charge. The torn shirt with missing buttons, the buttons on the floor near where Joy's body was found, her wound to the back of the head, and blood and hair on the stone fireplace would supply the probable cause for the manslaughter charge and together with the deliberation and intent would supply the probable cause for the first degree murder charge. Sandwiched in between was second degree murder, which required only a showing that Rolland *knowingly* caused Joy's death.

Rolland asked whether the officers would be allowed to testify as to what was told to them by third parties who were not sworn as witnesses, such as the Delajures. He thought that was hearsay and was not admissible in a court of law except in very rare instances.

It was explained to Rolland that the rules of evidence were tempered in a PH and that hearsay was admissible at the discretion of the judge. The defense could subpoena and call the Delajures, but it was unlikely that they would change their testimony and to call them would only bolster the prosecution's case.

Rolland asked if he would be called as a witness by the other side as in the civil trial since he was an "adverse party" so to speak. Lino explained that because constitutional rights, specifically the Fifth Amendment, applied in criminal cases, Rolland could not be compelled to testify and anyway it would be "foolhardy" for the defense to call him as its witness even if there was no Fifth Amendment.

The discovery had revealed that the neighbors who lived on each side of Rolland, Gary and Ann Anderson to the east and Dan and Lynn Staves to the west, had been interviewed by Deputies Milligan and Stanton and both sets of neighbors stated that they had not noticed Rolland or his car in the driveway at his home on the afternoon or evening of September 12. Also, the deputies had interviewed Lannette Castles, the receptionist/secretary/bookkeeper at Rolland's clinic, who told them that Dr. Dawson left the clinic at approximately 12:45 p.m. because he was not feeling well and didn't return the rest of the day. The autopsy listed the approximate time of death at 4:30 p.m.

Drew said normally the defense did not call witnesses at the PH because the proceedings were not like a trial or even a mini-trial. Even if the defense presented evidence that contradicted that presented by the prosecution that would only create a factual issue, which was required to be decided by the jury.

Rolland asked about introducing the polygraph results at the PH. Lino said polygraphs were not scientifically recognized and the results wouldn't be accepted either at the PH or at trial. Drew said they might try to get the results admitted at trial, but that would be a pretrial issue. He added that to offer it cold at trial in the presence of the jury would be grounds for a mistrial and would result in sanctions being imposed against the attorneys.

"What's the benefit of the PH then?" Rolland asked, shrugging his shoulders. "If it weren't for the Delajures' statements," Lino responded, "the court would probably bind you over on the lesser charge of manslaughter or maybe even criminally negligent homicide rather than on the murder in the first degree charge or even murder in the second degree."

"That would be quite a victory," Bodean volunteered. "As it is, I think that possibility is slim to nil." Both Drew and Lino agreed.

Drew noticed that Rolland's shoulders sagged as they had when Drew first visited him at the El Paso County Jail. Rolland then said he rued the day he ever took up with Carla. "When you disobey God's commands you get punished," he'd said dejectedly and contritely. "Don't you ever do it. You will live to regret it."

Lino said Rolland had nothing to lose by having a PH except that the press would be reporting on the evidence presented and portraying Rolland in an even darker light. Rolland said nothing could make him look any worse.

Drew was for the PH. They could subpoena Carla and Pierre Delajure and have them testify for the defense. He said there was an outside chance Carla, being advised of the penalties for perjury, "might fold." "That would wipe out at least the first degree murder charge then at both the PH and the trial," he added.

Rolland said that was a slim chance since she'd already perjured herself at the harassment trial by her lies. Lino wasn't so sure. It was decided the defense would subpoena both Carla and Pierre, move to sequester the witnesses so each would be unable to hear what the other had to say, and pray that Carla would "get religion" either out of fear of a perjury prosecution or because it was the right thing to do.

Even though subpoenas had been issued by the clerk of the county court, the subpoenas would not be served because Drew had received a telephone call from Norman Terrell telling him the prosecution would waive the death penalty if the defense would waive the PH. Terrell said Dayton wouldn't agree to lower the charge to manslaughter at least not at this juncture. Their investigator, William "Will" Rodgers, had talked to both Messers Evans and Wheaton and verified the speculative nature of the Delajures' sexual harassment accusations but Dayton said the Delajures' credibility "was a matter for the jury" and that that "was what a trial was for."

In speaking with Lino, Bodean and Rolland, Drew decided it was in the defense's best interest to waive the PH. Not having to worry about the death penalty was a fair trade-off for not putting the Delajures to the test. Their time would come. It was not the concession they had hoped for, but for now, it would do!

At first light on that cool October Colorado Springs Monday, with the sun playing peek-a-boo in the eastern horizon, Drew lay in bed wide awake. He had been awake now for almost two hours. He had a dream, still vivid in his mind, of Joy with babe in arms with her Technicolor turquoise eyes gleaming and fixed on him. She validated the decision to waive the PH and said it was only the first in a series of successes that would be experienced in his defense of her husband. What she next said disturbed him. "Have the spirit of God working within you today while you pray to him unceasingly."

Drew was puzzled. Today would be a "no brainer." All the defense had to do was waive the PH and set the first appearance date in district court. It would be highly unlikely that Rolland's bond would not be continued especially in light of Terrell's having agreed to it as part of the waiver stipulation. Drew, however, would take Joy's admonition seriously. She had been the guiding star throughout this whole ordeal so far.

As the defense team started to walk from the law offices of Quinlin, Devlin & Cummins to the El Paso County courthouse, Drew could see a small crowd assembling outside the main entrance to the courthouse. As they crossed the street and got closer they could see men and women, mostly women, gathered carrying placards some raised high above their heads. It was the local chapter of PROTECT (acronym for Public's Response On Treatment Endangering Children's Time-on-earth). Some placards read *Baby Killer* and some read *Death to the Mother Killer* while others read *Preserve Life of the Unborn,* and *The Baby Didn't Deserve to Die.*

As if Rolland didn't have enough guilt to bear already. But this was more than even Superman should have to endure. Rolland had been tried, convicted, and sentenced by public opinion at least by PROTECT.

It was a hostile group, and even though some shouted insults as the defense team passed, there was no violence. Rolland was identified by several as the baby killer, and he was the brunt of their wrath. Only Drew knew it was a case of mistaken identity.

As they sat in Judge Bernard Rigsby's courtroom, Drew and Lino on each side of Rolland and Bodean in the gallery, Drew hoped that Joy's foretelling didn't include any further surprises.

It was not like Judge Rigsby to be late. Drew thought it was inconsiderate for the judge to keep everyone waiting in nervous anticipation for so long. Then he noticed uniformed police officers outside in the corridor and two who entered and positioned themselves in back of the courtroom. When Judge Rigsby entered, he apologized for the delay and said there had been an incident involving the picketers but "the situation was now under control."

The courtroom had some spectators, in attendance. The press, of course, had their pocketsize notepads and pencils at the ready. Terrell was there by himself. Dayton's absence was conspicuous.

Rolland waived the preliminary hearing. Judge Rigsby made sure Rolland understood the nature of his waiver and almost seemed to be talking him out of it. He advised Rolland that he couldn't change his mind once it was waived. Rolland gave all the right answers. The PH was waived and the date for Rolland's first appearance in district court was set. District Judge Dorothy K. Beasley, it was announced, would be the judge assigned the case. *Oh great, a female judge,* Drew and Lino both said to themselves. The next court date would be November 10 at 9:00 a.m., and Rolland's bond would be continued to then.

Both newspapers carried front page stories of the wife and baby killer's court appearance. Photographs of the PROTECT protestors were featured as well with signs clearly visible for all to read. The television stations had footage of the spectacle and even captured a glimpse of the defense team running the gauntlet on its way into the courthouse. The images and commentary didn't generate any fans for Rolland.

The headline in the evening paper read: "Death of Wife Case Headed for Trial." The headline in the morning paper the following day read: "Doctor Faces Trial in Death of Wife." Not very ingratiating headlines both. It didn't take a rocket scientist to figure out what effect the adverse publicity was having and would have on Rolland's trial, not to mention his medical practice and maybe his personal safety.

The Conflict Within

It has been said that Nero fiddled while Rome burned. Drew felt he was a modern-day Nero and doing nothing while Rolland's life was crumbling around him. Nero didn't have a conscience, and it appeared neither did he. How could he be so calloused as to let Rolland burn or take the heat when he was the one responsible for the fire?

Drew had taken ethics in law school receiving high marks both semesters. He had also served on the ethics committee for the Colorado Bar Association. And, oh yes, he taught the law and ethics course at the local community college several semesters. Wasn't the term paper he had his students write one semester entitled "Conflicted Loyalties"?

Loyalty was not something new to his generation. Loyalty was an issue long before Judas or Brutus or double agents in the James Bond series. It has been a topic of discussion since time immemorial. Wasn't that part of the thesis in Plato's *The Trial and Death of Socrates*?

Drew thought about the Golden Rule, "Do unto others as you would have them do unto you." He wouldn't want to lose his reputation, his family, his license to practice law, his clientele, his friends, and his sanity, so why would he be silent and allow the doctor to lose his reputation, his license to practice medicine, his patients, his friends, and his sanity?

He thought about Kant's Categorical Imperative, "What if everyone did what I did or didn't do what I'm contemplating not doing?" What if everyone who accidentally killed another's wife and the baby in the womb let someone else take the blame like he was doing? It would be a hell of a world, wouldn't it?

The eighth commandment provides: "Thou shall not bear false witness against thy neighbor." Wasn't remaining silent tantamount to a lie? If you have a duty to speak, and you don't, isn't that a lie? By not coming forward with the truth, Drew felt he was perpetrating a falsehood, to-wit, indirectly saying that Rolland was the one responsible for Joy's death.

With a grandfather who was a Baptist minister and having studied the Bible earnestly during various periods in his life, various scriptures came to his mind, including the following: "A man cannot serve two masters: He will love the one and hate the other or hate the one and love the other."

There are conflicting or countervailing interests involved here, he said to himself. *They are on a collision course. You have to balance one against the other. Balancing competing interests is never easy especially here. It boils down to ruination of Rolland's life versus his own,* Drew thought. *When there are competing loyalties, which one trumps?* Drew had unwavering loyalty for his family. Should he not have unwavering loyalty for his innocent client as well? Shouldn't that reign supreme regardless of the cost?

There were trade-offs Drew had to consider. Under the circumstances, Drew could not have his cake and eat it too. Rolland could not be set free unless he was fortunate enough to be acquitted of all charges. If he wasn't acquitted, Drew felt, then he would face that awful decision whether or not to provide the information that would liberate Rolland and at the same time implicate and imprison himself. A terrible dilemma to be in. No win-win situation here. One would lose and the other would win; or the one would win and the other would lose. If Drew was straight forward and told the truth, Rolland would win and *he* would lose.

The ultimate sacrifice would be to die for a friend or in this case an innocent client. Since the death penalty was no longer part of the equation, Drew was not going to be required to lay down his life for Rolland literally but *only* figuratively. He would be only sacrificing his reputation and his relationship with his family and friends and maybe the rest of the world. Was he willing to give all that up for a cause—a cause to foster the administration of true justice? If he was, then the time was not now he decided.

His decision to postpone his decision and await the outcome of the case was worth the gamble. If Rolland was acquitted, then no one would be the wiser. If Rolland was convicted, then Drew would make that decision. Rolland's conviction then would be vacated, Rolland would be set free, and it would be Drew who would face the music.

A Tribute to Joy

After court on Monday, the defense team met at Drew's office. Drew related that, as they were leaving the courthouse, Terrell had asked him what Dr. Dawson wanted to do with his wife's body. He told Drew they had concluded the forensics and the body was still in the morgue. Drew said the defense might like their own expert to examine the body. That was all right with the DA's office.

Drew explained to Rolland that the severity of Joy's head wound was a very subjective thing and it was possible that another pathologist might find that the wound was consistent with an accidental fall. That would mean that death might have occurred through a noncriminal agency. Rolland said he agreed, and Lino and Bodean concurred.

Bodean had worked with a semi-retired pathologist, a former Adams County coroner now living in Denver, by the name of Dr. Homer Renning. Both Drew and Lino recognized the name. Bodean borrowed Drew's telephone, and about that quickly Dr. Renning was aboard. Drew telephoned Terrell and got the green light. The date and time would be Dr. Renning's call.

On Thursday, October 30, Dr. Renning performed an abbreviated autopsy focusing primarily on the head injury and cause of death. His conclusion as to the cause of death mirrored that of El Paso County coroner/medical examiner, Dr. Francisco Mendoza, "massive hemorrhaging of the brain due to blunt trauma." However, Dr. Renning, unlike Dr. Mendoza, found that the head injury "was consistent with trauma resulting from an accidental fall."

The defense team was ecstatic with Dr. Renning's findings. Even if the jury didn't know which expert to believe, that might just create enough reasonable doubt to go from murder one to manslaughter or criminally negligent homicide. After Dr. Renning submitted his written report, a copy was hand-delivered to the DA's office.

Rolland wanted the body cremated and internment at Faith Light Mausoleum. He also wanted to hold a special service at Sangre de Cristo Community Church, which was located at the base of Cheyenne Mountain near the famed Broadmoor Hotel. He said he wanted the pastor, Reverend Patrick Brennigan, to officiate and Drew to give the eulogy. Rolland said he would be too emotional to do so and, in light of having been charged with his wife's death, was uncertain what a friend or relative might say if asked to give the eulogy. Drew, when asked, was speechless and mumbled something like "okay" or at least that's the way Rolland interpreted it.

There were giant snowflakes falling on that otherwise mild November Saturday the first day of the month and appropriately designated All Saints Day. At 10:00 a.m. with the urn of Joy's ashes sitting on the altar, Reverend Brennigan was poised with prayer book in hand ready to officiate in accordance with the pre-ordained funeral ritual.

There were approximately thirty-five members of the Dawson and Armested families in attendance. Both of Rolland's parents were there; Dr. Earl Dawson and wife, Ethel; Rolland's two sisters and their families; and other relatives Drew had not been introduced to. Both of Joy's parents, Jonathan and Maureen Armested, were there along with Joy's brothers Ross, Raymond, and Ben together with their wives, and Joy's sister, Gayla, with her husband and oldest daughter, Kirstin.

Drew guessed there were at least another fifty to sixty friends, co-workers and others such as Drew's wife, Missy; Lino and his wife, Tammy; and Bodean and his wife, Natalie. There were doctor friends of Rolland's in addition to the clinic doctors. Drew did not recognize many of the names that appeared on the register.

Rev. Brennigan read from the scriptures, prayed over Joy's remains, and assured those assembled that she was a favored child of God and she was looking down with a smile assuring them that she was in a better place and would see them again some day.

Drew wasn't at all sure he should give the eulogy because he might be perceived as someone who didn't know Joy *all that well.* In his heart he knew he did and to pay tribute to this remarkable woman was a rare honor and opportunity to say to Joy's family and friends what he hadn't been able to say to Joy.

Drew could feel Joy's presence this day, and her image was as vivid as it had been the night before when he was awakened from a deep sleep.

"I am very grateful for your efforts on Rolland's behalf. We both know he is innocent. Please keep the faith. Everything is going to turn out all right in the end."

Drew felt relief and an indescribable calmness.

"I am anxious to hear what you have to say about me. I only wish I could be there in person." Her smile radiating and her eyes sparkling, she said, "Don't let my memorial be your farewell address."

Drew was agonizing over what to say and how to say it. It would have to be veiled and cryptic. Since Joy's death, he had become more philosophical and circumspect. It was as if he had entered into some spiritual or supernatural realm. He had found himself reading an old Bible he had in an old trunk belonging to his grandfather and had used it to prepare his eulogy. In one of her dreams, Joy had told him that the acronym BIBLE stood for *Basic Instructions Before Leaving Earth*. She said she would be lonely if he was denied admittance to the big court in the sky.

Drew had spent sixteen years in the courtroom, was an adjunct professor, and gave a lot of after-dinner speeches, but he had never been this nervous. Nothing had mattered this much before. He wanted this to be a perfect performance for *her*.

When Drew first stood, he broke the ice by reading Revelation 17:10: "Be thou faithful unto death and I will give thee a crown of life."

Then he said, "Family and friends of Joy Armested Dawson, on the wall in my office is a painting of a lioness and her cub in a grove of golden aspen. It is a beautiful painting. However, the beauty of the painting is not the landscape but the penetrating greenish-blue eyes of the lioness and those of the cub brilliant in the day's sun.

"Although I became acquainted with Joy mainly through her paintings and that one in particular, which was and is my favorite, I am convinced that those eyes were a self-portrait of the artist's own. Much like Leonardo da Vinci's *Mona Lisa* being his smile, those turquoise eyes are eyes of joy, Joy's eyes looking lovingly down on each of us.

"In preparation for what I was going to say today, I looked up the definition of *artist*. Webster's New World Dictionary defines *artist* as a person who does anything very well, with imagination and feeling. Not knowing Joy as well as some of you, I felt that described not only her as a professional but her as a person.

"Born Joyce Carol Armested on September 12, 1966, at Charleston, West Virginia, she was the youngest of five children. From day one, she was called 'Joy' by her siblings: twin brothers, Ross and Raymond, age six; brother Ben, age four; and sister Gayla, age two. Dr. Jonathan and Maureen Armested knew how to space their children.

"When Joy was almost ready to start grade school, the family moved to Columbus, Ohio, where Dr. Armested received a professorship and later a chairmanship in the department of business administration from which he recently retired after thirty-five years of service.

"Joy attended grade school and high school in Columbus graduating from Columbus High School with honors in 1984. Not only was she an exceptional student but an accomplished violinist and pianist as well. She was a thespian and lettered in swimming and track all but her freshmen year. How she was able to do all of that her family to this day still marvels.

"Joy showed promise as an artist and graduated *magna cum laude* from Columbus College of Art & Design. To become an artist was a fulfillment of a life-long ambition. As with everything, art became almost an obsession or a compulsion. She soon was not only painting but marketing at a master's price landscapes and seascapes that have become her legacy and will be enjoyed and cherished for generations to come.

"In 1991, while attending a banquet with her father honoring the class of 1981 at Ohio State University she was introduced to a dashing young medical doctor, who was celebrating his ten-year class reunion, Dr. Rolland J. Dawson. He was thirty-two; she was twenty-five. To make a long story short, in less than a year, she and her Prince Charming were married and rode off to

Boston, where they resided for the next five years before moving to Colorado in 1996.

"I forgot to mention that during her senior year at Columbus College of Art & Design, Joy was crowned Miss Ohio and appeared in the Miss America Pageant in 1988. She was known as much for her inward beauty and her philanthropic and altruistic endeavors as her outward beauty. And, oh yes, I forgot to mention that the year before she met Rolland, Joy dedicated twelve months to serving the disadvantaged at the Coritas Mission in the upper Appalachian region of the state of Pennsylvania.

"The spirit of Joy lives on in her music, her art, her love, and her inspiration. How can we go away and not say we were touched by her in some special way and will never be the same again because of her and her memory. Every rose we smell, every fresh breath we take, every delight in which we partake, and every smile and twinkling eye we see will be a reminder of her.

"When I was in college, I was a literature major. Three of my favorite readings included the following prose and poetry that fit the occasion. The first is from John Donne's 'Air and Angels': 'Twice or thrice had I loved thee/ Before I knew thy face or name, So in a voice, so in a shapeless flame/ Angels affect us oft, and worshipped he.'

"The second is from Shelly: 'For she was beautiful—her beauty made/ The bright world dim, and everything beside/ Seemed like the floating image of a shade.'

"The last is a poem by William Wordsworth: 'Though nothing can bring back the hour/ Of Splendor in the grass, of glory in the flora;/ We will grieve not, rather find/ Strength in what remains behind..../ In the faith that looks through death,/ In years that bring the philosophic mind./ And O, ye fountains, meadows, hills and groves,/ Forbade not any severing of our lives!/ Yet in my heart of hearts I feel your might;/ I only have relinquished one delight/ To live beneath your more habitual sway.'"

With that, Drew took a long deep breath and the long stem rose he had been holding and, bowing briefly before Joy's urn, gently placed it in front of the brass plate which read:

Joyce "Joy" Armested Dawson
Born September 12, 1966
Died September 12, 2008

Joy had been born and died on the same day of the month only forty-two years apart. Having been entombed with Christ by baptism, Joy, he knew, would walk in the newness of life.

Reverend Brennigan, in concluding the service, paraphrased a passage of scripture attributed to St. Paul. "Death has been swallowed up in victory. Where, O death, is your victory? Where, O death is your sting? Where is death's sting if the tomb is but a passage to a promised kingdom? The resurrection is God's seal upon the victory that his Son achieved. We rejoice in this promise and we thank you Lord for the vision of hope it has brought to our world."

Both daily newspapers carried front-page stories on Joy's memorial service the following day. The headline in the Colorado Springs *Times Herald* read: "Memorial Services Held for Slain Artist." The headline in the Colorado Springs *Star* read: "Accused's Attorney Gives Eulogy at Dawson Service." Local television stations carried the story on Sunday as well. Both newspaper accounts not only detailed the memorial service, but the chronology of events in the murder case starting with Dr. Dawson's discovery of his wife's body on September 12.

Particularly disturbing to the defense team were the editorials in both newspapers. The editorial in the *Star* was especially egregious and sparked the nasty flow of disparaging letters to the editor.

The editorial was captioned "Eulogy Defies All Belief" and read:

> On her forty-second birthday, local artist Joy Dawson's life and that of her unborn child were to be no more. Taken in the prime of her life and the promise of their first child, her doctor husband was charged in her death.
>
> The *Star*'s editorial staff is at a loss as to why the father to be was not also charged in the wrongful termination of his wife's pregnancy. Our local district attorney said Dr. Dawson could not be charged for criminal homicide because the fetus was not considered to be a "person" under Colorado law. We are not trained in the law, Mr. Prosecutor, but tell us why the termination is not considered to be at least criminal abortion.
>
> In case you forgot, the criminal abortion statute makes it a felony for any person to end or cause to be ended "the pregnancy of a woman by any means other than justified medical termination or birth." According to our reading of the statute, "by any means" infers just that. Intending to kill the mother, in our book, imputes intent to terminate the pregnancy. This is the doctrine of transferred intent is it not?
>
> There are a lot of things the editorial staff doesn't understand, the least of which is what kind of respect the doctor showed for his deceased wife in allowing the attorney who is representing him in defense of the murder charge to give the eulogy at his wife's memorial service. That takes the "guts of a burglar" and for that Dr. Dawson is awarded this publication's *Defies All Belief Award* for the year.

Entry of Plea

Although technically winter didn't begin for another six weeks, no one told the weatherman. Monday, November 10 was a cold, wintery Colorado Springs day. It wouldn't do any good to call the chamber of commerce. Winter road advisories were broadcast discouraging out of town travel.

When Drew arrived at work, he was glad that he had all-season tires and had already winterized his car. When he checked his phone messages, he had one from Rolland at approximately 7:15 a.m. saying that Monument Hill had been closed and he'd been re-routed back to Denver. He didn't think he would be able to make it to court.

Sticking his head into Lino's office, Drew said, "Why the hell didn't he drive in last night instead of chancing the weather? He knew we would be meeting at eight."

"The arraignment is not scheduled until nine. That's over an hour away. He may still make it."

"I guess his parents were flying out of DIA this morning heading back to Boston. I'm sure he was stretching out the good-byes in light of everything that's happened and not knowing what the future brings."

"I suppose you're right. But first things first. The bond is a fragile thing in murder in the first-degree cases, and if the defendant doesn't appear or the judge thinks the defendant might boogie, the bond will be revoked and guess who sits in the slammer pending the outcome of the trial?"

"As I recall, rule ten allows the court 'for good cause shown' to accept a not-guilty plea made by the attorney in a defendant's absence."

"True, but I prefer to have that made by a defendant himself and so does the judge. Besides, you know how temperamental Judge Beasley is. Let's just hope she didn't have an argument with her husband last night and awoke this morning with an attitude."

"I thought Mr. Judge Beasley was on the wagon."

"Wagon or no wagon, the Beas will still be on her high horse. She receives a vicarious thrill in bringing the 'male species' to their knees.

"Well, let's just wait in the conference room. I wanted to discuss some ideas I had regarding possible motions. Obviously, we need to change the place of trial. There is no way Rolland can get a fair shake here."

Drew and Lino gathered the Dawson file, which now consisted of a series of folders filling the file box, and carted it into the conference room. Nicole brought in the news that the roads were still closed and that Rolland had called saying he was headed back to DIA.

When Drew and Lino approached the El Paso County courthouse, they were met by only a few die-hard placardetuers. The two passed without incident. Only one made any effort to offend.

The much-too-big woman with a much-too-big mouth asked, "What'd you do with the baby killer?"

Chief Trial Deputy Terrell was already seated at the prosecution table again without his boss Norman Dayton. Not too many others were there to watch the Christians being fed to the lions. Terrell gave Drew a copy of the information containing the charges and a list of potential witnesses endorsed on the back. It mirrored the complaint with the exception of the designation. The original had already been filed with the clerk of the district court.

The bailiff called the court to order, announced the grand entrance of the judge, and then Judge Beasley looking around and, in a ponderous judicial voice, inquired "Where's the defendant?" Drew explained the reason for Rolland's absence and the judge, understanding the weather and road conditions between Denver and Colorado Springs, seemed to be appeased.

Both Drew and Lino had to chuckle when Judge Beasley entered and positioned herself at the bench. She was thick, not fat, appeared as though she had miniature shoulder pads under her black robe, with short-cropped black hair and glasses, she reminded them of the female version of U.S. Supreme Court Associate Justice Antonin Scalia. Only when she spoke could you tell the difference. And that was not merely because of the pitch of her voice.

Judge Beasley asked if the defense had received a copy of the information together with the list of witnesses. Drew announced that he had just been served with a copy of the same. The Beas, as she was referred to by the local attorneys, agreed to continue the arraignment to the following day at the same time but because the defendant had failed to appear, she would have to revoke the bond and issue a bench warrant for Rolland's arrest. However, because of the circumstances, she would stay execution of the warrant pending his appearance on the morrow.

Rolland when next he called was told of the status and consequences in the event he failed to appear as required the following day. He would be returning home ASAP and be at Drew's office first thing in the morning.

Rolland was ushered into Drew's office at 7:59 a.m., Tuesday, November 11. Joy's oil of the lioness and cub hanging on the wall again caught his attention. This time, his eyes teared and his lips quivered, and he said nothing for what to Drew seemed like an eternity. Rolland's eyes were locked in wonder as the turquoise eyes of the lioness were transfixed on him. When he moved, they seemed to move with him. Drew always experienced the same sensation.

When Joy was buried, the anguish caused by Drew was not buried with her. It survived and was now manifest in her grieving husband. It was not easy for Drew to sit and watch as the consequences of his deadly deception persisted.

Rolland struggled to regain his composure and after having done so stated, "I'm sorry. I don't know why Joy's oil has such an effect on me. I'm not usually so emotional. I watched as the oil progressed starting with the landscape. I remember Joy inserting the lioness and cub but had never seen the finished product."

"It's quite understandable," Drew said. "Looking into the turquoise eyes of the lioness is like looking into Joy's turquoise eyes."

Drew didn't realize what he had said but only later remembered the puzzled look on Rolland's face. In Rolland's mind, he wondered how Drew knew the color of Joy's eyes. Drew and Joy had never met, and Drew bought the painting from an art gallery. Rolland had never disclosed the color of Joy's eyes, and there was nothing in the prosecution's discovery documents that described the color. Even the photographs in the newspaper did not betray the true color. First at the funeral and now again, Drew had described Joy's most distinguishing characteristic— her turquoise eyes.

It was at that point that Rolland said he understood what Drew had said at Joy's funeral about the painting. "I guess you become acquainted with an artist through his or her creation much like knowing a writer through his or her writings."

"I think that's true. However, through that painting and what you've told me about Joy, I feel I've known her a lifetime."

"I just thank you again for the eulogy. There's no way that I could have done it. You truly were my 'mouthpiece' and spoke my heart. I thought everything you said was most appropriate."

"Thank you. I was moved by what Gayla and Ben said. I felt sorry for Joy's father being unable to speak. It's an emotional time for family."

Although on prior occasions, they had talked about arraignment and the plea Rolland would enter, they would go over it one more time. There were three possible pleas not counting the "not guilty by reason of insanity" plea, which was not appropriate in this case: Not guilty, *nolo contendere* (no contest), and guilty. Rolland would be entering a not guilty plea and requesting a jury trial. Drew explained that all motions had to be made within twenty days of the arraignment unless extended by the judge. That meant the next court date would be a hearing on the motions.

One more try at the arraignment. Lino had another matter in another court and wouldn't be accompanying them this day. Although it had quit snowing, the air was brisk, and they could see the frost of their breath as they exhaled. They could also see the same diehard placardetuers that Drew and Lino had seen the previous day plus several new ones. That was when Rolland nudged Drew and said, "Carla and Pierre have joined the diehards!"

Drew had the opportunity to see Carla and Pierre for the first time or so he thought. When he got a glimpse of Pierre now turned placardetuer, he recognized him as a man he had turned over to the feds in the late 1980s when he first started with the DA's office. Only, his name was not Pierre Delajure; it was Dominique Demarco. *I can't believe I still remembered his name after all these years*, Drew said to himself.

At the preliminary proceedings in district court, Drew acknowledged receipt of the information together with witness list, and he waived, on behalf of his client, a formal reading thereof. Judge Beasley insisted on informing Rolland of his constitutional rights even though Drew said Rolland would waive the formality as he had already been advised of his rights by Judge Rigsby in county court. The Beas began in her usual authoritative fashion.

"Dr. Dawson, you realize you need make no statement and any statement you make can and may be used against you?"

"Yes, Your Honor."

"You have a right to counsel. I see you have Mr. Quinlin with you today. Is he and will he continue to be your counsel?"

"Yes, Your Honor, along with Mr. Blankenship."

"If you're indigent, you have the right to request the appointment of counsel or consult with the public defender before any further proceedings are held. Understand?"

"Yes, Your Honor."

"Do you understand that any plea you make must be voluntary and not the result of undue influence or coercion?"

"Yes, Your Honor."

"Do you also understand that because of the nature of the charges you have a right to a jury trial and the right to a speedy trial?"

"Yes, Your Honor."

"Do you understand the nature of the charge and the possible penalties?"

"I do, Your Honor."

"Very well then, how do you wish to plead to murder in the first degree, a class I felony carrying a possible penalty of life or death?"

"Not guilty, Your Honor, and I request a jury of twelve."

"Your plea will be entered, and your request for a jury trial is hereby noted." And, turning to Drew, asked, "Mr. Quinlin, will you be filing motions, and if so, do you have an idea at this time what they will be?"

"Judge, we will be filing motions. At this point we anticipate filing a motion for bill of particulars and a motion for change of venue. Other motions will depend on what we receive by way of discovery and what our investigation discloses. We think a half day may be sufficient to hear all motions."

"Mr. Terrell, are you anticipating any motions that the prosecution may be filing?"

"Your Honor, depending on what we learn from our continuing investigation and what the defense generates by way of their motions, we may. But in answer to Your Honor's question, we anticipate none at this time. And we are comfortable with a half day setting."

"Very well, I'm looking at the court's calendar to see when we might have a four-hour block of time available. The earliest time I have is December 29 at 8:00 a.m. until noon. Is that agreeable, Mr. Quinlin?"

"Yes, Your Honor."

"And you, Mr. Terrell?"

"Yes, Your Honor."

"Very well, the defense shall have twenty days from this date, that is until December 1, to file their motions; and the prosecution until December 11 to file their responses and motions if any. Otherwise this court will be adjourned until December 29 at 8:00 a.m. Dr. Dawson's bench warrant is hereby rescinded and his original bond reinstated and continued to that date and time. This court is in recess."

Drew pulled Terrell aside and told him about Dominique Demarco, a.k.a. Pierre Delajure, and asked Terrell if he would check on Pierre's rap sheet and specifically if Pierre had a felony conviction. Drew said that he remembered Demarco was charged under the federal RICO (Racketeer Influenced and Corrupt Organizations Act) involving a pattern of criminality. Terrell agreed to check both the federal (NCIC) and state (CCIC) crime information centers for arrests and convictions and provide copies.

When Drew and Rolland returned to Drew's office, Drew explained what he had discovered and what it meant to the case. If Demarco, a.k.a. Delajure, had a felony and testifies at trial, that could be brought out and the jury would be instructed they could take the felony into account in assessing credibility. In other words, he told Rolland, the jury has the prerogative of discounting a felon's testimony.

Rolland's prosecution was continuing to be sensationalized in the press. Both local newspapers carried front-page headlines and stories of the day's events. The *Colorado Springs Star* headline that night read: "Plea Entered in Wife Killing Case." The *Colorado Springs Times Herald* the following morning headlined "Doctor Arraigned in Murder of Wife." *The Denver Post* carried a larger than usual account of the case, which was now receiving state-wide attention. What the defense team was not prepared for was the television coverage on the 10:00 p.m. news.

Disparaging the Living

On one of the local channels that wintery November 11 night was the teaser or promo: "Death of doctor's wife not isolated incident. Stay tuned on KSIR Channel 33 for details at 10:00 p.m."

When they had entered the El Paso County courthouse that morning, Drew and Rolland had noticed the crew had cameras rolling and reporters interviewing various placardetuers. With Carla and Pierre among them, Drew wasn't sure what would be on the news but wasn't expecting what he saw and heard.

Although the film showed various placardetuers, some with sound booms stuck in their faces including the implacable Pierre Delajure, the whole newscast consisted of a narrative by newsperson Julia Zoren. In her usual truculent manner, she lashed out at Rolland with scathing hostility.

"A case receiving much local attention is the prosecution of prominent orthopedic surgeon, Dr. Rolland J. Dawson, who has been charged in district court with murder in the first degree in the death of his wife and unborn child.

"On September 12, the battered body of Joy Dawson, a well-known local artist, was found in the parties' summer home in Black Forest north of Colorado Springs. The autopsy was performed by county coroner/medical examiner, Dr. Francisco

Mendoza, who attributed the cause of death to *foul play*. The autopsy also revealed that at the time of her death she was three months pregnant.

"The tattered shirt of Dr. Dawson was discovered by authorities at the scene. According to unnamed sources, buttons found near the body were determined to be those missing from Dr. Dawson's shirt. Dr. Dawson refused to make statements at the scene and instead called his brother-in-law attorney, Troy Campbell.

"There is public outcry and rage over no charges being brought in the death of the unborn child and the district attorney's office not opposing bond. 'If Dr. Dawson had been a janitor or a common laborer,' this newsperson was told by an irate placard carrier at the courthouse, 'he would not have received such favored treatment.' This newsperson shares their outrage and questions the motives of our elected prosecuting attorney."

While Ms. Zoren was narrating, a cutaway of Drew and Dr. Dawson running the gauntlet on their way into the courthouse, was shown on the tube.

"Dr. Dawson is pictured here with his attorney on their way to district court where Dr. Dawson entered a plea of 'not guilty' and requested a jury trial. Dr. Dawson is represented by Drew Quinlin, a former prosecuting attorney with the local district attorneys office and the successful defense attorney in the battered-wife syndrome case tried here in September.

"This station is particularly annoyed in this case by information heretofore not made public and learned by this station for the first time this morning while interviewing two of the protestors. The two, who have given permission to have their names used on this broadcast are local residents, Pierre Delajure and his wife, Carla."

With this, there was a cutaway of the Delajures being interviewed but with no sound. Instead Ms. Zoren narrated the following:

"According to court documents, Carla Delajure, seen here talking to this newsperson, filed a sexual harassment suit in 2006 against Dr. Dawson, which ultimately was resolved in his favor. Prior to the suit, however, Dr. Dawson reportedly told Ms. Delajure, while her husband listened in on an extension, that he, Dr. Dawson, had a 'fool-proof way to kill his wife so as to make it look like an accident.'

"So far, it appears, Dr. Dawson has been able to beat the system. But even Napoleon had his 'Waterloo.'"

Soon the telephone was ringing off the hook. First Rolland, then Lino, then Bodean, then Drew's father. While Missy watched and listened with Drew, she kept asking him how they "can get away with it." Now Rolland was asking the same question only with anguish, resignation and disbelief in his voice. It was agreed that Rolland and the defense team would meet at Drew's office at 8:00 a.m. the following morning and concentrate on damage control.

While thinking of Carla Delajure and now Julia Zoren, Drew had remembered from his school days the following from a poem of Tennyson:

Deforming and defacing, till she left
Not even Lancelot brave, nor Galahad clean.
For men at most differ as Heaven and Earth,
But women, worst and best, as Heaven and Hell.

Carla, relentless in her quest to do the good doctor in, had anything but a quiescent pawn in Julia Zoren. Carla's scurrilous attacks were expected but not the ignominious comments of a newsperson whose mantra was "fair and balanced." Drew mused that "fair and balanced" meant basically the same thing but now he knew why Julia Zoren didn't claim to be "fair and accurate."

With everyone assembled, it was clear that Rolland had a cause of action for libel, but was it viable? That was the question. The law of defamation could be traced back to ancient times. It allowed he who was defamed to avenge his honor and damaged reputation. How would that work under the current state of the law?

All agreed that even if KSIR retracted their libelous statement or issued an apology that would not restore Rolland's tarnished reputation. You can't unring a bell. Once a reputation has been damaged it can never be undone. Drew called it the Humpty Dumpty rule. "Once Humpty Dumpty has a great fall, you can't just glue all the pieces back together and have the same Humpty Dumpty," Drew said mournfully.

Lino recounted an incident when he was a deputy district attorney standing for the proposition that a damaged reputation is irretrievable especially for a professional.

He recalled that one of the deputies had had a case involving the prosecution of a local banker for aggravated robbery. The victim, a local socialite, identified the banker from a photographic lineup of individuals who fit the general profile of the perpetrator as described to the police. He, of course, was arrested and charged.

At the trial, she identified the defendant as the robber and when asked how she knew it was the same man said she had never had a gun pointed at her before and that they were "eyeball to eyeball" and his face was "forever etched" in her memory. "That was the man!" she proclaimed unhesitatingly as she pointed her shaking finger at the defendant.

The banker was convicted and sentenced to a prison term. He, of course, lost his job. His wife left him. The front page of the newspaper carried the headlines, story, and his photograph in numerous editions. If he had children, they would have been judged for the sin of their father. "You can imagine the fall-out," Lino said.

To make a long story short, the socialite returned to his office demanding to see "the district attorney himself." She thought the perpetrator was in prison and only moments before had seen him washing windows at the shoe store on the corner.

Investigators were dispatched to the store as the socialite identified him as the perpetrator. Unfortunately, it was not the same man she had identified from the photographic line-up or the man she identified in court or the man who had been sent to prison. It was the *real* perpetrator.

The district attorney's office then filed a *writ of habeas corpus ad prosequendum* and brought the convicted man back to court. Only this time it was to vacate the conviction, dismiss the charges, and set him free. His record being expunged and apologies made all around, he was sent away to live his life as if none of those unpleasant things had happened.

"Are you saying that's what's going to happen to me if and when I'm acquitted?" Rolland wanted to know.

"Not necessarily," Lino said. "But the mere fact you've been charged and prosecuted, whether or not you are convicted, will leave some doubt in the public's mind."

"But I never told Carla, nor did I tell anyone or even think it, that I had a 'fool-proof' way to kill my wife 'and make it look like an accident.' For Carla and Pierre to make that statement and for KSIR to repeat it, isn't that libel?"

"Truthfulness is always a defense," Lino said. "That wouldn't apply here since the statements are false. But how do you prove a negative? You can only hope Carla and/or Pierre recant. Otherwise, it is your word against theirs. There are two of them and only one of you, and presumably you have a motive to lie to save your skin. They have no motive or at least it would be perceived or postured that way."

"That sure is a poor system. I think I like the ancient way of avenging one's honor and settling the dispute through a duel at sunrise. At least I would have a—excuse the pun—fighting chance that way."

It was time to educate Rolland on the law of libel. On the conference room white board, Drew wrote the six elements of libel: publication; of defamatory statements; that are false; of and concerning the person defamed; the defamer is at fault; and the defamed person's reputation has been harmed.

He explained to Roland that there were four possible defendants: Carla Delajure, Pierre Delajure, Julia Zoren, and KSIR. KSIR would have the "deep pocket" in the event of a judgment in Rolland's favor although Ms. Zoren would no doubt be covered under some type of insurance policy. "The Delajures were most likely judgment proof," he added.

Rolland asked if KSIR by merely repeating what the Delajures told them would still be liable. In other words, they didn't initiate the defamatory statements; they merely quoted the Delajures.

Lino responded, "There is what is called the 'republication doctrine,' which says the repeater is as liable as the originator. Even if they attribute the source to someone else, as they did last night, KSIR is still liable for the false defamatory statements."

Drew, continuing in true professional vintage while still standing at the white board, wrote: *public official, all-purpose public figure* and *limited-purpose public figure* in a row on the left side of a vertical line he drew. On the right side, he wrote *private figure*. He then underlined *private figure* and drew a vertical line down from the middle. On the left side of that vertical line, he wrote *involving matter of public interest or concern*; on the right side of that vertical line, he wrote *not involving matter of public interest or concern.*

He then explained to Rolland that with regard to all categories except *private figure not involving matter of public interest or concern* the plaintiff had to prove *actual malice*. Drew then wrote *actual malice* on the white board and defined it as knowledge of falsity or reckless disregard for the truth. In other words, the defendant lied or was aware of probable falsity or entertained doubts as to the truth. With regard to a private figure *not* involving a matter of public interest or concern, all the plaintiff had to prove was simple negligence by a preponderance or greater weight of the evidence, the standard in an ordinary civil case.

Drew went on to explain to Rolland that the burden of proof in the other categories was proof by "clear and convincing evidence," a greater burden than even in a criminal case where the proof was "beyond a reasonable doubt."

"Where do I fit?" Rolland asked.

"With regard to a private figure involving a matter of public interest or concern," Lino said, "Colorado is unique in that respect. Normally, a pure private figure is slotted in the last category and has special treatment. As a result of *Walker v. Colorado Springs Sun, Inc.*, a 1975 Colorado Supreme Court Case, however, a private person in Colorado who sues for libel involving a matter of public interest or concern is treated like a public figure with the higher proof requirements and greater burden of proof."

Bodean, not wanting to be outdone, said, "In other words, Rolland, you would have to prove those statements were false; the Delajures, Zoren, and KSIR would not be required to prove that the statements were true. Also, you would have to prove that they acted with actual malice."

"The reason being," Drew added, "the statements involve a matter of grave public interest or concern. That having been said, it doesn't mean we shouldn't hold Channel 33's feet to the fire. I think the piece Zoren did was despicable and was not 'fair and balanced' or more appropriately 'fair and accurate.'"

"That airing together with the newspaper accounts," said Lino, "certainly shows irresponsibility on the part of the media, and if that doesn't enhance our chances to get a motion for change of venue granted, nothing will."

"Reputation is an idle and most false imposition; oft got without merit, and lost without deserving," Drew quoted from Shakespeare.

It was decided that Drew would fax a letter to KSIR demanding that they preserve the offending tape and put KSIR on notice that Dr. Dawson intended to file a civil action naming Ms. Zoren and the station as defendants. In the interim, an effective retraction and public apology was in order. In the fax he would request a copy of the tape and that the station have their attorney contact him. He would also send a hard copy by registered mail, return receipt requested.

Both Drew and Lino had already taped the offending segment. It was nice to have had the advance promo so that they would have everything at the ready. So even if a Rosemary Wood was working at KSIR and the offending tape was erased by mistake, Drew and Lino would still have a copy.

On that November Wednesday at 1:30 p.m., Drew received a telephone call from Steven Wickershire, the attorney who represented KSIR. He was at the station sitting with the manager Mike Millan. Steve had reviewed the tape; it was sitting on the table in front of him. He and the manager would be receptive to meeting with Drew to discuss the matter if Drew was so predisposed. Drew arranged to meet them at 4:00 p.m.

At 4:00 p.m., Drew and Lino arrived together at KSIR. The receptionist said as soon as Mr. Wickershire arrived the manager would be available. In the interim, they were shown where the coffee was located and told to help themselves. They were ushered into a rather drab conference room. Television sets with the current Channel 33 programming were positioned in the common areas. They saw personnel working but not the incomparable Julia Zoren.

Wickershire and Millan, with coffee cups in hand, steam heralding their recent fill, entered the room. Lino recognized Mike from Rotary Club and any confrontation there might be was stymied at least for the moment.

Mike was dapper in his navy blue suit, white starched shirt, and silver black-flecked tie. With an arrogance born of old family wealth, he took charge of their meeting. Though he didn't lead in a dictatorial or overbearing fashion, they knew by whose rules they would be playing.

It was Mike who spoke first. "Gentlemen, I can understand your consternation. Even though what I am about to say may be construed as an admission against the station's best interest, I feel compelled to speak my mind. Julia's news reporting in question was admittedly slanted and not 'fair and balanced.' It certainly was not up to the high standards indigenous to KSIR."

Both Drew and Lino nodded their approval but did not interrupt. Mike continued: "Julia might have been careless in relying on untrustworthy sources and in not checking with obvious sources, but her indiscretions, according to Steve here, did not amount to actual malice."

"Your client fits in the same category as a celebrity," Steve said to Drew and Lino, "and at the very least, as a limited purpose public figure where the matter involved is of great public interest and concern. Dr. Dawson, in order to succeed in a libel suit, must prove that KSIR acted with actual malice. That is, that the station either deliberately lied or acted with willful disregard for the truth."

Seeing that Drew and Lino were not the least bit convinced or appeased, Mike interjected the sixty-four-thousand-dollar question: "What do you want our station to do?"

Lino, since he knew Mike, spoke first. "It's obvious the errant newscast has compromised Dr. Dawson's Sixth Amendment rights and has torpedoed Dr. Dawson's ability to receive a fair trial in El Paso County. That having been said, Dr. Dawson never made the statements attributable to him, and for Ms. Zoren to infer that the Delajure's statements were not recent fabrication and not due to 'sour grapes' is tantamount to 'reckless disregard for the truth.' The Delajures are still reeling from their failed extortion attempt and contrived harassment action and are using your station to perpetrate their fraud. I guess that makes KSIR a complicitor whether wittingly or otherwise."

It was Mike and Steve's turn to sit and listen, and, somewhat nervously, they did.

"If Ms. Zoren had bothered to check," Drew said, "she would have discovered two critical facts. First, she would have found Pierre's credibility questionable. Secondly, she would have found that Dr. Dawson had passed the polygraph denying ever having made the alleged statements as well as any involvement in his wife's death. Why is Ms. Zoren so bent on destroying Dr. Dawson and his reputation? What kind of axe does she have to grind?"

Mike and Steve dodged both questions. Instead Steve asked. "You still have not answered the question. What do you want the station to do?"

Sensing that the tone of Steve's question might be considered contentious, Mike asked, "Are you seeking a qualified retraction or apology of some sort or maybe Julia's 'head on a platter'?"

Lino said, "Let me answer that directly. You are correct. Mike asked the same question moments ago, and we skirted it. I guess we came in here having made up our minds to bring a libel suit. Maybe there is more than one way to skin a cat. I can't speak for Drew or Dr. Dawson, but I think a retraction or at least a qualified retraction to our liking might be a good place to start. That should also be accompanied by some sort of apology to appease our client." He turned to Drew. "What do you think?"

"We did come here looking for blood and perhaps Ms. Zoren's head on a platter. I, for one, don't think Ms. Zoren is a sparkling ambassador for your fine station. Much like the one free dog bite, I think the station is now on notice as to her 'dangerous propensity.'" She is now a liability.

Mike said nothing and let Drew and Lino vent. He was a seasoned negotiator; that was obvious. Mike was not ready to challenge them to a duel unless he had no option.

He volunteered, "As I previously stated, we have been told by Steve that legally we are probably on solid ground. However, I am looking at the ethical angle and want the station to be both responsible and responsive. If it's a qualified retraction and apology you want, I can do that. The future employment of Ms. Zoren, however, is something I need to visit with Steve about."

Drew then suggested that he, Lino, and Steve formulate an acceptable retraction and apology and go from there. That would give both sides an opportunity to regroup. They would still like a copy of the offending newscast. Mike tossed Lino an envelope and said, "This one's on the house." Mike said he was late for an appointment and suggested the legal brain trust stay and formulate a retraction.

After a little wrangling, the three attorneys agreed on the following phraseology:

"KSIR aired a segment on its 10:00 p.m. newscast on Monday, November 11, 2008. The segment was based on an interview of two individuals participating in the PROTECT protest on the steps of the El Paso County courthouse in connection with the *Dawson* murder prosecution. The statements attributed to Carla and Pierre Delajure were purely their own. KSIR has no independent knowledge as to the truthfulness of those statements nor as to the credibility of the two individuals who made them.

"Dr. Rolland Dawson denies he made the statements attributed to him, and KSIR has no independent knowledge that either he did or didn't. Any statements made by KSIR to suggest otherwise were unintentional and should be completely disregarded. We publicly apologize to Dr. Dawson for the misunderstanding and ask our viewing and listening audience to afford him the presumption of innocence to which he is entitled under our system of justice."

The attorneys agreed that they would submit the proposed retraction statement and apology to their respective clients and if accepted by both would be aired on the 5:00 p.m. and 10:00 p.m. newscasts and at least on two successive nights starting immediately. It was also agreed that someone other than Julia Zoren would issue the official statement.

Both Mike Millan and Dr. Rolland Dawson agreed to the retraction statement and apology. The prerecorded statements were presented by Mike himself on Thursday and Friday nights. After Wednesday's newscast, Julia Zoren was released by KSIR Channel 33 and Steve Wickershire, when asked, referred to her as a free agent.

Although the retraction statement and apology were intended to correct the misconceptions created by the KSIR newscast, it was uncertain that they did. As Drew was heard to say, "You can glue the pieces of a damaged reputation back together, but it will never be the same—it will always be damaged." It was still problematic that Rolland would receive a fair trial in El Paso County. Both Drew and Lino felt he couldn't.

Sea of Desperation

With all the adverse publicity and a decline in his production at the clinic, it was only a matter of time before Dawson, Tagert & McKinnin Orthopedic Services, LLC voted to expel Rolland from the LLC and buy him out in accordance with the provisions of the LLC's operating agreement. However, because he was the original founder of the clinic, he was given an option to voluntarily disassociate, which he agreed to do. His disassociation would be effective at midnight on November 30. The clinic would thereafter be known as Tagert & McKinnin Orthopedic Services, LLC.

Having been an orthopedic surgeon for over twenty years and the son and grandson of orthopedic surgeons, the disassociation from the clinic he founded was more than Rolland could handle. His house of cards had been tumbling down now for the past sixty-five days and at noon on the sixty-sixth day: November 17, when he failed to emerge from his office to attend a meeting with the clinic's attorney and the other members, his staff became concerned. When Lynnette Castles, the clinic's receptionist, knocked on the door and there was no response, she used a pass key to gain admittance. There lying on a leather couch with an empty bottle of Trazadone and water glass turned on its side was a comatose Dr. Rolland J. Dawson.

Rolland was rushed to the ICU in the hospital where he was known only too well. There his stomach was pumped, and he was placed in a special ward and put on suicide watch. It would be days before he realized what he had done, and Rolland would never remember intentionally trying to end his life. He told his parents when they arrived that even though he had reached the deep depths of despair and desperation he had not consciously willed his demise. He said that before he would do such a thing he would say his good-byes and make peace with the Lord.

It was another several days before he could have visitors other than family, and even then that was restricted. Although both Drew and Lino came to visit, only one was allowed in at a time. Lino was the first to go in and then Drew. Drew couldn't bear to look into the eyes of the man whom he had pushed overboard into the sea of desperation.

Drew had hoped that Rolland would be acquitted, and then he wouldn't have to reveal the great nightmare. Drew hadn't counted on Rolland's life being irrevocably destroyed. Even if he revealed his deep, dark secret now, it might be too late. In any event, it would just be a tradeoff: Rolland's vindication for Drew's head on a platter and untold heartache for the whole Quinlin clan. Drew's life was already ruined, even if it was not visible to anyone else, and it would never be the same. What about those other innocent lives? If Rolland didn't recover, then he was not trading lives; he was only condemning to despair, the same fate as Rolland's, Missy, Molly, Karen, Kevin, his parents, loved ones, and friends. If he could just trade his life for theirs and Rolland's, he would do it in a heartbeat. Now all he could do was pray for Rolland's restoration. He thought of the utilitarian approach he taught his students in his ethics classes: the greatest good for the greatest number. At least that was the rationale for his procrastination in not turning the windmill right side up at this time.

Rolland had been diagnosed with having Major Depression Disorder (MDD). His psychiatrist, golfing partner, and best friend, Dr. Hans Bookerton, said that this had been brought on by the onslaught of negative events, hopelessness, helplessness, frustration, guilt, regret, anger, anxiety, self-hatred, disgust, and paranoia.

So deep was the sea of desperation that he became agoraphobic (feared being in public places), anhedonic (was unable to express pleasure), and psychotic (had lost contact with reality). In other words, Rolland had hit rock bottom, and there was nowhere for him to go but up.

Many experts in the mental health field, some he had known for years, formed a support group that would reverse the trend that had pervaded Rolland's life the past seventy-plus days. Psychologists, psychoanalysts, and psychotherapists (including Dr. Bookerton) would be his constant companions whether he liked it or not. All were determined to extricate him from his self-imposed entombment.

Drew was included in Rolland's list of rescuers. Drew liked to quote from Rickard Lovelace and, when he thought of Rolland's self-imposed exile, thought of the following verse:

> Stone walls do not a prison make
> Nor iron bars a cage;
> Minds innocent and quiet take
> That for an hermitage;
> If I have freedom in my love,
> And in my soul am free;
> Angels alone, that soar above,
> Enjoy such liberty.

Drew himself was a prisoner. He was imprisoned within his soul. Not just because of the great nightmare but because of the great injustice he had perpetrated on Rolland. The only way he himself would ever be extricated, and then not completely, would be by extricating Rolland. The jaws-of-life were in his hands, and it was within his grasp to unlock the doors of liberation.

On Monday of Thanksgiving week, Rolland and his mother and father came by the office on their way to Boston, where Rolland would spend Thanksgiving and Christmas with them and be with friends and family. He would be gone five weeks on doctor's orders. He would be stopping by the pharmacy for a two-month supply of antidepressants. With the district attorney and the bondsman both having agreed to Rolland's out of state travel, it was approved by the court.

Drew and Lino had greeted Rolland and his parents with heartfelt embraces, which were just as enthusiastically reciprocated. Reuniting the defense team was a solemn and emotional event and sealed a bond between them that would never be broken. Rolland looked better than Drew and Lino had seen him at any prior time. Being with his parents and his failed check-out attempt being perceived as a mandate to stick it out, he boasted of having a new lease on life. He did not appear to be as anxious (actually *frantic* would have been a more descript word).

His psychoanalyst had administered a series of tests. One was a life stress test that weighted certain stresses in his recent past. The accumulated score was measured on a graph starting with no adverse reaction to severe problems. Rolland said "he was way over the top; off the chart completely."

The "death of a spouse" was weighted the highest at one hundred points; other high point getters were being charged with a serious crime, being fired from a job, losing one's livelihood, losing one's reputation, change in living conditions, fear of incarceration, lack of purpose in life, change in sleeping habits, upcoming holidays without a spouse or loved ones, change in social life, change in eating habits, decrease in physical activity, coping with disappointments, and coping with false accusations. All that Rolland needed to break the bank was three hundred points. His score, which he didn't divulge, he admitted was much higher than that.

Rolland said he came to grips with his destiny when he was "on the fringe of taking that giant step." He realized that there was a greater power with a greater plan in a greater universe than his own. He said there were three words that his psychotherapist wanted transmitted to his brain: tranquility, serenity, and peace. He said he has been ordered to think only good thoughts and expect only good things.

Rolland's father said he needed to instill into his son the art of forgiving and forgetting. He quoted from Colossians 3:13: "Bear with each other and forgive whatever grievances you may have against one another." He also quoted from the psychologist, William Jones: "The essence of genius is to know what to overlook."

"In other words, never look back."

Drew, who prided himself on his own quotes, was impressed.

Rolland's mother got into the act and quoted Ephesians 4:32: "Be kind and compassionate to one another, forgiving each other, just as in Christ, God forgave you."

"Wow," Lino said, "I didn't know anyone could outdo Drew, our firm's resident allegory guru, but now I've just met two who did." And turning to Drew, he said: "What say you, oh literate one? Don't tell me you've run out of fables."

"Where do you want me to start?" Drew asked. "Let me quote from Matthew Arnold first: 'And we forget because we must and not because we will.' Do you want another one?"

"Oh please," replied Rolland's mother.

"Don't encourage him," Lino said.

"Okay, this one's from the Bible, the book of Philippians, but I don't remember the chapter and verse like you do. 'Forgetting those things which are behind, and reaching forth unto those things which are before, I press toward the mark.'"

"That's a great quote," said Rolland's father.

"I'm surprised you didn't have a Shakespearean quote, genius," Lino taunted.

"I thought you'd never ask," Drew replied. "'Oh! That I were as great/ As is my grief, or lesser than my name,/ Or that I could forget what I have been,/ Or not remember what I must be now.'"

With that, Rolland removed his white handkerchief and waving it above his head said, "Enough already, I surrender."

The laugh that followed was food for the soul. Nothing had been funny for a long, long time; not for Rolland, not for Drew, not for anyone connected with the great nightmare.

It wouldn't be possible, at least for Drew, not to look back, and it wouldn't be probable for Rolland, once he knew the truth, to forgive Drew. Drew would have the ominous task of rectifying the great deception, and the longer he waited the more difficult it would become.

Live by the Sword;
Die by the Sword

On the day following Rolland's suicide attempt, the defense team met to discuss the possibility that Rolland might be incompetent to proceed. The issue, of course, did not become ripe until November 17, when the suicide attempt was made, because Roland's mental condition was not suspect prior to that time.

In Colorado, no person may be tried, sentenced, or executed if such person is incompetent to proceed at any stage of the proceedings. That is to say, if Rolland were found to be mentally incompetent to proceed, the motions hearing and the following proceedings would all be stayed or suspended until he had been restored to competency.

If Dr. Bookerton had made a determination that Rolland did not possess "the appropriate level of understanding necessary for meaningful cooperation with his attorney" and was otherwise incompetent to proceed, the defense would file a motion to suspend the proceedings for that reason. The court would then make a preliminary finding as to whether Rolland was or was not competent to proceed. If the court felt the information was inadequate to make a determination, it could order an independent psychiatric examination. At the hearing held thereon, the court would then make a final determination. The burden of proof, of course, would be on the defense if they were asserting incompetency.

If Rolland was found to be competent, then the proceedings would resume just as if the issue was never raised. If Rolland was found to be incompetent, then he would be committed to the custody of the department of human services, who would then designate the state facility that would be responsible for Rolland's care and psychiatric treatment. There he would remain until he was restored to competency. At such time as he was found to be restored to competency, he would be reinserted into the court proceedings, and his prosecution would resume.

After Rolland and his parents left Drew's office, Drew called and spoke with Dr. Bookerton. Rolland had given Dr. Bookerton permission to speak with Drew and/or Lino. Dr. Bookerton basically gave Rolland a clean bill of health and opined that Rolland was competent to stand trial.

The competency aspect went by the wayside as did any consideration of a not guilty by reason of insanity (NGI) plea. There was no evidence that Rolland was insane at the time of the alleged commission of the offense. Besides, the NGI plea had to be made, if it were to be asserted, at the time of the arraignment.

With regard to the insanity plea, Colorado followed what was called the M'Naghten Rule. The applicable test in Colorado was as follows:

> A person who is so diseased or defective in mind at the time of the commission of the act as to be incapable of distinguishing right from wrong with respect to that act is not accountable. But care should be taken not to confuse such mental disease or defect with moral obliquity, mental depravity, or passion growing out of anger, revenge, hatred,

or other motives, and kindred evil conditions, for when the act is induced by any of these causes the person is accountable to the law.

On this Tuesday of Thanksgiving week, the defense team was finalizing their motions that were due on December 1. Because of the number and complexity of the motions, it was decided to list the proposed motions in the order of importance on a flip chart. Bodean was conscripted to be the scribe. Although their order of importance was debated, the following were listed:

- Motion for bill of particulars
- Motion for change of venue
- Motion to exclude evidence
- Motion to suppress statements and evidence
- Motion to exclude public and media from pretrial hearings
- Motion for restrictive orders
- Motion to permit view of premises
- Motion for additional discovery
- Motion for disclosure of felony convictions
- Motion to permit polygraph results

The defense team, minus their star player, then proceeded to address each motion in the order presented.

The motion for bill of particulars was the *first* to be discussed. Requiring the DA to specify the exact time of death and exactly how Rolland was alleged to have killed Joy was critical in establishing alibi and in establishing defense's accidental death theory.

The motion required the DA to specify and provide to the defense the exact date and time of the alleged offense and, the precise manner in which the offense charged was alleged to have been committed.

"The county coroner," Drew ventured, "has established the time of death at 4:30 p.m. Rolland didn't arrive at the Dawson Chalet until 7:15 p.m. If those times can be proven, then there is no way Rolland could have caused his wife's death accidentally or otherwise." Drew lamented the fact, however, that Rolland's neighbors, the Andersons and the Staves, hadn't seen Rolland or his car during those critical times.

Bodean said he had interviewed Gary and Ann Anderson and Dan and Lynn Staves and they had confirmed that the Dawsons infrequently parked in the driveway and normally parked in their triple-car garage. They didn't see him come or go, which was not unusual, and didn't know he had come home sick that afternoon, or they would have checked in on him. The houses sat on multi-acre lots that were fenced and arranged for privacy. There were no busybodies in the neighborhood. All were too absorbed with their own lives, and none had the proclivity to keep track of what everyone else was doing. "In other words," Bodean said, "they can neither confirm nor deny the times Rolland came and went that afternoon and evening."

"We," Drew said, "nonetheless will still file Rolland's notice of alibi unless somehow Dr. Mendoza changes the time of death. Even though we have no corroboration, Rolland was home sick with the flu from approximately 1:00 p.m. on September 12 until 7:00 p.m. when he left to check on Joy. He didn't arrive at the scene until 7:15 p.m."

Dr. Mendoza had ruled out an accidental death and attributed the trauma that caused Joy's death to force inconsistent with a fall. Dr. Renning, on the other hand, had opined that the head injury was consistent with an accidental fall. All agreed the bill of particulars provided by the DA would not be inconsistent with Dr. Mendoza's and the prosecution's pathologist, Dr. Bellamy's, conclusions. The jury would be required to choose between the three competing determinations. If they believed Dr. Renning, Rolland in all likelihood would be acquitted. Dr. Bellamy might be the swing vote, they speculated. His opinion, however, seemed for the most part to match that of Dr. Mendoza.

The motion for change of venue was the *second* to be discussed. Drew said that that might be the most critical motion of all and would probably be granted in light of the intense and widespread adverse publicity that the media had generated.

The grounds averred in seeking to have the location or place of trial transferred from El Paso County to a neutral county, were listed as follows:

Defendant could not receive a fair, impartial, and expeditious trial in El Paso County, as guaranteed by the Constitution of the United States and the Constitution of the State of Colorado.

The citizens of El Paso County have been prejudiced against defendant because of adverse pretrial publicity. The defense would reference the aforesaid prejudice by the dozen affidavits they would attach that Bodean had obtained.

The pretrial publicity, consisting of news releases, radio and/ or television broadcasts were massive, pervasive, and prejudicial. They would attach a summary of the newspaper headlines, clippings from the two daily newspapers together with photographs and a transcript of the KSIR Channel 33 newscast. They were considering offering the film of the Julia Zoren telecast and the qualified retraction and apology. The film was certainly the best evidence.

The twelve affidavits followed basically the same format. Each affiant, under oath, deposed and said:

    CARROLL MULTZ

He/she was a resident and citizen of the County of El Paso, State of Colorado; he/she was over the age of eighteen years and otherwise qualified to serve as a juror; he/she has resided in the county from the time of Joy's death up to the present time; he/she is a regular subscriber to either or both the *Colorado Springs Times Herald* and the *Colorado Springs Star* both local newspapers with a county-wide circulation; he/she reads the newspapers every day and has read numerous accounts in one or both of the aforesaid newspapers purporting to state facts implicating Dr. Rolland J. Dawson; and, he/she has watched television programming and newscasts purporting to state facts implicating Dr. Rolland J. Dawson including the Julia Zoren telecast at 10:00 p.m. on November 11, 2008, entitled "Death of Doctor's Wife Not Isolated Incident."

From the print and electronic accounts, he/she is of the impression that Dr. Rolland J. Dawson has violated the criminal laws of the State of Colorado; it would be difficult if not impossible to erase such impressions from his/her mind if called as a juror and even if instructed by the judge to do so; the aforesaid publicity for the most part has been adverse to Dr. Rolland J. Dawson; and, he/she is prejudiced against Dr. Rolland J. Dawson as a result of the foregoing.

His/her opinions and prejudice is shared by a majority of the citizens of El Paso County with whom he/she visits and speaks; the matters involving Dr. Rolland J. Dawson, as aforesaid, have been the topic of conversation in the community; he/she does not feel Dr. Rolland J. Dawson could or would receive a fair, impartial, and expeditious trial in El Paso County as a result of the pretrial publicity; such publicity was extensive in quantity and in dissemination and distribution in El Paso County; and such publicity was and is prejudicial to Dr. Rolland J. Dawson.

"Did the qualified retraction and apology nullify the sting of the Julia Zoren newscast?" Bodean asked.

"Definitely not!" Lino said. "Telling the viewer and listener to disregard the previous broadcast would be like trying to unring a bell. It's just not possible."

"I agree with Lino," Drew added. "I think the jury pool is tainted and it's impossible to rehabilitate their thinking once they've made up their minds. They're already walking into court thinking, *Where there's smoke, there's fire*. In other words, they feel the district attorney's office wouldn't be bringing criminal charges against Rolland unless he was guilty."

The defense team, it was obvious, were not functioning well without their star player. Rolland's attempt on his life and now his absence made his defense more mechanical, abstract, and problematic. Somehow their heart was more with Rolland than in preparing his defense.

Trying to bolster morale, Lino said, "I think our motion for change of venue will be granted. I wouldn't be surprised if the DA didn't oppose it. Neither Dayton nor the Beas want to spend the time, energy, and expense on a trial that will just be reversed by the 'Supremes.'"

Drew agreed. "The Beas takes pride in never having been reversed. Rolland's Sixth Amendment rights certainly have been compromised by the demonstrations and all the adverse publicity Rolland's case has generated. The Colorado Supreme Court seems to go out of its way to make sure an accused's constitutional rights are safeguarded."

Bodean asked the two where the case would likely be tried if the motion were granted. "I can't imagine it being transferred to Teller County," he said.

"It could be Denver or Pueblo," Drew responded. "Either probably would be better than here. Denver would be the least tainted and, therefore, is preferable."

The motion to exclude evidence was the *third* to be discussed. Bodean asked if it was necessary to file the motion to exclude evidence. "The prior sexual harassment civil suit has absolutely no bearing on the case, and the DA's office certainly wouldn't risk reversible error by trying to get that into evidence, would they?"

"Let me answer that," Lino said. "The prosecution can introduce evidence of other acts of a defendant only to show a common plan, scheme, design, *modus operandi*, motive, opportunity, intent, or absence of mistake or accident. Or it could be offered in rebuttal, if we introduce evidence of Rolland's good character. And we don't intend to do that. The answer to your question is no; anything dealing with the sexual harassment of Carla is absolutely inadmissible. However, so that it is not even proffered, it needs to be eliminated before we even reach trial."

"We don't want to have our resources taxed, not to mention our minds," Drew said. "We need to, as Lino pointed out, eliminate any diversions in advance. At least this way, we will find out if the prosecution intends to pursue it, and I can't imagine they will."

Lino then added, "The statement attributed to Rolland of knowing how to get rid of his wife and 'make it look like an accident' is more problematic. Drew and I disagree on whether that is admissible. Drew thinks it is too remote in point of time and the product of recent fabrication. I feel it is admissible subject to being challenged on cross-examination. However, we both agree the Beas will admit it."

"Our motion to exclude evidence," Drew added, "not only targets the possible sexual harassment connection and the statements allegedly made to the Delajures but that portion of the autopsy referencing the discovery of a 'fetus.' Such evidence is not germane to the issues in the case in any respect and would only tend to inflame the minds of the jurors. It's probative effect would be outweighed by its prejudicial effect. Therefore, I think that portion of our motion excluding reference to the fetus will be granted along with exclusion of the sexual harassment reference. The statements allegedly made to the Delajures was more than two years before Joy's death and I think stale. However, like Lino, I don't think the Beas will rule in our favor on that one."

The motion to suppress statements and evidence was the *fourth* to be discussed. "By the way," Drew said, "the evidence and statements we are seeking to suppress are the shirt and buttons and Rolland's admission that the shirt was his. The only evidence of a physical nature tying Rolland to Joy's death is the shirt. And the only evidence that it was Rolland's shirt is his own statement."

"The sheriff's deputies pretty much covered their tails," Lino said. "Rolland was not 'in custody' at the time he summoned them to the scene, and, until they found the shirt which Rolland said was his, Rolland was not a suspect. In fact, even after they found the hair and blood spot on the fireplace, there was no evidence of foul play. It was only after the potential shirt connection did one of the deputies leave the room and call his commander. When he came back, few questions were asked. Rolland was not taken into custody, and, in fact, he called his brother-in-law attorney, Troy Campbell."

"Our contention," Drew countered, "is that the sheriff's deputies didn't have permission to search the room where the shirt was found and, even though the shirt may have been in plain view, it was not even suspected of being in any way involved in or connected to Joy's death until it was wrongfully examined. Since the sheriff's deputies neither had a search warrant nor permission, the search was unlawful as well. Since it was the fruit of an unlawful search, it is inadmissible in evidence and should be suppressed."

When Lino started to interrupt, Drew said, "Let me finish. After they found the torn shirt, they focused in on Rolland. He became a potential suspect if the shirt was his. That's evident from the offense report because after his admission, one of the deputies left the room to call his commander. Their whole tone and demeanor changed. Even then, they didn't advise Rolland of his rights, and though the succeeding questions were sparse, they continued asking questions. Rolland's admission and succeeding responses should be suppressed."

"As you know," Lino said, "Rolland was not under arrest; he was not in custody. That is to say, his freedom of movement was not curtailed in any significant way, and therefore the deputies were not required to advise him of his rights. Not only could he leave, he did leave. He was not arrested or taken into custody until days later. Remember, I'm on Rolland's side, and as much as I hate to admit it, the law is not on our side."

Bodean said, "For whatever its worth, I agree with Lino. By taking or accompanying the deputies to the place where Joy's body was discovered was, what I was taught, implied consent. Rolland took them through the back door, through the kitchen where the shirt was hanging on a chair in plain view. He could have objected or refused to answer their questions about the shirt, but he didn't. Since he could come and go as he wished, there's no way he could be deemed to have been 'in custody' so as to invoke the requirement that he be read his right to remain silent and so on. The investigation hadn't really focused on him, and once it had, they asked questions the answers to which they must have deemed inconsequential because they were not included in their report."

"The police academy taught you well, my son," Lino said, complimenting Bodean, who had been a cop in his "previous life."

Drew admitted he didn't have any false expectation that the motion would be granted as to either the shirt or Rolland's admission. But, in the event of a conviction, Drew said, they needed to preserve the record for appeal anyway.

The motion to exclude the public and the media from pretrial hearings was the *fifth* to be discussed. "The whole purpose of excluding evidence of Rolland's sexual harassment case, termination of Joy's pregnancy by her death, and the statements Carla and Pierre Delajure say Rolland made about knowing how to get rid of his wife so as to make it look like an accident are so that evidence, if suppressed or restricted, doesn't reach the jury," Drew said.

Drew then added, "That's the purpose of *in camera* hearings. By closing the pretrial hearings to the public and the media, or at least certain phases thereof, there is little likelihood prospective jurors will be exposed to evidence that's been predetermined to be inadmissible. In other words, the media, for example, can't print something they haven't heard. Whatever the media obtain legally, normally they can print or broadcast."

"Doesn't the judge have the power," Bodean asked, "to close judicial proceedings to both the public and the press if it might compromise a defendant's right to a fair trial? At least that's what we were taught at the police academy when I was on the other side."

Lino offered to field Bodean's question. "Pretrial matters such as motions are considered public record and 'presumptively' open to inspection by the public and the press. Hearings on those motions similarly are 'presumptively' open to the public and the press. That means that access must be afforded to the public and the press unless it can be shown that there is 'substantial probability of harm to a defendant's right to a fair trial.'

"The United States Supreme Court has made it clear that a motions hearing and the like normally must be open to the public and the press if that type of hearing has traditionally been open and access will play a positive role in the judicial process.

"That having been said, when a defendant seeks closure, as in our case, he or she has an uphill battle. It can be done, but the defendant must show that there is an overriding interest to protect such as the right to a fair trial and that there is a 'substantial probability' that that interest would be harmed if the proceedings are not closed.

"That's only the beginning of overcoming the hurdle. If the court finds that there are trial alternatives that will cure the harm such as *voir dire*, change of venue, and admonitions to the jury, it will deny a defendant's request for closure. The latter would be considered least drastic measures."

"To phrase it differently," Lino continued, "when it comes to resolving the conflict between the media's First Amendment right to a free press and the defendant's Sixth Amendment right to a fair trial, the courts will bend over backwards to find a compromise solution. Closure is only a matter of last resort. And, if the court grants the request for closure, it will not necessarily be to the whole hearing or motion but only to those portions compromising defendant's right to a fair trial."

"The decision of the trial judge," Drew interjected, "is subject to close scrutiny by the appellate courts, however, so that in the event of an appeal by the party against whom the judge ruled, the appellate courts will have something to review. For that reason, 'a closure order' must fully articulate the alternatives to closure and the reasons why the alternatives would not adequately protect the defendant's rights."

"So the most that would be closed to the public and press," Bodean summarized, "is evidence relating to the sexual harassment suit, the 'death' of the fetus, and perhaps the alleged statements made by Rolland to the Delajures."

"Maybe that part of the motion relating to the admittance of the shirt and Roland's admission of ownership would be included as well," Lino responded.

Noticing that Bodean still had a puzzled look on his face, Lino asked, "Why are you looking at me funny?"

"Hasn't the jury already been exposed to what we're trying to keep from them?" Bodean asked.

"What do you mean?" Lino asked.

"Well, they already know Joy was pregnant when she died. They already have access to the court records of the sexual harassment trial. And the Julia Zoren newscast on Channel 33 pretty much broadcast for the world to see what the protestors had printed on their signage as well as the Delajures' publication of Rolland's boasting of being able to get rid of his wife and making it look like an accident."

"Bodean," said Lino, "you make a persuasive argument, and that is probably what the Beas will say in denying our motion. 'The cat is already out of the bag.'"

"Our motion for a gag order may be a better alternative," Drew volunteered. "In fact that's the next motion on our list."

"Before we go there," Lino interjected, "what do you all think of seeking closure during the jury selection process?"

"Where are you going with that?" Drew wanted to know.

"Well," said Lino, "because of the intense and widespread pretrial publicity and the perceived public opinion against Rolland, the prospective jurors might be less candid in answering our questions during jury selection, especially if the press is present. Remember the defendant's request for closure in the Martha Stewart case in 2004? Her attorneys succeeded in having *voir dire* closed."

"Remember," Drew reminded Lino, "the U.S. Court of Appeals reversed the trial judge's ruling. Besides, if we follow your logic, wouldn't the jury in attempting to comport with public opinion tend to slant their answers so as to be construed anti-Rolland? I thought that is what our law professors called a *non sequitur*."

"You're right," Lino admitted and, turning to Bodean, said, "See why we keep him around? He sometimes has a way of bringing us back to reality."

"Touché," Drew chided. "Is it okay if we continue to the next motion?"

"Of course," Lino said, hanging his head in feigned embarrassment.

The motion for restrictive orders was the *sixth* to be discussed. Drew, since he had the reins, would ride this horse. "I think it would be fair to say we're more concerned about what the media prints and broadcasts than what Dayton and his office makes public or tells the press. Dayton is careful not to generate a reversal by his pretrial or trial statements, but, unfortunately, information prejudicial to the defendant is found in various investigative reports before it even reaches him. The press usually has access to those reports.

"In the Nebraska Press Association case that Lino and I are familiar with, the United States Supreme Court in 1976 set out the guidelines for the courts at all levels to follow in the issuance of restrictive orders or 'gag orders' against the media. In fact, I have a copy of that case in front of me. Basically, it says in terms, Bodean, you or any layman can understand: a gag order aimed at the media is permissible only where the 'gravity of the evil, discounted by its improbability, justifies such an invasion of free speech as is necessary to avoid the damage.'"

"Hey, wait a minute," Bodean objected. "The U.S. Supreme Court insults my intelligence by making it so simplistic. However, since Lino might not understand, please explain it."

Drew continued, "A gag order is deemed to be what we call 'prior restraint.' It is a violation of the free speech requirements of the First Amendment and is, therefore, unconstitutional unless—unless it can be constitutionally justified. And it can be constitutionally justified only if: intense and pervasive publicity will inevitably result, no other alternative measures will mitigate the effects of that publicity, and the gag order will insulate prospective jurors against exposure to such publicity. A gag order is the exception rather than the rule and gag orders, as you know, are issued sparingly.

"I also pulled *Colorado v. Bryant*, a 2004 Colorado Supreme Court case which may help you better understand the current state of the law with respect to restrictive orders. It held, in essence, that a prior restraint (gag order) is constitutional if it: serves to protect a state interest of the 'highest order'; is narrowly tailored to serve that interest; and, is 'necessary to protect against an evil that is great and certain' and that cannot otherwise be protected by less invasive means."

Drew went on to explain: Kobe Bryant was a star Los Angeles Lakers basketball player receiving knee treatment at a Colorado ski lodge. On June 30, 2003, he had a sexual encounter with a nineteen-year-old female employee of the lodge. Bryant claimed it was consensual; his accuser claimed it was rape. The incident was reported to authorities and criminal charges were brought against Bryant. At a pretrial hearing closed to the press and the public, the defense sought to obtain and be allowed to introduce in evidence at trial the sexual history of the accuser. This was opposed by the prosecution under the Colorado rape shield statute. The accuser's identity was also sought to be protected by the prosecution under another Colorado statute.

Prior to the rulings, a transcript containing, among other things, the accuser's name and sexual history was accidentally sent to various news organizations. Upon learning of the mistake, the trial judge issued a gag order prohibiting the news organizations from publishing or revealing the contents of the transcripts and mandating destruction of the transcripts and all copies thereof. The news organizations sought to have the gag order set aside. On July 19, 2004, the Colorado Supreme Court, by a split decision, upheld the gag order.

"The media is still reeling from the decision claiming that the gag order constituted a prior restraint and therefore was an unconstitutional abridgement of the First Amendment right of a free press," Drew said. "Specifically the media argued that they had lawfully obtained truthful information about a matter of public significance and therefore should have been able to publish it. Amazingly, the trial court ultimately allowed the media to publish the contents of the transcripts with the exception of the victim's identity and sexual history and in the end charges against Bryant were dropped at the request of the victim."

The motion to permit view of premises was the *seventh* to be discussed. "Really, this is to obtain an order allowing the jury to view the 'crime scene' although it may be more appropriately labeled the 'accident scene,'" Lino said.

Lino continued, "We allege in our motion that a view of the actual scene of the alleged crime is relevant to the issues presented in the case and is substantive evidence. We also allege that a view of the actual scene will enable the jury to better understand and apply the evidence.

"I think it is critical to our accidental death defense that the jury see that it is more probable than not that Joy tripped on the low hearth that extended out into the room from the fireplace and fell backwards, hitting her head against the jutting stones of the fireplace itself. These photographs Bodean took are great in showing the rise of the hearth but the best evidence would be for the jury to see it and judge it for themselves. In fact, it would not hurt if one or two found themselves tripping over the lip as Dr. Mendoza did."

Drew surmised that Dayton and Terrell would be filing a similar motion as well and if they hadn't already drafted the motion would probably confess the defense's motion. To view the scene was more traditionally a prosecution rather than a defense motion.

Bodean said he had video of the alleged crime scene that might be proffered if the Beas, in an effort to save time and expense, denied their motion.

The motion for additional discovery was the *eighth* to be discussed. Although the defense had filed their original discovery motion in county court it was the usual practice to file one in district court once the case was bound over at the preliminary hearing. Since the DA was already under a continuing duty to provide discovery, this was considered a perfunctory gesture.

The motion for disclosure of felony convictions was the *ninth* to be discussed. Bodean asked Drew and Lino if they had heard back from Terrell regarding whether or not Pierre Delajure had a felony conviction. Lino said when he was at the courthouse on another matter with Terrell that Terrell had mentioned that Pierre was part of the witness protection program as a result of having blown the whistle on his confederates and that that was the reason for his change of name. He said he had not heard back from the feds as to whether he could reveal whether or not Dominique, a.k.a. Pierre, had been convicted of a felony and if so what felony.

"For impeachment purposes," Drew said, "we will need that information. Without Pierre and Carla's testimony, there is no basis for a murder conviction at least certainly not for murder in the first degree."

"The instruction to the jury regarding the felony conviction almost seems to say, 'If a witness has been convicted of a felony, it is likely that he is also a liar.' That would obviously discredit Pierre's testimony. The only problem," Lino continued, "there is still Carla's testimony."

"Who knows," Drew said, "Carla may also be a convicted felon. Our request is for disclosure of felony convictions of all prosecution witnesses, not just Pierre."

They speculated that the DA would file a motion for protective orders to keep from having to blow Pierre's cover and that by hiding behind the United States Federal Witness Protection Program they would be opposing disclosure of Pierre's suspected felony conviction, if any there be.

Since the Colorado rules of criminal procedure required the prosecuting attorney to provide to the defense "any record of any prior criminal convictions," for any witness the prosecution intended to call, Dayton would have no choice. If he called Pierre, then he needed to disclose any felony conviction.

The motion to permit polygraph results was the *last* to be discussed. Bodean wondered about the purpose of filing the motion to permit polygraph results. The courts had not recognized polygraph results as scientifically reliable and had summarily denied the request. "Wasn't that a waste of everyone's time?" Bodean asked.

Both Lino and Drew responded. If polygraphs were not scientifically reliable or recognized then why did the FBI, CBI, and other law enforcement agencies use them? They certainly had been used as a basis of deciding whether or not to file criminal charges or pursue a suspect. Why weren't they reliable as an indicator of innocence as well?

Drew stated that courts change their minds all the time. With the same constitution and everything else being equal, the United States Supreme Court in *Brown v. Board of Education of Topeka* expressly overturned its own precedent, which had upheld the constitutionality of "separate but equal" segregation in *Plessy v. Ferguson*. They had the courage to do it there so why not again and maybe even by the Beas?

Bodean said he wasn't disagreeing with the prevalent use of polygraphs and said if administered properly could provide a useful tool in ascertaining whether someone was telling the truth. He was only questioning the reluctance on the part of the courts to accept them.

Bodean said he did investigations for employers and knew they were used by federal, state, and local governments; various security firms; firms engaged in manufacturing and distributing controlled substances; and businesses investigating internal theft. "If they're unreliable, why do government and private industry go to all that time and expense?"

"There is a spin-off effect," Drew said. "Even though we're not doing it for that purpose and feel it should rightfully be considered by the jury in determining innocence or guilt, the judge will know Rolland passed and so will the district attorney. Up to this point, all that everyone has heard is all the bad things about Rolland. They've not been exposed to the possibility that Rolland may be innocent. Oh, yes, innocent!"

"I'm convinced," Bodean said.

As the defense team minus one put the finishing touches on the ten motions they would have Nicole type, all the exhibits to be attached were organized and segregated according to the motion to which they would be attached. Bodean listed the sixteen headlines that appeared on just the front pages of the local dailies and gave them to Drew to be attached to their motion for change of venue. They consisted of the following:

Local Artist Found Dead
Death of Local Artist under Investigation
Artist's Death Suspicious
Coroner's Report Issued in Death of Artist
Autopsy Ordered by DA in Death of Artist
Pathologist Report: Dead Artist Was Pregnant
Husband Charged in Death of Artist Wife
Doctor Free on Bond in Death of Wife
Doctor Charged with Capital Murder

Doctor Could Receive Death Penalty in Death of Wife
Death of Wife Case Headed for Trial
Doctor Faces Trial in Death of Wife
Memorial Services Held for Slain Artist
Accused's Attorney Gives Eulogy at Dawson Service
Plea Entered in Wife Killing Case
Doctor Arraigned in Murder of Wife

The criminal rules required the defense to certify their list of potential witnesses and defenses and file them with the court as well as to provide a copy thereof to the prosecution. Even though a defendant is not required to testify, Rolland headed the list of defense witnesses. The other potential witnesses were: Dr. Homer Renning, Conrad Jenkins, Gary Anderson, Ann Anderson, Dan Staves, Lynn Staves, and Lannette Castles. Just in case evidence of the sexual harassment connection crept in, Preston Evans and Darren Wheaton were also endorsed.

It was explained to Rolland that if a witness was not listed, he or she would not be allowed to testify. That was true for the prosecution as well. The only exception was rebuttal witnesses.

The certification of defenses really applied to affirmative defenses such as self-defense, defense of third parties, and so on. Because the rules didn't specify *affirmative defenses,* Rolland's *defenses* were listed as follows: not at the scene at or about the time of death; did not cause death directly or indirectly; and death was accidental or if not accidental was caused by someone else.

The next phase of the great nightmare and the great deception would be the motions hearing. This was considered one of the most critical phases because the rulings of the court would be something the defense would have to live with through trial and maybe the rest of Rolland's *life*. This is what speakers at defense trial seminars had reference to when they said: "You live by the sword, and you die by the sword. You live by the rulings on the motions, and you die by the rulings on the motions." Only time would tell whether the defense in the prosecution of the doctor in the death of his wife would live or die by the rulings the Beas would render on its motions.

The First Thanksgiving without Joy

Outside, it was a miserable Colorado Springs wintery day this Thanksgiving. Inside with the warmth of the huge crackling fireplace and the hospitality of the Stephen R. Quinlin family, the hostile weather went unnoticed or at least ignored.

Drew's father and mother, though now in their late sixties, still lived in the palatial estate originally developed by Drew's grandfather, Franklin E. Quinlin, the founder and architect of both the mansion and the forerunner of Quinlin, Devlin & Cummins. The estate consisted of twenty-six acres and sat at the base of Cheyenne Mountain bordering the exclusive Broadmoor complex.

The two-story rose-colored sandstone building with its carriage house and guest cottage looked more like a private boarding school than a residence. And, as one entered through its stately black iron gates supported by the massive sandstone pillars on each side, he felt as though he were indeed entering the grounds of a private boarding school or something of equal importance.

Drew's favorite part of the Quinlin mansion, although he didn't call it that, was the large two-story ornate ballroom with oak floors and paneled walls. It even had a functional built-in organ that his mother played. Beatrice, or "Becky," as she was called, did not look at all like her name implied. Drew's mother was trim and stood all of five feet four inches tall. Two inches of that were her heels. She had a rather angelic face, ingratiating smile, penetrating dark eyes, and a grace reminiscent of Princess Diana. The only thing that hinted of her age was the color of her hair—powder white.

Drew was a momma's boy and actually a daddy's boy as well. Since he had no siblings, Drew was and would continue to be the center of his parent's affection and attention. The heir apparent of the Quinlin dynasty, both at home and at the office, he was their favorite son, as his father used to say with a twinkle.

No different this day. Drew, Missy, Karen, and Molly had spent the night at Grandma and Grandpa Quinlin's home Thanksgiving eve. Thanksgiving was Grandma Quinlin's favorite time to play hostess. She loved to entertain. Only on this special day would the number of guests be restricted by her "short list." Only the "close circle of intimates," as she called them, would share in this national day of Thanksgiving.

Like family and on the guest list were the firm's named partners, Bernard "Bernie" Devlin and wife, Amber; and Edward "Ed" Cummins and wife, Kathy. Lino was a senior partner and had for a number of years been considered a part of the Quinlin inner circle. He, his wife, Tammy, and daughters, Emily, age seventeen, and Kelsey, age fifteen, arrived in time to help Grandma Quinlin.

Although Becky usually had professional help for the Quinlin social events, Thanksgiving was different, and she was the self-appointed "chief cook and bottle washer." But she always had a lot of help with Missy, Amber, Kathy, and Tammy. Karen, Molly, Emily, and Kelsey rounded out the kitchen crew. It was a family affair, and even the men were known to roll up their sleeves on occasion and "do their fair part."

Becky's youngest sister by several years, Abbie, often mistaken for Becky and vice versa, lived across town and spent a lot of time at the Quinlin estate. A spinster, she was Drew's second mother as she often bragged. Drew was as fond of Abbie as she was of him. From childhood days, he could confide in Aunt Abbie and she honored the confidentiality of their discussions. When she arrived and she and Drew hugged and kissed, he for a fleeting second considered pulling her aside and sharing the secret of the great deception. He got cold feet even though the opportunity presented itself later that day. Maybe sometime, but not now.

Drew had been feeling great guilt this holiday, not like the last two Thanksgivings when he looked into Missy's loving eyes seated next to him at Pop's large table knowing that he had been cheating on her. It was different this year. He was visualizing Rolland sharing Thanksgiving with his parents. But for all it was a Thanksgiving without Joy. *When the Dawsons say their Thanksgiving prayer, what will they thank God for?* Drew asked himself.

There were two people Drew missed this holiday season: one was his son, Kevin, a third-year law student at the University of Montana Law School in Missoula, Montana. The other was Joy, whose turquoise eyes he was always staring into even when his eyes were closed. Kevin had called and talked to the family earlier. Joy would not be calling and talking to her family or anyone else this day, thanks to him. If only he could turn back the clock and put Joy back into the holiday season.

Lately, when he thought of Joy, he thought of Rolland. He could not think of one without the other. In his mind, they were inextricably intertwined. They were as much a part of each other as he and Missy. He could not forgive himself for the havoc he had created for Rolland.

Drew had been reading more and more from the Bible each passing day. He had now memorized Matthew 19:4-6: "At the beginning, the Creator made them male and female.... They are no longer two, but one. Therefore what God has joined together, let man not separate."

He had disobeyed God's command at about every level. The more he read the Bible, the more transgressions he uncovered. He revisited the Ten Commandments and recounted the two proscriptions against committing adultery and bearing false witness against his neighbor. He had committed adultery with Joy. By withholding truthful information from Rolland, he was living a lie. And, if the truth were known, he was guilty of theft. He'd stolen Rolland's wife's affection and love "something more valuable than gems." And the other commandment "Thou shalt not kill." That one he didn't want to think about.

It was a tradition for the man of the household to carve the turkey. Drew's father had that honor. Part of the ceremony was the sampling that accompanied the ritual. Drew always wondered if there would be any turkey left to eat with the mashed potatoes and gravy, dressing, multiple vegetable dishes, candied sweet potatoes, cranberry slices, olives, stuffed celery, fruit bowls, and hot homemade rolls with melted butter. Drew also marveled at how everyone always had room to sample the pumpkin, mincemeat, apple, and pecan pies.

It was also tradition for Abbie to be in charge of preparing the Thanksgiving prayer and have copies properly appended to each place setting. The Quinlin family, actual and extended, read the current year's Thanksgiving prayer with reverence and feeling:

Dear heavenly Father,

We gather together this Thanksgiving Day to praise you for who you are, Lord, and to thank you for all you have done for us this year. You are the Creator of life and Father of us all, and we thank you for creating such loving family and friends. You are our Protector, our stronghold and our shield, and we ask you to keep our family, friends, and military safe as we miss being with them this holiday. God, you are our Provider. Jesus, you are the Bread of Life. Holy Spirit, you are the air we breathe. We praise you for bringing us together this day, for providing this beautiful meal for us, for giving us health and life. We ask for your blessing upon us, Lord, as you are the author and perfector of life. We are especially thankful for your mercy upon us, Lord, that Jesus died for our sins so that we might live together forever in heaven.

In the precious name of Jesus Christ our Lord, we pray. Amen

Connecting the Dots

Rolland had called Drew and Lino inquiring if they had a good Thanksgiving. He said it was good to be back in Boston renewing old acquaintances and visiting the old haunts. He and the family had had a good Thanksgiving. Rolland's two sisters and their families had made the holiday all the more special. He missed Colorado Springs and was on the mend.

Drew and Lino now on a speakerphone, filled Rolland in on the latest developments. They had received the DA's bill of particulars. The DA had, as expected, specified the time of death as "approximately 4:30 p.m." and the exact cause of trauma to the head as an "excessive push or use of an unknown blunt object."

"What about our motion for change of venue?" Rolland asked. "Are they still digging in their heals?"

"Not surprisingly," Drew said, "the DA's office is stubbornly opposing our motion. Their brief in opposition contends that such a remedy 'is a drastic measure that does not justify the expense and inconvenience.' Almost mockingly, they assert that any prejudicial publicity 'can be rectified by less drastic measures such as extensive *voir dire* to screen prejudicial jurors, a continuance to allow public sentiment to subside, an admonition to the jury not to rely on anything other than that which is presented in the courtroom and to put out of their minds any preconceived notions they might have, sequestration which will prevent any further prejudicial pretrial publicity, and, possible change of venireman that is, import a jury panel from outside the community where they have not been exposed to any prejudicial pretrial publicity.'"

Rolland laughed out loud after he was told what the DA had offered as possible alternatives to a change of venue. "Is he really that naïve?" Rolland jibbed. "Where are we going to find twelve deprogrammed robots?"

"Dayton just wants twelve people who will be fair and impartial to his side. That's all," Lino said.

Drew added, "If it weren't for all the picketing and all the publicity given to the placardetuers and, of course, Julia Zoren's op-ed, I think it would be a toss-up. As it is, I don't see how Judge Beasley has a choice."

"I don't think the Beas, as you call her, likes men, and certainly not who she perceives to be a wife and baby killer," Rolland said soulfully. "I still shudder when I envision her steely accusatory eyes looking at me with disgust."

"Now you know why we didn't waive a jury," Drew said. "Let us fill you in on the DA's response to our other motions. Dayton has opposed our request for disclosure of felony convictions, at least as it applies to Pierre Delajure. He claims that under the United States Federal Witness Protection Program, he is not authorized to give out that information. Our position, of course, is that Dayton has two choices: either divulge that information or don't call Pierre as a witness."

"It sounds as if Pierre has a felony conviction to me." Lino added, "Otherwise Dayton wouldn't have taken the protective posture that he has and risk not being able to call Pierre at all."

"What about our attempt to keep out the evidence about the sexual harassment suit and the testimony about the fetus?" Rolland asked.

"Dayton confessed that portion of our motion seeking to suppress the harassment evidence," Drew said. "So that's out. But he opposed the suppression of the testimony regarding the termination of the fetus. We don't know what the Beas will do with that."

"That's pretty damaging testimony, isn't it?" Rolland queried.

"Absolutely," Lino responded. "Our position, of course, is that the prejudicial effect far outweighs the probative value. You're not charged with any crime involving the fetus. The inclusion of that evidence is designed only to inflame the minds of the jurors. I think it would be reversible error for the Beas to allow it. I can't understand Dayton wanting to risk a reversal by trying to get it admitted."

"You said not to get my hopes up regarding admission of the polygraph results. Do the two of you still feel that way?"

In unison, both Drew and Lino said yes.

"What about excluding the admission of my ownership of the blue flannel shirt and the shirt itself? I hadn't been advised of my rights, and what evidence is there that there's a connection to Joy's death?"

Lino responded, "Since you were not a suspect and not in custody, your admission as to ownership of the shirt will come in. Since the shirt was torn and the missing buttons found near Joy's body as well as matching fibers on her person, there is a nexus. The jury will be allowed to consider that evidence and give it whatever weight they determine."

"By the way," Drew said, "after we received Dayton's bill of particulars, we filed our notice of alibi stating that at 4:30 p.m., the time of Joy's death, you were not at the scene but at home sick in bed; that you didn't arrive at the scene until approximately 7:15 p.m."

Rolland, hesitating for a long moment, said, "There's something that I keep mulling over in my mind, and for the life of me don't know how it fits into my case. When I arrived at our summer home at 7:15 p.m. and tried to revive Joy, I removed a turquoise necklace from Joy's neck thinking it might be restricting her breathing and stuck it in my pocket. It was one I'd never seen before, and I forgot about it until after I was interviewed by the deputies."

"Was it one that might have been left at your summer place?" Lino asked.

"It looked expensive, and I'm thinking of having it appraised when I return to Colorado Springs. The stones are almost identical to the color of the eyes of the lioness in the painting hanging in Drew's office. If it had been at our summer place, I would have noticed it. I might not have taken any particular note except for the fact that the day of Joy's death was the day of her forty-second birthday."

Drew's face blanched. He began stammering over the speaker phone and choking and immediately left the room. Drew couldn't give her anything in writing, such as a card. He had found the turquoise beads in a jewelry store, and even though they were expensive, they matched her eyes, and when he placed them around her neck, the sparkle in her eyes was more brilliant than even the beads.

After he hung up with Rolland, Lino remembered being with Drew not too many months before when Drew had purchased a necklace just like the one Rolland had described. When Drew returned, Lino asked, "What did you do with the turquoise necklace you purchased?"

Drew, still pale and trying to regain his composure, stammered, "Don't ask!"

Lino really didn't need an answer. He was already connecting the dots.

Rekindling the Fire

Drew and Missy had not had the intimate relationship the last several years that they had grown to crave and relish. Missy told one of her closest friends, Charlotte Ferrington, that during the last two and a half years they had grown apart. She knew it wasn't the seven-year itch because they had been married twenty-three years.

Missy was born Melissa Jean Morton August 29, 1963, in Spokane, Washington. Her father was a geologist, and her mother was a language teacher. Her brother Mark, now a contractor in Coeur D'Alene, Idaho, just across the Washington border, was born in 1965. A sister, Terry, was divorced and living in Tacoma, Washington, with her two teenage sons, Donald, age nineteen, and Tagert, age sixteen. Terry was born in 1967.

Missy's father, Dr. Prescott "Pres" Morton, had been teaching at the University of Montana in Missoula, Montana, and had only recently retired. Her mother, Marlys, taught in the drama department at U of M and was scheduled to retire this coming May.

Missy and Drew met after a college play in which Missy starred during their freshmen year at the University of Colorado. Drew was on the CU golf team when they met, and Missy was eager to learn the game. Drew was tall and athletic, and so was Missy. They were a perfect match and shared fraternity and sorority life together. Missy reminded Drew of "Audrey Hepburn but a few dress sizes bigger." And that's how he described her to his parents before he brought her home during Christmas break of their freshmen year. There was an instant affinity between Missy and Drew's parents. In June of 1983, at the end of their sophomore year, Missy and Drew were married.

Missy was the dark version of Joy. Missy had dark, penetrating eyes and a broad smile. Her pitch-black hair she wore long but usually brushed in a braided bun or ponytail. She looked great in an evening gown, but to Drew, even greater in tight blue jeans. She turned a lot of heads, and Drew always felt like the big man on campus whenever she was at his side.

Kevin was born in 1984, and Drew and Missy had decided he was the only child they were going to have. Karen was a surprise some years later as was Molly. They wouldn't trade any of their children for the world, and their children had pretty much been the center of Drew and Missy's life. That is until a little over two and one-half years ago when Drew got derailed by his high-profile itinerary.

Drew was scheduled to be in Aspen on Thursday, December 11, to appear in district court on a felony disposition. Drew and Missy's favorite sport, next to golfing and tennis, was skiing. Aspen and Steamboat Springs were their two favorite spots. What a great opportunity to mix pleasure with business. Karen and Molly would stay with Drew's parents. For the first time in a long time, Drew and Missy could be alone and attempt to rekindle the fire.

Since Drew would need to be in court first thing Thursday, they would drive up Wednesday afternoon and stay at the

Hotel Jerome, their usual lair. That would give them Friday and Saturday to ski Aspen and maybe Snowmass. They would also have time to eat at their favorite dining spots along and around Galena Street in downtown Aspen. Aspen was a playground for the rich and the famous, and with the average home prices in the millions, they figured they would have to mortgage their home if they stayed more than a few days.

Though the drive to Aspen was just a little over 155 miles, with icy roads and falling snow, they had been on the road for over four hours.

The Hotel Jerome was well known to Drew. He had been introduced to skiing at an early age by his parents and had been on the CU ski team. In fact he had trained for the U.S. Olympic team but because of academic problems was "encouraged" by his father to prioritize his activities in favor of "academic achievement." Instead of a career, skiing remained recreational, and Aspen for the most part was the family's favorite playground and the Hotel Jerome their favorite home away from home.

The Aspen ski tradition remained with Drew, and it became a ritual with Missy, Kevin, Karen, and Molly as well. In fact, when Drew was a prosecuting attorney, most of the conferences and seminars sponsored by the Colorado District Attorney's Association were held in Snowmass just outside Aspen. Periodically, they would be held in his other favorite winter playground, Steamboat Springs.

Drew knew the Hotel Jerome like the back of his hand. He was intrigued by the founder of the hotel, the man responsible for helping put Aspen on the map, Jerome B. Wheeler. Apparently, Jerome was a third cousin of Ralph Waldo Emerson, but his real claim to fame was marrying into the Macy's Department Store family and ending up running the entire operation. Like General Palmer, Jerome had served in the Civil War, and his legacy was his vision and philanthropic and altruistic bent.

With the funds from a silver mine discovery, Jerome built a four-story sandstone hotel in the heart of the city. The Hotel Jerome with all its majesty, where Drew and Missy were now checking in, was opened on Thanksgiving Eve 1889. It had been remodeled and restored many times over the years, but its furnishings and decorations continued to reflect the style of the times.

After Drew and Missy unpacked, settled in and showered, opened the bubbly and toasted, and turned their elegant room into a honeymoon suite, they would embark on a romantic journey whose echo, if recognized, would be heard around the world. Dawn would break with Drew and Missy still entangled in each other's arms—just like old times.

Drew was careful not to wake Missy as he prepared to leave for court. Although he was not due in court until 9:00 a.m., he had arranged to meet at the Pitkin County courthouse first with his client at 8:00 a.m. and then the district attorney at 8:30 a.m.

His client, a public employee for a number of years, had been caught with her hand in the cookie jar to the tune of $10,000. It was an open-and-shut case. There had been a full confession, absolute *Miranda v. Arizona* compliance, no loopholes. Ms. Hickendill would be pleading guilty to the charge of felony embezzlement of public moneys in return for probation, one hundred hours of community service and restitution. It would be a no brainer.

Although he had not had a lot of cases in Pitkin County, he had been a special prosecutor there many years before and on occasion had business in the courthouse. There were two features that distinguished this courthouse from the others with which he was familiar. One was its impressive and ornate cupola, and the other was the silver figure of the Lady of Justice standing on a pedestal above the main entrance.

It wasn't so much what the Lady of Justice had but what she didn't have. Although the traditional Lady of Justice is depicted with a blindfold, this one had *no* blindfold. Instead of administering blind justice, this one was administering justice *with her eyes wide open!*

The Pitkin County courthouse was dedicated in February 1891 at a cost of $77,272. The courthouse was three stories tall with a half story underground. The half story above ground and trim were of peachblow sandstone quarried in the Frying Pan Valley. The remaining two stories were of brick construction. Inside, the fine oak details for the most part had retained their original character. Recent repairs and renovations had made it more functional without compromising its authenticity.

Drew met with Ms. Hickendill, a matronly woman in her midfifties who looked every bit like the local librarian but was in reality a thief. She was prepped; she would do just fine.

Next was the predisposition meeting with the district attorney, Mike Cassidy. Although he was term limited, Mike and Drew's paths had crossed a number of times. Mike had also been a deputy and later a chief deputy before becoming the DA. They had done some seminars together and taught at the police academy in Golden at the same time.

Their reunion would not be the same without reminiscing about their old cases. Since they were on Pitkin County turf, they had to discuss two of the local most notable. Ironically, the two incidents occurred within a period of one year of each other.

In 1975, the notorious Ted Bundy had been arrested, charged, and convicted in the death of a Utah woman. While serving his sentence, he was extradited to the Aspen area to stand trial in the death of a local woman. While using the Pitkin County courthouse law library, he jumped out of a second-story window and escaped. He was later apprehended and placed in what was thought to be a secure facility in Glenwood Springs, located some forty-two miles northwest of Aspen. After sawing through the welds of a metal plate in the ceiling of his cell, he again escaped. Ultimately, he was apprehended, tried, and convicted.

It was no doubt as the result of his improbable escapes that Bundy became known as the serial killer who had nine lives. Drew still shook his head over all the law enforcement blunders and wondered how many young girls' lives would have been spared if law enforcement had just done its job.

The other case, of course, was the 1976 shooting death of champion skier Spider Sabich. Claudine Longet, a former French actress and singer, and ex-wife of singer Andy Williams, had been charged with murder in the second degree, a felony, in Spider's death. At trial, Claudine apparently convinced the jury that the gun had a hair trigger and that the death was an accident, as she was found guilty only of reckless endangerment, a misdemeanor. She was sentenced to serve thirty days in jail.

It was now time for court. Judge Tillman Grevier, a retired district court judge riding the circuit, handled the disposition on special assignment. Everything went according to the script, and Drew was soon back with Missy.

When he arrived at the Hotel Jerome, Missy was in the lobby waiting to greet him. With a steaming hot cup of black coffee in one hand and the day's issue of the *Denver Post* folded in the other, she greeted Drew with an inviting kiss.

"Hello, darling," she said in a tone he had not heard in way too long. "Why didn't you wake me?"

"Snuggles," Drew said, calling Missy by a name coined before they were married and not used for a while. "I didn't want to invade your solitude. Since you were in la-la land, and presumably still dreaming of me, I didn't want to pervade your paradisiacal slumber."

Missy set the coffee and paper on the counter as Drew set down his briefcase and the two hugged and didn't seem to want to let go. They might have stood there longer had it not been for the hotel clerk. "Mr. Quinlin, you have a telephone call. You can take it at the front desk if you wish."

The half door was open, and Drew took the call that turned out to be from Mike Cassidy, the prosecutor in the case he just finished. Mike said he and his wife, Kaitlyn, whom Drew and Missy had met, wanted them to be their guests that evening at the Wheeler Opera House. Mike and Kaitlyn had two extra tickets, and Mike apologized for not thinking of it sooner. While Mike articulated the proposition, Drew repeated it so Missy could hear. Before Drew could ask, Missy enthusiastically nodded her affirmation.

Drew and Missy thought they might get in at least a half day of skiing. They thought they would ski Buttermilk this day, but with the theater offer (and acceptance) and the shortened day, they aborted the idea. Instead, they would have brunch at Poppycock's, a restaurant that served breakfast all day that was located not far away on East Cooper Avenue.

Breakfast was Drew's favorite meal, and at home that was the one meal the family enjoyed together. Missy's crepe suzettes were to die for. Hot porridge with melted butter and cinnamon were a close second. Then the traditional breakfast of eggs, bacon, sausage or ham, with hash browns, grits or cornmeal (which Missy's mother called "polenta"); and of course, toast, biscuits, or homemade cinnamon rolls were not too shabby either. Drew's mother and her sister, Abbie, said breakfast was the most important meal of the day and never let him skip it when he was growing up.

Breakfast and dinner were the time for family conversation and exchanging reports of the day. Drew's father also used it as a time to discuss his cases and quiz Drew on what had appeared in the daily news and not just on the sports page. Also, Drew was called upon to give his status report at dinner time concerning his daily chores. His father was a stern taskmaster and exacted full compliance. Excuses for failure were unacceptable.

Drew and Missy had never been to Poppycock's before. It turned out to be a delightful place, and they vowed to return. The old-fashioned oatmeal pancakes and special formula cappuccino together with the doting attention cried out for a heavy tip. What a way to start out this special weekend of reconciliation, they both agreed.

Drew humored Missy by shadowing her as she made her visitation at almost every fashion shop, gift shop, boutique, and anywhere and everywhere that had a functional cash register. They did not return to the hotel empty-handed as would be confirmed by their credit card statement at the end of the month. The beneficiaries of Missy's spending spree were of course Karen, Molly, and Kevin, mom and pop Quinlin, mom and pop Morton, and Missy's best friend and next door neighbor, Charlotte Ferrington. Missy thanked Drew for his unusual patience and promised him a special treat.

Drew and Missy had lunch at the Cantina early afternoon and spent the few hours they had left of the day relaxing and catching up on their reading. Even Drew felt peace these precious hours. He thought about Rolland and prayed the same serenity would encircle his client.

Drew and Missy met Mike and Kaitlyn at Bentley's Bar in the rear of the Wheeler Opera House. They could enjoy happy hour and catching up on the latest before watching Brandi Carlile perform. Missy had her album *The Story*, and all were looking forward to what turned out to be a spectacular performance.

The Wheeler Opera House was located in the heart of Aspen. It was another creation of Jerome B. Wheeler. The same Jerome

B. Wheeler for whom the Hotel Jerome had been named; the same one who was responsible for the Midland Railroad having been built. The opening night of the Wheeler Opera House was April 23, 1889. It was described by the *Aspen Democrat Times* as "the prettiest little structure of its kind between Pueblo and Salt Lake City."

While at the theater, Drew, more out of curiosity than interest, asked Mike about available real estate. Mike mentioned that Prince Bandar, the former Saudi ambassador to the United States, had his modest 56,000-square-foot bungalow on the market. The price tag: a modest $135,000,000. Drew wasn't sure with two teenage daughters to send through school and all that they could afford to purchase it "at least not at this time."

Drew recalled a time some years before when he flew into the Grand Junction Airport and being allowed to stick his head in the door of Prince Bandar's jet parked on the tarmac with three of its uniformed crew awaiting the arrival of the Prince. The jet was similar to Air Force One and had to land and take off at the Grand Junction Airport because the Aspen Airport was too small. The jet was at the ready to fly to Dallas so that the Prince could attend a Dallas Cowboys football game.

While Drew and Mike discussed "important matters," the ladies were engaged in what Drew and Mike teasingly called "lady talk." Missy recounted the last time they were in the Wheeler Opera House. It was to watch a local resident, John Denver, perform in concert. It was right after he wrote one of his songs about his hometown. She couldn't remember whether it was *Aspenglow* or *Starwood in Aspen*. Kaitlyn said her all time John Denver favorite was one he wrote in 1974 "Annie's Song." There was no disagreement there!

With its redundancy of snowfall and being surrounded on three sides by mountains: Red Mountain to the north, Smuggler Mountain to the east, and Aspen Mountain to the south, the Aspen area had been a skiing paradise just waiting to be developed. The Lord had provided the natural resources; now it was up to man to take advantage of it.

On Friday, Drew and Missy skied Aspen Mountain. Finding that the Crystal Palace, one of their favorite dinner theaters, had closed earlier that year, they dined at the Cache-Cache after their day on the slopes. They reminisced about ski days bygone when their single $96 ski pass would have paid for the entire family. Drew remembered his father talking about a 1985 anti-trust case that went all the way to the U.S. Supreme Court, *Aspen Skiing Co. v. Aspen Highlands Skiing Corp.* Apparently, the owner of three of the four major downhill ski areas in Aspen was sued by his smaller competitor for refusing to continue to participate in a jointly offered "all Aspen" six-day lift pass. The "little guy" won because the refusal to cooperate had an anticompetitive effect on the market and was deemed to be a violation of the Sherman Antitrust Act.

On Saturday, they skied Snowmass. Although there were dining spots of note close by, they returned to Aspen and the Hotel Jerome. After shedding ski wear and warming the bones with a steam bath, they ventured down the street to the Steak Pit known for its custom cut steaks, fresh fish, and authentic seafood dishes.

On Sunday, after a brunch at the Hotel Jerome, they made the return journey home. They had left Colorado Springs on Wednesday as Drew and Missy Quinlin, and they left Aspen and returned to Colorado Springs on Sunday, not just in name, but as Mr. and Mrs. Quinlin.

No Joy This Holiday Season

The ground was blanketed with snow as far as the eyes could see. In fact, from the time they left Colorado Springs, Colorado, and landed in Missoula, Montana, they wondered if the creator had run out of the deep rich colors with which to paint the landscape they had enjoyed less than six months before. No fear of not having a white Christmas here.

Pres and Marlys picked them up at the Missoula Airport. Both the home team and the visitors were relieved that the several delays occasioned by the weather had expired and the rumor of cancellation had not materialized. They were sorry to learn that Missy's sister, Terry, and her teenage boys, Don and Tagert, had thought best of the situation and rescheduled their visit until spring. Karen and Molly were particularly disappointed they would not be seeing their cousins.

Not knowing for sure whether they would be spending Christmas with Missy's parents, the usual miscellany of gifts had been shipped in early December. Usually, Christmas was spent in Colorado Springs with Christmas morning being occupied with the discovery, assembly and testing of Santa's gifts and the afternoon with gift exchange and dinner with Drew's parents. With Kevin attending law school at the University of Montana and living with Missy's parents, this would be the second in a row of the Christmases they spent in Missoula.

Kevin was spending Christmas break not law clerking as he had in the past but with a fellow classmate and her family in Spokane, Washington. Kevin had been dating Connie Collins since first enrolling in law school at the U of M, and Kevin and Connie had an announcement they were expected to make when they arrived Christmas Eve.

The Morton's rambling log ranch-style home was located on an eighty-acre tract east of Missoula just outside the city limits. It had a horse set-up with a self-supporting hay meadow. A number of horses were kept in a sheltered corral a short distance from the Morton's home. The six-bedroom home was supplemented by a guest cottage with all the amenities. These were the quarters provided to Kevin while attending law school. Being with his maternal grandparents and being semi-independent was the major part of the lure to the U of M Law School. Having a built-in summer job of caring for his grandparents' champion horses was a childhood dream come true.

As they turned onto a private lane leading to the massive lodge pole arches framing the gate to Morton Ranch, they were struck with awe at the winter wonderland snowscape that unfolded in front of them. Drew could see Joy capturing that scene on canvas with the late sunrays casting their golden hue with the Big Sky blue of Montana heaven dominant overhead.

The Morton Ranch was dotted with clusters of rich green pines burdened but graceful under a heavy blanket of white fluff. Near the front of the Morton home were two huge live pines with Christmas lights all aglow. In the middle of the two was a nativity scene with life-sized figures fashioned out of plywood. The caption on the side of the manger read "Joy to the World." The Mortons had outdone themselves this Christmas as was evident when the Quinlins entered the interior.

The living room was two stories tall with balconies on both sides of the massive moss rock fireplace. Drew's mind took him to a chalet in the Black Forest where he envisioned a similar scene although here there was no limp body of an artist for him to leave behind.

The huge pine positioned indoors was just as impressive as the two standing guard outside. The number of presents at the base of the tree made Drew feel guilty when he thought of the children around depressed regions of the world who would not be opening even a single gift.

Drew was having a rough time reconciling his experiencing joy while thinking of Joy and wondering what Rolland was experiencing this holiday season without joy or Joy. The signage on the manger outside bothered him and was a painful reminder of what the world needed and what he took from this world. It wasn't right for others to suffer for the terrible mistake that he had made. Both his grandfathers had taught him that for every action there was a reaction and for every cause there was an effect. He thus learned at an early age that for every act of indiscretion there was a consequence. And at many a sentencing he had heard the judge say, "You play, you pay." There was always a price to pay. There were no free lunches. He knew there would be a payment that would be exacted of him. He just didn't know when or how much. There was judgment that awaited him.

While Drew was pondering his fate, he felt a tap on the shoulder.

"Here, let me help you with that," he heard. Turning around, Drew peered into the eyes of his brother-in-law, Mark, Missy's younger brother, who was reaching for one of the bags with which Drew was struggling.

"I didn't know they had bell captains here," Drew said as the two shook hands, slapping each other on the shoulder with their free hands.

Mark led Drew into the large bedroom that would be Missy and Drew's for the next several days. Missy and Mark's wife, Mary Jo, had already found each other as had Karen and Molly. Warm exchanges, hugs, and giggles all around.

Of course, favorite Uncle Mark diverted the attention of Karen and Molly. The girls loved their uncle Mark, and he loved them. Mark and Mary Jo had no children, much to their consternation, much like Rolland and Joy. Karen and Molly were the daughters that Mark and Mary Jo never had and Missy's sister's two sons, Don and Tagert, were the sons that Mark and Mary Jo never had. It was unfortunate that Terry and the boys wouldn't be here this Christmas.

Christmas Eve brought the merriment that more than met expectations. It was all the more special with the announcement that accompanied the arrival of Kevin and Connie. The family had met Connie on several occasions and would welcome her with open arms as their daughter-in-law. In fact, they felt Kevin was fortunate to have captured such a prize. The diamond she sported was every bit as large as Missy's. Kevin must have cashed in his childhood bonds and dipped into his college fund. Connie was radiant, and Kevin seemed very pleased with himself having Connie at his side. Karen and Molly had already adopted Connie as their big sister.

With so many of their favorites around, Karen and Molly were like honey bees going from one flower to the next. Drew was immersed in the love and joy of this blessed Christmas season relishing the excitement of the events from which lasting memories would be built. Not far from his mind, however, would be a different type of joy, a Joy who would not be found in this holiday season.

Setting the motions hearing the Monday after Christmas was not such a great idea after all, Drew thought as his plane was preparing to land in Colorado Springs. It would have been nice for Missy, the girls, and him to have stayed in Missoula at least through the weekend.

Drew's parents met Missy, the girls, and him at the airport after a short delay. The Quinlins would have their family Christmas celebration on Sunday. However, on Saturday, Drew would be meeting with the defense team, including Rolland, in preparation for the motions hearing. Fortunately, what little that needed to be done after he left for Montana was attended to by Lino and Bodean.

A New Day's Dawning

Drew had convinced himself that the great nightmare was something that could be swept under the carpet if not forever for the moment at least. If Rolland were acquitted, the dirt need never be exposed. He would challenge his legal talents to the outer limits and beyond in seeking justice for his client. He had no "Plan B" and prayed none would be needed.

It was the kind of day the natives wished they lived in the Bahamas. There was nothing tropical or weather friendly about this first Saturday after Christmas. You could pick your tee time at the Kissing Camels Golf Course this day.

When Rolland arrived, he had to be let in the door of Quinlin, Devlin & Cummins. The other members were in the reception area comfortably seated in the leather chairs sipping piping hot coffee and partaking in the assortment of pastries Bodean had graciously provided. They were waiting for the man of the hour, the man whose fate was finally in their hands.

It was almost a makeover they all thought as Rolland entered. No, it *was* a makeover. Rolland had shaved his graying facial hair, had shed his glasses in favor of contacts, and sported a prep school haircut. He was almost unrecognizable in his sporty attire and resembled the *after* photograph in a weight loss commercial. It was obvious he had been lifting weights and that was the first the other members of the defense team had seen him walk with his chest out and shoulders back.

"You must be Dr. Dawson's nephew," Lino said, extending his right hand. The others just stood and stared.

Rolland ignored the hand and instead gave Lino a robust hug and proceeded to do the same with Drew and Bodean.

"Welcome back," Drew said. "We missed you."

"I missed you all too," Rolland replied.

"We're not going to ask you how you've been," Lino said. "We can see for ourselves you've been faring fairly well."

"Underneath my boorish facade was a man waiting to be set free. I have played the part orchestrated by my father and by my mother to some extent and have spent my whole life being a pleaser. I've never really been me. It has taken professional help to find a way to finally set the captive free.

"Being charged in Joy's death really leaves me with two choices. I can either give up and surrender, as I had made up my mind to do, and be a quitter. Or I can be my own man and face head-on the assault I know is coming. I've never been a quitter, and the only way I can beat the odds is to fight the good fight."

Still, neither Drew, Lino, nor Bodean said anything.

"There is a stronger force than me. By putting my fate in God's hands, I know he will champion my cause. 'If God is with me, who can be against me.' With his help, through the three of you, I know I will succeed. He is a 'just' God, and I know to borrow your mantra, 'justice will ultimately prevail.'"

Drew didn't doubt for a minute that justice would ultimately prevail, but his quandary was "in what form and when?"

Rolland set the tone for the motions prep that was to follow. His attitude was contagious before, and it was even more contagious now. The defense team was firmly headed in the right direction.

The hiatus in the proceedings was proving to be a productive respite. The time with family and the inspirational effect of Christmas had put everything in perspective. They had a challenge to face and Rolland's destiny, with a little help from above, was in their hands.

Rolland then produced three small obviously jeweler-wrapped boxes and presented one to each of the three who were still reeling from Rolland's miraculous transformation. "A belated merry Christmas," he said, as each was handed and opened his respective gift.

It was not long before they donned their respective solid gold chain and medal of the Good Shepherd, the ultimate executor of justice, that would henceforth serve as a reminder of the source of the strength and power from which they would draw as they embarked upon the journey of court battles that were beyond even their wildest imaginations.

Following the order presented in Rolland's absence in preparation of the pretrial motions, the defense team prodigiously proceeded.

The bill of particulars was moot in-as-much as the prosecution had specified or particularized the exact time the offense was alleged to have been committed and, as well as they could, the manner in which death occurred. As a result, the defense had filed their notice of intent to assert alibi as a defense. Rolland couldn't have committed the offense because he was at a different location. Unfortunately, it could not be corroborated by anyone else's testimony.

The motion for change of venue was a defense motion, and therefore, the defense had the burden of convincing the court that Rolland could not receive a fair trial in El Paso County because of the prejudicial impact of the pretrial publicity. The defense would also have to dispel the myth advanced by the prosecution that certain trial-level remedies could reduce the impact without having to change the place of trial.

The defense team had twelve affidavits to support their contention that the pretrial publicity had compromised Rolland's right to receive a fair trial as guaranteed by the Sixth Amendment to the United States Constitution. In addition, all twelve had been subpoenaed to appear at the motions hearing so that the defense could amplify upon their assertions and make them available for questioning by the court and the prosecution.

All were convinced the requisite pattern of prejudice could easily be established by the massive and persuasive newspaper, radio, and television coverage of the case beginning with Rolland's arrest. The challenge, however, was to convince the court that not only did the potential jurors have a preconceived notion of guilt but that such opinions could not be set aside despite their good intentions to the contrary and the judge's admonition to set aside their preconceptions and judge the case solely on the basis of the evidence presented at trial.

The other trial-level remedies the defense team discussed that were options were change of veniremen, that is import jurors from an untainted and under-exposed locale; continuance, that is continue the trial to some future date when the locals had forgotten about the case; and sequestration of the jurors once they were selected so as to keep them in seclusion and insulated from further out-of-court publicity.

CARROLL MULTZ

Change of venireman was certainly the next best option to a change of venue they agreed. However, the jury would still be exposed to trial publicity unless they were locked up and shielded from the print and broadcast media. A continuance, they felt, could not erase their strong and deep impressions and, even if dimmed by time, would be revived by their exposure to the case. The jurors would not be able to sort out what they had heard outside the courtroom from what they heard at trial.

Sequestration of witnesses might prevent the jurors selected from hearing the current views regarding the trial, but the defense team wondered how the jurors could erase from their minds the dominant influence of the knowledge that had been acquired outside the courtroom as a result of the intensive and wide-spread pretrial publicity.

Drew would be presenting three landmark cases handed down by the United States Supreme Court in the 1960s. He was also prepared to make the economic argument that it would be cheaper in the long run to change the location of trial now than to have a conviction reversed because of a violation of Rolland's Sixth Amendment rights to a fair trial in not granting his motion.

The prosecution had already confessed that part of the defense's motion to exclude evidence pertaining to the prior sexual harassment civil suit. Lino speculated that the prosecution had done so to avoid a reversal in the event of a conviction and, even if they hadn't, the Beas, would in all likelihood, be ruling against its admissibility.

Lino said he would be handling the motion to exclude evidence. The defense, he said, would be seeking to exclude evidence pertaining to discovery of the fetus and the statements allegedly made by Rolland to the Delajures. He felt the defense had a good chance of succeeding on exclusion of testimony regarding the fetus but not with regard to the statements made to the Delajures. Nonetheless, he would be arguing that the statements were recent fabrication and, therefore, not competent evidence. He would also argue that the statements, if made, were stale and, therefore, too remote in point of time from utterance to date of death.

Lino pointed out that he would also be handling the motion to suppress statements and evidence. This motion was somewhat similar to the motion to exclude evidence but was directed at evidence allegedly obtained as a result of police misconduct. He was not confident, nor was Drew that the defense would succeed in having suppressed the blue flannel shirt, cloth fragments, and buttons or Rolland's statement that the shirt was his.

Drew then discussed the next two motions that were on their list: motion to exclude the public and media from pretrial hearings and motion for restrictive orders. He explained to Rolland that these motions would be made in the disjunctive and at the beginning of the motions hearing.

"The very first thing we will do on Monday is ask Judge Beasley to exclude the public and the media from at least those portions of the hearing dealing with the exclusion and suppression of statements and evidence. Specifically, we are targeting the evidence of an unborn child, Rolland's alleged statements to the Delajures, his statements regarding the shirt and admission of the shirt itself.

"Should we succeed in having that evidence excluded or suppressed, it will all have been in vain if such evidence is subsequently publicized by the media. Also, if the public is allowed to attend the evidentiary hearing, they will have been exposed to evidence that is to be excluded and you know how fast gossip spreads in high profile cases such as this."

"It will spread like wildfire," Bodean commented. "Although," he added, "much of what may be suppressed has already been printed and broadcast. Isn't the cat pretty much already out of the bag?"

"Rolland, we argued this in your absence," Lino said. "There is no question as Bodean suggests that potential jurors have already been exposed and, in great doses, to what we're trying to keep from them. However, if our motion to change the venue to another county fails, then we need to minimize the sting of exposure by some type of damage control. In other words, we cannot afford any further exposure. And preventing the media from reporting on and the public from hearing further damaging and inadmissible evidence mitigates what we consider inescapable—and that is an unfair trial."

"It is clear," Drew added, "that the only way for you to receive a fair trial is to have the trial transferred to another area. Lino will be trying to convince the court of that, and we're hopeful the judge will agree. However, we can't put all our eggs in one basket and count on that. The district attorney is opposing our motion contending that there are other less drastic options, as he describes it. We think that jurors do try to be fair but that their human frailties would interfere with their ability to set aside their predisposition or allow them to disregard what they have heard outside the courtroom in making a decision. For Dayton and Terrell to suggest that jury selection, for example, would identify biased jurors and weed them out or instructions from the court to set aside their biases would rehabilitate jurors defies all common sense. It is ridiculous!"

"The judge might buy it," Lino interjected. "However, I think for her to deny our motion for change of venue would be reversible error. I can't imagine any appellate court upholding a conviction based on the hostile environment permeating this case."

"They would have to completely disregard the Sixth Amendment," Bodean said, shaking his head.

"I'm confused," Rolland said. "Why would the district attorney chance a reversal by opposing the motion for change of venue when reversal is inevitable and would result in a retrial—

assuming, of course, I am convicted? Does his office need the extra work and expense?"

Drew and Lino began to respond at the same time. Drew motioned to Lino to go ahead.

"Dayton and Terrell are on the proverbial horns of a dilemma," Lino responded. "They have already been publically chastised for not seeking the death penalty in your case and for not filing some type of charge relating to the unborn child. If they don't oppose the motion to change place of trial they will be perceived as having folded or caved in."

"You mean branded as quitters or cowards," Bodean stated.

"I think," Drew said, "Dayton and Terrell are counting on the Beas granting our motion. I think this is their way to shift blame and come off the good guys. Dayton is the consummate politician and, as Lino said, is on the horns of a dilemma. Only, I say that for a different reason. He is damned if he opposes our motion and it is denied because he risks a reversal, and he is damned if he doesn't oppose it and it is granted because that greatly enhances the possibility of an acquittal."

Drew went on to explain that if the media and the public were not excluded from evidentiary or suppression phases of the hearing, the defense would be asking the Beas to issue a gag order or a restrictive order to ban the publication or broadcast by the media of the evidence restricted or suppressed. That was an option that the court had at its disposal.

The only problem, Lino pointed out, was that gag orders flew in the face of the First Amendment right of freedom of speech and freedom of the press.

Drew added that the defense would have to persuade the judge that a gag order was justified because the intense and pervasive prejudicial publicity was inevitable, there was no other reasonable alternative to mitigate its effect and the gag order would effectively attain its intended result that is to keep prejudicial material from reaching prospective or potential jurors. Gag orders were the exception rather than the rule, Lino reminded Rolland.

Rolland was briefed on the remaining motions and wanted clarification on the motion regarding the disclosure of Dominique a.k.a. Pierre's convictions, if any. It was explained to him that the prosecuting attorney must provide not only any record of felony convictions but any record of any prior criminal convictions of any person the prosecuting attorney intended to call as a witness in the case. If Dayton refused to make such disclosures, Rolland was so advised, Pierre would be prevented from testifying.

Not having been involved in the preparation of the motions, Rolland was unsure how knowing Pierre had been convicted of a felony would help. Lino explained that if Pierre has been convicted of a felony and testified at trial, the defense could confront him with the felony when they cross-examined him. "He will be testifying under oath, and if he lies that is perjury, a felony in itself," Lino said. "If he admits the felony, the jury will be instructed by the judge that they may take that into account in assessing his creditability. What that means is that the testimony from a suspect is suspect and the jury has the leeway of disregarding that testimony or giving it whatever weight or credence they deem appropriate."

Drew told Rolland that in all likelihood he would testify in his own behalf. Even though a defendant has a Fifth Amendment right not to testify, Rolland had nothing to lose and everything to gain by testifying. He was innocent, and he "would proclaim his innocence from the rooftops."

Bodean added that he felt that the statement attributed to Rolland as having been made to his paramour about knowing a way to get rid of his wife and making it look like an accident was the most damaging evidence in the case. It would be Rolland's word against the Delajures'. With Pierre's testimony being neutralized and maybe even eliminated, it was still Rolland's word against Carla's. One against one with the tie going in his favor theoretically would nullify the prosecution's so-called "evidence of motive or premeditation."

"But then again," Rolland said wistfully, "they might choose to believe Carla."

Lino suspected that without Pierre at her side and looking over her shoulder, Carla might be more apt to tell the truth. Drew agreed that that might occur or that they may be able to discredit her enough on cross-examination to create at least a reasonable doubt in the minds of the jurors. All, however, agreed that that might result in the charges being lowered from murder in the first degree and possibly murder in the second degree to manslaughter or criminally negligent homicide.

Rolland appeared confused. "I've been charged with murder in the first degree," Rolland said, "not with murder in the second degree, manslaughter, or criminally negligent homicide. Isn't it all or nothing?"

Drew interposed, "Murder in the second degree, manslaughter and criminally negligent homicide are what we call 'lesser included offenses.' You are charged with murder in the first degree, a class one felony, which requires deliberation and intent to cause death. Murder in the second degree is a class two felony if caused knowingly or a class three felony if caused upon a sudden heat of passion. 'Knowingly' means that the perpetrator was aware that his conduct was practically certain to cause the result.

"On the other hand, manslaughter is a class four felony and only requires that the perpetrator act recklessly in causing the death of another. A person is deemed to have acted recklessly 'when he consciously disregards a substantial and unjustifiable risk that a result will occur or that a circumstance exists.'

"Now, criminally negligent homicide is a class five felony and only requires criminal negligence. That meant a gross deviation from the standard of care that a reasonable person would exercise."

Both Drew and Lino agreed with Rolland, that the degree of culpability required for murder in the second degree, manslaughter, and criminally negligent homicide were somewhat blurred and both knew this explanation as to the respective differences did not appease Rolland. All, however, recognized that all were felonies, but the penalties were significantly different.

In answer to Rolland's query as to the differences, Lino stated, "Murder in the first degree is a capital offense, specifically a class one felony with a possible penalty of life imprisonment or death. Murder in the second degree, is either a class two or class three felony depending on the circumstances. A class two felony carries a penalty of from eight to twenty-four years in the Colorado State Penitentiary. A class three felony, on the other hand, carries a possible penalty of four to twelve years."

"So if I were found guilty of the lesser included offense of criminally negligent homicide, that would mean the jury felt I had not caused Joy's death intentionally, knowingly, upon a sudden heat of passion or recklessly, correct?"

"They would be conveying the message," Lino said, "that the prosecution proved that you caused Joy's death but that you did so with criminal negligence and not with any higher degree of culpability. You then would be sentenced to a minimum of one year and a maximum of three years in the Colorado State Penitentiary. You could receive probation and not have to serve any penitentiary time."

"What if we appealed the verdict and the conviction was reversed? Upon retrial, could the prosecution reinstate the murder charge and we just start all over again?"

"No," Lino responded, "the most you could be prosecuted for under that scenario is criminally negligent homicide. You would be deemed to have been placed in jeopardy on the other homicide charges. The Fifth Amendment to the U.S. Constitution says you can't be tried twice for the same offense. The Latin maxim is *non-bis in idem*."

The defense team thought they were ready for the Monday challenge. It was ordained that all meet at the law offices of Quinlin, Devlin & Cummins at 7:30 a.m. and proceed to court from there.

Before the defense team disbursed, Rolland stated he had something to reveal that he said he was embarrassed about primarily because it was a test of his faith and trust or rather a lack thereof in regard to his wife's pregnancy. Apparently, while in Boston he succumbed to a fertility test as part of a general physical exam. He indeed was fertile and felt guilty about even questioning his wife's lack of fidelity. Drew was frozen in his seat. Joy's unborn child may have been Rolland's! That was something Drew had not considered.

Non Exemplis Sed Leqibus Judicandum Est

(Not by the Facts of the Case, but by the Law Must Judgment Be Made)

It was 7:45 a.m. on that frigid post-Christmas December morning when the defense team arrived at the steps of the El Paso County courthouse. They were blocked from entry by an unruly group of protestors carrying placards with the usual hate messages. They spotted two agitators in the crowd who they instantly recognized as Pierre and Carla Delajure.

Pointing in Rolland's and Drew's direction, Pierre yelled: "Here comes the wife and baby killer and look who's following behind—our notorious defender of the guilty."

"If you're looking for justice," a woman shouted, "we'll give it to you."

Another at the top of her lungs screamed: "Woman haters."

The sudden roar of frenzy drowned out all else, and the buzz of the crowd intensified as the defense team made its way through a hostile and resistant crowd. Lino later summed it up best: "Unwittingly, we were thrust into the middle of a beehive and soon found ourselves being surrounded by a swarm of angry bees."

Whatever the metaphor, the defense team was rightfully in fear for their lives. If it had not been for the swift action of the courthouse security and the arrival of local police authorities, it is uncertain what would have happened to Rolland, Drew, Lino, and Bodean. As it was, all four emerged with all the scrapes and bruises reminiscent of a school ground brawl.

The most serious injury was to Bodean's left eye, which almost immediately turned color and closed. Rolland's suit coat was literally torn from him and between Drew's dangling lapels and Lino's bare knees peering from the ragged edges of his suit pants not to mention Bodean's torn shirt, the defense team might have been mistaken for hobos who had just tumbled off a moving railroad car. It took some doing to make themselves presentable for court.

The inside of the courthouse was beginning to swarm with uniformed sheriff's deputies. It appeared that those, both inside and outside, who failed to heed the deputies' admonition to disperse, were being placed under arrest.

Bedlam was reigning supreme, and the court personnel were closing and locking their doors. Once order had been restored and the crowd dispersed, the doors to judge Beasley's courtroom were opened. It was already 8:30 a.m., and those entering the courtroom were being screened. Only those with court business were allowed admittance. The presence of the deputies in and around the courtroom provided some comfort to the defense team.

Judge Beasley's bailiff summoned the attorneys on both sides into her chambers. Both Norman Dayton and Edward Terrell were representing the prosecution; Drew and Lino were there representing the defense. Rolland remained in the courtroom with Bodean as did the lead investigator for the district attorney's office, William "Will" Rodgers.

Judge Beasley said she wanted to discuss the issue of courthouse security in chambers for obvious reasons. She asked Drew

CARROLL MULTZ

and Lino if they would waive the presence of Rolland during the ensuing discussion. They willingly obliged.

"In my seven years as a judge," the Beas began, "and a prosecuting attorney for five years before that, I have never witnessed such an outlandish and volatile situation. To be honest, it frightened me to death. The only way I was able to avoid being enmeshed was by entering the courthouse through the after-hours rear entrance. Even then, I wondered if maybe it was not safe to enter."

Looking at the torn and tattered appearance of Drew and Lino, the Beas shook her head. "I watched from my window as the two of you and your client tried to make your way through the protestors. Needless to say I was and still am shocked at the display of hostility and unabashed abuse to which you were subjected. That should never happen in a community such as ours. In behalf of our otherwise law-abiding citizens, I apologize."

"It'll only add spice to our memoirs," Drew commented. "I'm sure we look worse than we feel."

The Beas's smile was curt, but Drew and Lino both knew her concerns were sincere. Continuing, she said, "The long and the short of the matter, is that, utilizing the inherent power of the court, I will be entering a temporary restraining order against the PROTECT group and any other organization similarly inclined to obstruct justice in the same or similar fashion. The temporary restraining order will allow representatives to come in and advance any reasons there be for not making my order permanent. I can envision the First Amendment Coalition and sister organizations seeking to intervene (join the controversy), arguing that such an order is unconstitutional."

Dayton said he would vigorously prosecute the offenders on the various criminal citations that might be issued such as obstructing government operations, obstructing a peace officer, resisting arrest, failure to obey a lawful order, intimidating a witness or juror, inciting a riot, engaging in a riot, disobedience of public safety orders, disorderly conduct, obstructing passageways, disrupting lawful assembly, trespass and interference with public buildings, harassment, loitering, stalking, unlawful conduct on public property, and failure or refusal to leave premises or property upon request of a peace officer.

Dayton was reminded by Drew and Lino to add assault and battery to the list. Their investigator, they said, was sporting a black eye as they spoke after having been struck by one of the protestors. The placards the protestors carried contained potently criminal hate and threat messages that fit other criminal statutes, they added.

Judge Beasley made it clear that such unlawful conduct could not and would not be tolerated. The problem was one of commonality, and she sought their input in rectifying a problem that cast a bad light on the judicial system. The courthouse should be a safe haven and a place for peaceful resolution of disputes.

All were amazed at the take-charge attitude of the Beas.

While in chambers, it was agreed that the motions hearing would be continued until 8:00 a.m. the following morning. Judge Beasley said she would continue other matters on her docket that conflicted giving priority to the motions hearing and exhorted the attorneys to go forward and do likewise. Judge Beasley then extolled the attorneys for their discretion in not making a bad situation worse.

The two local newspapers added to the list of headlines and articles comprising the supporting documentation and evidence of massive and pervasive prejudicial pretrial publicity. The first page of both newspapers carried banner headlines, enlarged action photographs, and extensive print including interviews of some of the demonstrators. Television stations statewide had extensive coverage, which they titled "breaking news." If the readers and viewers were not convinced of the lynch mob mentality of the community and the sentiment of hostility toward the artist-wife killer before, they were by the time court started the following morning.

The El Paso County courthouse was buzzing with excitement when Rolland and the defense team arrived for court early that December Tuesday. Representatives of various law enforcement agencies made their presence known, and no incidences were apparent. Spectators were limited by the seating accommodations, and the security screening resembled that of Denver International Airport. The Beas's "no tolerance policy" was being implemented with military precision. The defense team only hoped Rolland would not become the ultimate target of the "blame game."

Rolland and the attorneys on both sides had barely taken their seats when Roxanne Drexel, Judge Beasley's new clerk, ushered them into chambers as mandated by the Beas. Regal in her black robe and seated in her extra-large high-back black leather chair behind an extra-large, cluttered, dark, ornate desk, the Beas motioned for everyone to be seated. She ignored the patronizing "Good morning, Your Honor" greetings that were being sporadically emitted by this group of unworthy. Drew thought to himself that she probably would have responded had they said something more appropriate, such as "Good morning, Your Eminence" or maybe "Good morning, Your Excellency; What can we your humble servants do to serve you?" She must have suspected what Drew was thinking because she gave him her patented disapproving glance.

In an authoritative tone, the Beas announced that she didn't conduct "star chamber" proceedings and that the defense's request to conduct an in-chambers hearing on their motion to exclude the public and the media from those portions of the motions hearing dealing with the exclusion and suppression of statements and evidence would be summarily denied without argument. Before Drew could articulate a request that the record note defense's exception to the ruling, the Beas interrupted, stating that the record would reflect the defense's exception.

Directing her attention specifically to Drew, the Beas stated, "Mr. Quinlin, the Court is not indicating at this time how it will rule on the suppression issues, only that the Sixth Amendment to our United State Constitution affords not only the accused a right to a public trial but inferentially the public a public trial, if you will, as well. The media have the same right; no more, no less. In addition, the First Amendment is the fountainhead of what we call freedom of the press including the electronic media as well. The last I looked, that amendment has not been repealed.

"Today this Court is going to be called upon to reconcile or balance Dr. Dawson's right to a fair trial as guaranteed by the Sixth Amendment with the media's rights afforded by the First Amendment. You have to appreciate the predicament faced by this Court. Whatever rulings I make with respect to your motions will receive strict scrutiny by the appellate courts. I'm on the proverbial horns of a dilemma. Regardless of my rulings, someone and maybe everyone will challenge them.

"That having been said, the Court doesn't feel the media have an absolute or unfettered right under the First Amendment to do, say, print or broadcast whatever they want. Nor do I think the First Amendment should be the preferred one or trump the Sixth Amendment or any other conflicting rights. What I am saying is that I have the onerous task of reconciling the right of freedom of the media with the right of an accused to receive a fair trial.

"Some people want the news; all are entitled to it. The conduit between obtaining the news and transmitting it to the public is the media. The freedoms we enjoy, therefore, are dependent upon the freedoms afforded the media. The rights afforded the media by virtue of the First Amendment must remain inviolate. As has been said, 'an informed citizenry is an effective citizenry.' For the foregoing reasons, the Court, in advance of the hearing on defense's motions is hereby summarily denying Dr. Dawson's motion to exclude the public and media from the ensuing motions hearing as well as denying the request for issuance of restrictive orders specifically the issuance of a gag order aimed at the media. In case my ruling is not clear, both the public and the media shall be allowed to attend the remainder of these proceedings. And they shall have the right to report the news as the framers of our Constitution intended."

Drew, rising quickly to his feet, said, "Your Honor, might we briefly be heard?"

Judge Beasley, slowly removing her spectacles and looking directly at Drew, replied, "Mr. Quinlin, unless you can convince me that the circumstances here are extraordinary, and do so in quick order, you will be wasting your time and mine. You may proceed."

"Judge," Drew began, "there are indeed extraordinary circumstances here. The print and broadcast media have run amok with the coverage in this case. The massive and pervasive prejudicial pretrial publicity has already ensured that Dr. Dawson will not receive a fair trial in this end of the state. Uninhibited, unabated, and unrestricted, the media will only exacerbate the situation. The only way to reign in the media and control this runaway freight train is for Your Honor to issue a restrictive order.

"This case reminds me of the case of *Sheppard v. Maxwell* where, in 1954, another doctor was charged with the murder of his pregnant wife. His name was Dr. Sam Sheppard. A television series and a movie called *The Fugitive* resulted from the improvident rulings or lack of the trial judge limiting the publication and broadcast of prejudicial pretrial publicity. After a lengthy and expensive trial, Dr. Sheppard was convicted. However, the United States Supreme Court in 1966 reversed the conviction on the grounds that Dr. Sheppard had been deprived of a fair trial because of the massive and pervasive nature of the pretrial publicity. The United States Supreme Court criticized the trial judge for not controlling the flow of the prejudicial pretrial publicity by the media.

"In another United States Supreme Court case, *Nebraska Press Association v. Stuart*, decided in 1976, a landmark case, the High Court set forth the criteria in determining whether restrictive orders issued against the media violated their First Amendment rights. The Court ruled it didn't where intense and pervasive publicity is a certainty; where other reasonable alternatives would be ineffective; and where the restrictive order would effectively prevent the harm sought to be prevented (to wit: insulate the jurors from exposure to the prejudicial information).

"Judge, the facts in this case fit the criteria in the Nebraska Press Association case. The law, facts, and justice cry out for your intervention in this case. Don't allow the media to usurp the prerogative of the jury and thereby deny Dr. Dawson his constitutional right to a fair trial.

"We are also asking Your Honor to reconsider your denial of our motion requesting closure of the hearing on the remainder of the pending motions. Some of the spectators crowded into your courtroom may be prospective jurors or the telegraphic network of the information they obtain here. Word of mouth accounts for the exponential exposure to all types of information, and what is not yelled from the rooftops will be disseminated in the media's 'breaking news.'

"Your Honor, should Dr. Dawson be fortunate enough to have you suppress some of the evidence considered highly prejudicial to him, such evidence will nonetheless reach the jury albeit individually through the print and electronic media. Neither side expects or wants to select an illiterate jury, that is one that is deaf, dumb, and blind and doesn't read the newspapers, watch television, or listen to the radio. That would not be a realistic expectation anyway, as every citizen in our community has been exposed to the pretrial publicity in this case.

"At trial, it will be futile to tell them to disregard what they have been exposed to outside the courtroom and consider only the evidence admitted at trial. How will they be able to make a distinction as they deliberate? How do you unring a bell?

"As Your Honor is aware, the United States Supreme Court case of *Press-Enterprise v. Riverside Superior Court* has established a test for courts to use when deciding whether a hearing or portion thereof should be closed to the media and the public. It is based primarily on whether an overriding interest is likely to be harmed if closure is not ordered. The overriding interest in this case, of course, is Dr. Dawson's constitutional right to a fair trial, which we submit he will not receive if closure is not ordered."

As Dayton rose to respond, the Beas, addressing him, said, "Unless the prosecution joins in the request to exclude the media and the public from the motions hearing and the request for a restrictive order on the media, Mr. Dayton, you need not respond."

"The prosecution is not in favor of either," Dayton said, somewhat subdued.

"Very well, since the defense has not advanced any justifiable or compelling reason that requires the court to reverse its prior rulings, the rulings stand. Unless the circumstances change drastically and journalistic excesses become prevalent, no gag order will be issued herein. In the interim, the remainder of the motions hearing shall be open to the media and the public. The Court will take a ten-minute recess at which time all parties will reconvene in the courtroom ready to resume where we left off. This Court is in recess."

As the defense team left the Beas's chambers, Lino whispered to Drew, "Looks like we struck out the first time at bat."

"There are still nine innings in this ball game," Drew quipped. "We still have several opportunities to get a hit and maybe even a home run."

Rolland, overhearing the conversation, said, "Not with this umpire."

Although the courtroom was filled to capacity, it was unusually quiet and serene. Security was tight, and none of the previous troublemakers appeared to be present. The courtroom appeared to be filled with the curious rather than the condemners.

The Beas seemed to take a businesslike approach to the hearing. After outlining her *in camera* rulings, she proceeded to quiz the attorneys about whether motions or parts thereof had been resolved and what stipulations could be made if needed. She stated that a bill of particulars had been filed by the district attorney pursuant to the defense's motion and that the defense had filed a notice of alibi as a result thereof. Both sides acknowledged the above, and the defense acknowledged that it was satisfied with the specifications in the bill of particulars.

The Beas, "to avoid wasting the court's time and everyone else's," as she phrased it, was prepared to make rulings without evidence or argument on various motions or parts thereof. First, she categorically denied the motion to permit polygraph results on the grounds that polygraphs were "not scientifically recognized." Second, with regard to the motion for additional discovery, she ruled that the parties were already under a continuing obligation to provide discovery in accordance with the rules of criminal procedure, and she would issue no orders extending that requirement. Third, as for the motion for disclosure of felony convictions, she stated that the prosecution would be required to make disclosure no later than thirty days before trial of all felonies for any witness that would be called in their behalf and that there would be no exceptions regardless of the circumstances. Fourth, with regard to the motion to permit view of the premises, she said she would take the motion under advisement and, depending on the photographic depiction of the premises as presented at trial, would entertain such a motion at a later time.

The Beas then addressed the motion to exclude evidence. "Because the prejudicial effects of the evidence related to 'a fetus' far outweigh its probative value, such evidence will be and is hereby ruled to be inadmissible at all stages of this case. Dr. Dawson is not charged with any offense related to the fetus nor is such evidence relevant to the charges he is currently facing." Dayton was then asked if he was still opposing the defense's motion to exclude evidence relating to the previous harassment incident. When Dayton responded in the negative, the Beas ruled that any evidence related thereto would likewise be inadmissible.

As was anticipated by at least part of the defense team, the Beas ruled against them and their attempt to exclude the statement Dr. Dawson allegedly made to Carla Delajure to the effect that he knew how to get rid of his wife and "make it look like an accident." In making her ruling, the Beas justified it by saying the statement went to Dr. Dawson's state of mind and his motive and if it was shown that he was present at the moment of his wife's death and somehow involved, whether or not her death was deliberate or accidental. The Beas also ruled that the statement was not too far removed in point of time and therefore not stale.

It was obvious to everyone at the defense table that Drew reeled from the ruling. It was a tough pill to swallow. That evidence provided the deliberation needed to prove murder in the first degree. Drew knew the end was drawing near as his client's fate was knocking loudly at his front door. It was also tugging at his heart. D-Day had arrived; the day to make the much-belated revelation.

The defense was asked to proceed in support of their motion to suppress statements and evidence. Both Deputies Milligan and Stanton testified, though not in the presence of each other, as Lino had asked for a sequestration of witnesses. The purpose of the sequestration rule was to keep witnesses from fashioning their testimony to conform to that of those who preceded them.

The two investigative deputies testified consistently and without major discrepancies. Both established that they were the first law enforcement officers on the scene; that they had been dispatched to the scene pursuant to a telephone call by Dr. Dawson upon his discovery of his wife's lifeless body; that they found buttons near the body and fabric fragments in the decedent's hands that were later determined to be from a blue flannel shirt hanging on a chair in the kitchen some ten feet from the body; that upon asking Dr. Dawson whose shirt it was, he stated it was his; that they asked him no further questions; that at the scene he was not taken into custody; that he was not placed under arrest at that time; that he was free to leave if he wanted to which he ultimately did; that they never advised him of his Miranda warnings; that he gave permission to take the shirt; that the shirt was in plain view; and that they seized it without a search warrant.

After attorneys for the respective sides made the usual arguments, Lino in support of suppression of the shirt and admission of ownership and Terrell in opposition thereto, Judge Beasley denied the motion in both respects. In support of her ruling, she recounted the deputies' testimony to the effect that they were summoned to the scene by Dr. Dawson; that he invited them in; that they observed the buttons and fabric fragments in plain view as well as the damaged shirt; that Dr. Dawson had not been placed under arrest or taken into custody at the time of his admission to ownership of the shirt; that no questions were asked of the doctor after his admission; and that under the totality of the circumstances the deputies were not required to advise Dr. Dawson of his right to demand a search warrant. "The statement and evidence were legally obtained and will, therefore, be admissible in evidence at the trial herein."

Live by the sword; die by the sword. So far the defense had little to show for the hard work invested in preparation for the motions hearing. *What is determined here*, Drew thought, *will determine the success or failure at trial*. Even though the Beas's adverse rulings might be the ammunition for reversal of any conviction upon appeal, that was little consolation now. Everything was riding on the all-important motion for change of venue.

After the midmorning recess, the defense team was instructed to proceed on their remaining motion. They were reminded by the Beas that since it was their motion, they had the burden of proving its worthiness (i.e., convincing the court that it should be granted).

Drew called as witnesses Laura Barnsley and Stan Finlin, two of the twelve citizens who had provided affidavits in support of the defense's motion for change of venue. Each testified that their exposure to the pretrial publicity via the newspaper and television had convinced them of Dr. Dawson's guilt; that unless it was proven that someone else committed the murder, they as jurors, would find Dr. Dawson guilty; that their neighbors with whom they spoke felt the same way; and that they doubted Dr. Dawson could receive a fair trial in El Paso County.

Upon cross-examination by Dayton, both testified that if they were selected as jurors and were instructed by the court to disregard their preconceived notions and judge the case solely on the evidence produced at trial, they probably would be able to do so. When asked further by the Beas as to whether *they* could afford

Dr. Dawson a fair trial both said they "thought *they* could." And, when asked by the Beas whether they could be fair and impartial if selected, each said, "Yes."

Looking in Drew's direction, the Beas asked, "Mr. Quinlin, does the defense intend to call any other witnesses who have submitted affidavits?"

"We do, Your Honor!"

"That will be unnecessary. In the interest of conserving time, the court will take judicial notice of the fact that their testimony would coincide with that stated in their affidavits. I assume the prosecution has no objection."

"No objection," Dayton responded.

"Very well. Mr. Quinlin, does the defense have any other witnesses they intend to call?"

"At this time, Your Honor, we are prepared to call the editors of both newspapers published in the county as well as the manager of KSIR Channel 33."

"Maybe we can circumvent their testimony by an offer of proof. Through them what do you intend to show?"

"Your Honor, the editors would lay the foundation for the introduction into evidence of the newspaper accounts attached to our motion for change of venue. They would also testify as to the exact extent of their respective newspapers' countywide circulation. The station manager for KSIR would lay the foundation for the admissibility of the newscast featuring the interview of Pierre Delajure and the editorial comments of Julia Zoren."

Addressing Dayton, the Beas asked, "Does the prosecution have any objection to the admission of the newspaper accounts or the KSIR film?"

"No, Your Honor. The prosecution has no objection."

"In light of the offer and there being no objection, the tendered articles and film will be admitted. No foundation therefore need be established."

The Beas then took a brief recess while she reviewed the film and read the proffered newspaper articles. Upon returning, she asked, "Mr. Quinlin, does the defense have any other evidence to present in support of its motions?"

"Your Honor, the defense has no other evidence to present."

"Very well. Mr. Dayton, does the prosecution intend to call any witnesses?"

"We propose," Dayton responded, "to call three witnesses who will testify that they are residents of the county and have read the newspaper accounts and viewed the television coverage of the case. Unlike the defense witnesses on direct, they will testify that they have not made up their minds to Dr. Dawson's innocence or guilt and could give him a fair trial."

"Unless the defense has an objection, I will consider Mr. Dayton's statements as an offer of proof and will treat the same as if the witnesses had so testified."

"I guess turnabout is fair play," Drew said. "The defense has no objection."

"The court will now hear final arguments," the Beas said. "Since the defense has the burden of proof with respect to the pending motion, we will start with defense counsel."

Drew, feeling the pressure and more nervous than usual, began, "May it please the Court. No one could argue that the proper forum for a criminal prosecution is the courtroom, not the media. Unfortunately, Dr. Dawson has already been tried and convicted by public opinion as a result the massive and pervasive prejudicial pretrial publicity. This is without him having had his 'day in court' and without the public hearing his side of the story.

"The slant of the news coverage in this case has painted a picture characterizing Dr. Dawson's wife's death as a criminal homicide. What happened to the concept of fair and accurate reporting? Has even one media outlet explored the possibility that Mrs. Dawson's death may have been accidental? Has anyone here even heard the term 'accidental' used in connection with this case?

"My point is this. The awesome power of the pen has transformed a private misfortune into a notorious crime. Let's face it; the death of a pregnant wife is sensational news. This case is not the only pregnant wife case to receive massive and pervasive prejudicial pretrial publicity. We don't have to think very far back to the Scott Peterson case or maybe that of the Sam Sheppard case, the latter being one of the most famous cases involving the prosecution of a doctor in the death of his pregnant wife.

"Because of the damning pretrial publicity, the Scott Peterson case, as the court might recall, was moved some fifty miles away to avoid a reversal in the event of a conviction on the basis of a tainted jury pool. It was patently obvious that Peterson could not receive a fair trial in the locale where the crime allegedly occurred. By the way, he was ultimately convicted, and to my knowledge, the conviction has not been reversed.

"The Sheppard case is more like the Dawson case. Not only do both involve the prosecution of medical doctors for the deaths of their pregnant wives but the whole media coverage in both focused almost exclusively on damning material that incriminated the doctor husband. The media in both cases drew and has drawn unwarranted inferences from the so-called evidence. As in the Sheppard case, 'much of the information thus disclosed was inaccurate, leading to groundless rumors and confusion.' The prospective jurors had been so pervasively exposed to the prejudicial pretrial publicity, as they have in the Dawson case, that they were unable to afford Dr. Sheppard a fair trial as guaranteed by the Sixth Amendment.

"The proof was in the pudding. Without a change in venue, it was a slam-dunk case for the prosecution. Upon review by the United States Supreme Court, however, Dr. Sheppard's conviction was overturned. At the retrial, where this time he received a fair trial, he was acquitted.

"In the Sheppard case, the United States Supreme Court focused on the impact of pretrial publicity and the trial court's duty to ensure that the defendant receive a fair trial. The court then noted: 'Due process requires that the accused receive a trial by an impartial jury free from outside influences. Given the pervasiveness of modern communications and the difficulty of effacing prejudicial publicity from the minds of the jurors, *the trial courts must take strong measures to ensure that the balance is never weighted against the accused.*'

"Your Honor, we're asking you to follow the admonition issued by the Supreme Court of the United States in the Sheppard case and the other two cases decided in the 1960s as cited in our brief specifically *Rideau v. State of Louisiana* and *Irvin v. Dowd.* As was stated in the Rideau case: 'Any subsequent court proceedings in a community so pervasively exposed to such a spectacle could be but a hollow formality.'

"Because there is a reasonable likelihood that the prejudicial pretrial publicity in this case will prevent Dr. Dawson from receiving a fair trial, we're asking you to transfer it to another county, a county not so permeated with publicity. None of the other trial-level remedies the prosecution is about to advance will effectively mitigate or lessen the impact of the pretrial publicity.

"Judge, the defense is not asking you to go to extremes as the court did in 1997 in the Oklahoma City bombing case when the place of trial was moved from Oklahoma City to Denver but only to move the case from within our state from a county pervaded with an atmosphere of bias to one with an atmosphere of neutrality. Thank you."

The Beas, looking at her watch, said: "Mr. Dayton and Mr. Terrell, the court has another matter requiring its attention and is therefore going to take an early recess for lunch. The court will reconvene at 1:30 p.m. at which time the prosecution can present its argument in opposition to the motion for change of venue. This Court is now in recess."

When court reconvened at the start of the afternoon session, Dayton was already poised at the podium ready to do battle. He must have had raw meat for lunch as he was more aggressive than usual and appeared somewhat agitated. It was obvious he did not want the Beas to grant the motion for change of venue.

After ceremoniously greeting the Court, he said, "I guess I have a greater faith in the citizens of our great county than does Mr. Quinlin. If Dr. Dawson can't receive a fair trial in El Paso County, he can't receive a fair trial anywhere. Although our office has not won a conviction in every criminal prosecution we've pursued, we always felt the jurors carefully and dispassionately considered the evidence in light of the instructions on the law as given by the court and rendered what all of us considered to be a fair and just verdict.

"The jurors are clearly the pulse of the community. They didn't select the venue for a defendant to commit a crime. In fact, they would much prefer that their county be crime-free. When a defendant commits a crime in the county, it is he or she who picks the forum, not the other way around. A defendant cannot have his cake and eat it too. A defendant cannot victimize a citizen in El Paso County and then find a more favorable county to be tried. He or she makes a choice, and he or she should think twice before committing a crime in our county."

Jumping to his feet, Drew protested, "Objection, Your Honor, Mr. Dayton is assuming facts not in evidence. In fact, the contrary is true. Mr. Dayton is the one who selected the forum, not Dr. Dawson. Dr. Dawson did not file the charge, nor did Dr. Dawson commit any criminal acts let alone any in El Paso County. Mr. Dayton's speculation and conjecture do not rise to the level of proof."

"Overruled, Mr. Quinlin. There are no jurors here to be prejudiced, and the court can sift through the wheat and the chaff." Turning to Dayton, the Beas said, "You may continue, Mr. Dayton."

"From Mr. Quinlin's argument, it appears he is convinced his client cannot receive a fair trial in El Paso County. It wasn't only the prosecution witnesses but the two defense witnesses as well who testified herein that they could afford Dr. Dawson a fair and impartial trial. Correct me if I'm wrong, but I didn't hear either of the defense witnesses say they could not set aside their preconceived notions or that they could not decide the case solely on the evidence presented at trial.

"Judge, even if they had testified to the contrary, they are only a few out of thousands of prospective jurors. The only way to tell if the prospective jurors are biased is to ask them that during jury selection. A few do not a community make."

"Objection," Drew interposed. "No one believes himself or herself to be biased or prejudiced. Even if that were not the case, it would be naïve to believe that he or she would ever admit it. Besides, it is not governed by a subjective assessment but based on an objective standard."

"Overruled. Counsel have wide latitude in final argument—especially argument to the court. Mr. Dayton, you may continue."

"As an elected official, I would be remiss in not weighing the impact a change of venue would have on the community. A change of venue is inconvenient and costly. All of the participants, except possibly Your Honor, but including the attorneys, witnesses, and others would have to be transplanted and transported to some distant jurisdiction. Nor does it appear economically feasible to import jurors from some distant jurisdiction in an effort to find twelve jurors who have not been exposed to the case.

"To ensure that Dr. Dawson receives a fair trial in El Paso County is to find a more suitable trial-level remedy. *Voir dire* or jury selection, for example, will weed out those who have strong biases from those who don't. Admonitions from the court not to read newspaper stories or listen or watch broadcasts about the case and to consider only evidence presented in the courtroom have proven effective. Also, seclusion or sequestration of the jury so as to keep them insulated from exposure to further out-of-court publicity is another means to mitigate or lessen exposure.

"It is the prosecution's position that a change of venue is a remedy of last resort and certainly not warranted in this case. The cure the defense is asking for is extreme and would be akin to asking a doctor to cut off the patient's head to cure a headache. The question is: do we want to fill the jury box with informed and intelligent jurors, or do we want to fill it with ignoramuses as the defense apparently suggests?"

When Drew started to stand to offer rebuttal, the Beas, motioning him to remain seated, stated, "I've given this matter considerable thought, done extensive research on the subject, and listened carefully to your respective positions. I am prepared to rule on the pending motion. As the Chief Justice of United States Supreme Court stated in *Nebraska Press Association v. Stuart*, cited by both parties in their briefs, 'pretrial publicity—even pervasive, adverse publicity—does not inevitably lead to unfair trial.' I do not find that there is a reasonable likelihood that prejudicial pretrial publicity in this case is such as to prevent Dr. Dawson from receiving a fair trial. Moreover, jury selection will allow the attorneys to identify those prospective jurors who cannot set aside their preconceptions and judge the case solely on the evidence presented at trial. Jurors who evince bias or prejudice and are resolute regardless of the evidence presented can be challenged for cause by either or both attorneys. Remember there is no limitation on the number of challenges based on

CARROLL MULTZ

cause, and bias or prejudice is a statutory ground to have a juror excused in this state.

"It defies all logic that of the thousands of available prospective jurors in this county that we will be unable to find and select twelve who can be fair and impartial. The trial-level mechanisms at our disposal, as outlined by Mr. Dayton, are designed in such away as to ensure that every accused, including Dr. Dawson, receives a fair trial from his or her peers. I, too, feel there will never be any twelve people better suited to sit as jurors in this case than those residing in this county. For the foregoing reasons, Dr. Dawson's motion for change of venue is denied.

"By the way, Mr. Quinlin, the Oklahoma bombing case is distinguishable from the present case in that it was a federal prosecution and the magnitude of the trial required facilities that were not available in the state of Oklahoma. The change was not to accommodate the defendant but to accommodate the court."

Without taking a breath, the Beas asked the attorneys to take a look at their calendars and assist the court in selecting a trial date. The defense team was too numb to do anything else. The Beas said that anytime within six months from the date of arraignment would be within the speedy trial period and that the earliest two-week block that she had available were the weeks commencing March 16 and March 23. She first asked if the attorneys felt two weeks was a realistic estimate of the length of the trial and whether the attorneys were available on those dates. Surprisingly, both sides answered in the affirmative, and the trial date was set.

The Beas said she usually commenced the first day of trial at 9:00 a.m. with the attorneys meeting in chambers for last-minute "housekeeping matters" at 8:00 a.m. Drew and Dayton nodded their acquiescence. She also indicated that because of the unusual circumstances of the case and her willingness to be flexible that the parties should reserve a court date in the event it was needed for emergency pretrial matters on Monday, February 16 at 10:00 a.m. that could serve as a status conference and a bond return date for Dr. Dawson as well. All were in agreement. Dr. Dawson's bond was continued to that date. The prosecution left the courtroom jubilant while the defense team retreated in total defeat, disgust, and disappointment.

As the defense team marched from the courthouse to the offices of Quinlin, Devlin & Cummins, it resembled in no small respect that of a funeral procession. There was no joy or Joy in Mudville because Casey, mighty Casey, had struck out. "In baseball parlance," Bodean was heard to mutter, "it was a 'shut out'— no make that a 'no hitter.'"

It had been a day made in hell. In fact, everything surrounding the case was a nightmare they hoped would soon end. The adverse ruling on their motion for change of venue was like jumping with a failed parachute. The result was inescapable. With a biased jury, their trial efforts will be in vain. Hopefully, the Beas had made erroneous rulings that rose to the level of reversible error. The defense team was convinced that any conviction of Rolland would be overturned on appeal. Then the case would be retried but next time by an impartial jury whose minds would be free from the dominant influence of knowledge acquired outside the courtroom and free from strong and deep impressions that close the mind.

In the Wake of Disaster

This cold snowy final day of the year was not as somber as the defense team had envisioned. The day after the motions hearing proved to be the best time for the motions hearing post-mortem.

Bodean and Rolland had met for breakfast at the Antler's Hotel; Drew and Lino had been playing catch-up at the law offices of Quinlin, Devlin & Cummins since before 7:00 a.m. When they all met in the conference room at 8:30 a.m., they were over their crying spell and the doom and gloom following the announcement of the rulings in the motions hearing miraculously disappeared. They had expected the worse but weren't ready for it when it came. Now they were facing reality and hoping the wounds would heal.

"Now we've got them right where we want them," Rolland said with a broad grin. "We will get that free bite out of the apple you all have been talking about," he continued. "Whatever happens at trial will be for naught because Judge Beasley has given us a free pass for a reversal. Right? And whatever charges I am acquitted of can't be resurrected on the retrial. So what do I have to lose?"

When neither Drew nor Lino responded, Bodean did. "It seems to me that the more trials we have and the more shots we have, the greater the likelihood of compromise verdicts. Rolland and I discussed double jeopardy at breakfast. He certainly is correct when he says he can't be tried twice for the same offense. So if he is found guilty of some charge and not guilty of the others, he can only be retried on the charge of which he has been found guilty. Also, I'm sure the Beas will be gun shy once she is reversed and will bend over backwards to avoid a repeat performance. Instead of resolving the close questions in favor of the prosecutor, she'll opt to err on the side of caution. I can't imagine that once she is scolded by the Supremes that she will again jeopardize her reputation. Judges pride themselves on not being reversed."

"Rolland and Bodean have a way of jolting us back to reality," Lino said to Drew. "I cried myself to sleep last night," Lino said, "and now I'm laughing thinking how cleverly we've painted the Beas and the prosecutor in the corner."

"Not only did the prosecutor and the judge not know it, but we didn't either—that is, not until now," Drew said, finally managing a smile. "I can't believe our strategy worked," he added mockingly. All finally had something to laugh about.

"I have my doubts about jury selection," Lino said. "I don't think *voir dire* is an effective tool to weed out biased jurors. If they don't want to sit, they know how to posture their answers to questions asked by the prosecution, defense, and court in such a way as to guarantee their rejection. On the other hand, if they want to be selected, they know the right responses everyone is looking for. Obviously, every juror, even those who have already made up their minds, believe in their heart of hearts that they will be fair and impartial jurors."

"Everyone has his or her own biases and prejudices, and it is inevitable that those biases and prejudices will creep into every decision he or she makes," Bodean said. "The right thing is what a person is programmed to believe is the right thing, not necessarily what in fact is the right thing."

"What I'm afraid of," Lino said, "is that with the media and public present during jury selection, the prospective jurors will be playing to the crowd. In other words, they may not respond to questions candidly but, because of a feeling of crowd pressure, express the popular view."

"I can see where a potential or prospective juror's responses could be influenced by peer pressure or the presence of the media and the public," Rolland said. "But how can you ascertain the truth? How do you know whether they are malingering and when they are not? You can't unscrew the top of their heads and look in. And I know you can't require that they be polygraphed or injected with truth serum. Are you really groping without a realistic expectation of success? I guess what really bothers me is that my fate will be placed in the hands of jurors who are unwilling to reveal their true biases and in their minds have already convicted me."

Drew reentered the mix. "Who do the three of you think you are—the quintessential philosophers of the Common Era? You know that *voir dire* is presumptively open to the media and public and that hell would freeze over long before the Beas would issue a closure order. The Beas is familiar with the Martha Stewart case where the trial court granted Stewart's attorneys' request for closure during examination of prospective jurors because of their fear the jury would be hesitant to tell the truth with the media and public present. But the Beas also remembers that the appellate court reversed the rulings stating: 'It is difficult to conceive of a potential juror who would be willing to reveal potential bias against the defendants in their presence, but not in the presence of reporters.'"

With that, Drew shoved a copy of the 2004 decision of *ABC Inc. v. Stewart* across the table in the direction of Lino and Bodean. "Other courts have held just the opposite," Lino countered. With that, Lino retrieved a manila file folder from a pasteboard box near his feet and, pulling a stack of neatly stapled sheets, launched the legal missile in the direction of Drew.

"Counselor, there are two sides to every issue, and there's always a court opinion out there to support any given position. I have just provided you with a federal case decided in 1998, *U.S. v. King*, in which the trial court ruled to the contrary. The court in that case said: 'Prospective jurors, if made aware that their views will be publicly disseminated in the next day's newspapers or on radio or television broadcasts, will be under pressure not to express unpopular opinions relevant to their choice as trial jurors.'

"That expresses my sentiment exactly on how a prospective juror will react during the jury selection process in our case," Lino added. "I think we would be remiss in at least not making the request. Even though we know the Beas will deny it, I feel certain the inevitable failure of *voir dire* to accomplish its intended purpose will only bolster our argument ultimately for reversal in the event of any conviction. I may be wrong, but I am certainly not in doubt."

"Now you see why we have Lino working on this case," Drew said in a complementary tone.

"Speaking of accumulating error for reversal," Bodean said, "we have two more front page headlines and stories to add to the list. I assume everyone read last night's edition of the *Star* and this morning's edition of the *Times Herald*. Clipped and presented to the group were the entire articles from both local newspapers. The headlines in the *Star* read: 'Evidence of Fetus Ruled Inadmissible in Murder of Wife.' The headlines in the *Times Herald* read: 'Key Evidence Suppressed in Prosecution of Doctor.'

"The good news is that the headlines make it look as though the defense won the motions hearing," Drew said. "The bad news is that everyone is going to read each article to see what evidence is to be kept from the jury."

"At the trial," Lino added, "the readers who make up the jury pool are then going to be admonished to disregard what they read and 'judge the case solely on the evidence presented at trial.'"

"No wonder everyone is disenchanted with our criminal justice system," Bodean said and then added: "It is too pathetic to provide comic relief. Why can't the judiciary descend from their ivory towers and temper their decisions with plain ordinary common sense? I remember one jury trial where the judge admonished the jury to disregard an objectionable statement at trial and, when asked by one of the jurors 'What statement?' the judge repeated the statement."

"Informed, courageous, and practical judges would put the appellate courts out of business, and lawyers specializing in appellate work would be unable to send their kids to expensive private schools," Lino said with sarcasm dripping from his voice, "if judges were informed, courageous, and practical."

"Remember, criticizing judges is a 'no-no' and is disrespectful. There are bad apples in every barrel. I have found judges for the most part to be honorable, dedicated, and competent," Drew said. He then added, "Some of my best friends are judges."

"Easy for you to say," Lino jibbed. "You were a municipal judge, and your grandfather once upon a time had been a trial judge as well as an appellate judge."

"I can't imagine Drew or his grandfather not granting our motion for change of venue and not transferring the case to a virgin community," Bodean said.

"Maybe the Beas will come to her senses before it is too late," Rolland added morosely.

For the moment, a strange silence permeated the conference room. Rolland and the rest of the defense team were lost in careful reflection and deep meditation when Nicole returned with steaming coffee and fresh baked cinnamon rolls. "Did you put yourselves in some type of hypnotic spell or trance by all your ponderings?" she queried. "Maybe some caffeine and pastries will extricate you from your self-imposed exile from reality."

Surprisingly, not even Bodean had a reply.

Their post-mortem of the motions hearing had been a therapy session of sorts. They came with feelings of anger, disappointment, rejection, and failure and left with confident expectancy. The real enemy was themselves and in order to overcome the obstacles they faced they would need a major attitude adjustment. To emerge triumphant would require just a little more effort. If they believed in their client's innocence then they must believe that justice would ultimately prevail. The ultimate power was on their side.

It was New Year's Eve. Soon the old year would be behind them and the New Year with all its promises lay in front of them. They prayed they would be up to the challenges that would be inextricably intertwined in the defense of Rolland and that they could and would overcome the barriers of public opinion that had been erected against him. Hopefully, the eyes, ears, minds, and hearts of the jury would be receptive and Rolland would be afforded the fair and impartial trial to which he was entitled and truly deserved.

Celebrating a Joyless New Year

The uncertainty of the new year was on everyone's mind as the bewitching hour drew near. Drew's attention was not on the present but on a time when the New Year's celebration started early at the Dawson Chalet in the Black Forest. In his arms ringing in the new year was a turquoise-eyed wildcat—wild with anticipation and excitement. There was Joy in his life then; there was no Joy now. He knew there was no one else to blame for her absence and the guilt this night was overwhelming.

"Hey, where's the usual exuberance?" Missy asked as the clock struck twelve.

"You can't see it because it's too dark," Drew said, "but hopefully you can feel the love I have for you and have always had and will always have."

With that the two held each other tightly and danced in the New Year.

Although Drew was not totally surprised, he was tentative and embarrassed when Paul Creaton, leader of the Paul Creaton Band, announced that Drew would be joining them to play Drew's latest musical composition "It's You I See." With everyone applauding their enthusiastic approval and Missy pushing him toward the stage, Drew mounted the piano bench, and with the wind and percussion instruments providing the harmony and Paul the vocal, Drew played an inspired version of the song he'd written shortly after Joy's death. The melody was described by Missy and Rolland as haunting. The lyrics were as follows:

I knew better than to walk away
Even though you begged me to stay
I saw that look in your eyes
Even then I didn't realize...that

No matter what path I take
Or what direction I go
All roads lead to you
How can it be
That no matter where I look
It's you I see
Yes, it's you I see

You knew that I couldn't stay away
That I would come back another day
I heard that sound in your voice
It was clear I had no choice...because

No matter what path I take
Or what direction I go
All roads lead to you
How can it be
That no matter where I look
It's you I see
Yes, it's you I see

You know it's difficult for me to say
That I need you each and every day
Once I felt that love in your heart
I knew we could never be a part...because

No matter what path I take
Or what direction I go all roads lead to you
How can it be
That no matter where I look
It's you I see
Yes, it's you I see

Oh, I've been to many continents
Crossed many seas
Looked into many eyes; heard many voices;
And touched many hearts
But no matter where I am or
No matter what I'm doin'
I can never be free...because
Every time I close my eyes
It's you I see
Yes, it's you I see

There was thunderous applause. Drew, who had been a member
of the original group, then played several more of his composi-
tions and then exited the stage and went to be with Missy, Rolland, and fellow firm members and their spouses.

The law firm's New Year's celebration at the Broadmoor Hotel
had been an annual event initiated by his grandfather, observed
by his father, and now embraced by him. Former firm members
and their spouses kept the history of the firm alive, and the old
war stories became more magnified and glorified with each year's
recitation. It was always interesting to learn how they did it in
the good old days and how the legal system has now gone to hell
and back in a hand basket.

The Broadmoor Hotel has always been considered a hotel
and resort *par excellence.* Its beginnings were in 1891, and its climb
to grandeur started in 1918 when Spencer Penrose, upon striking
it rich with his mining claims at Cripple Creek, built the luxury

no expense-barred hotel and resort in southwestern Colorado Springs located at the base of Cheyenne Mountain and in the shadows of Pikes Peak.

In fact, the Penrose Room, where the festivities were being held for Quinlin, Devlin & Cummins this transitional day, was reputedly the only five-diamond dining in the state.

As Drew sat marveling at the architecture, he thought back to the days of his youth when his parents and grandparents would bring him there to observe elegant swans, geese, and wild birds that graced the lake of the Broadmoor Resort and the paddle-boats available at the concession stand. When he grew older, he would swim in the large swimming pool, play tennis on the assorted courts, and caddy for his father and grandfather on the three eighteen-hole golf courses. Since the age of thirteen, he had been a member of the Broadmoor Golf Club and was one of its most active and proficient players.

"Why so pensive?" Missy asked. "You appear light years away."

"You know nostalgia sets in about this time every year."

"So what is it you're resurrecting from the past? You seem more preoccupied than usual."

"I was thinking that growing up in the backyard of the Broadmoor was normally only something folks dreamt about. I feel very fortunate to have had such devoted and generous parents and to have had the opportunities I was afforded. If it weren't for my parents, I wouldn't be here today."

"In more ways than one. Are you wondering why God picked you? Don't you think you are deserving?"

"Frankly, I feel a little guilty and undeserving. Not too many young people could boast they had ice skated at the old Broadmoor World Arena with the likes of Peggy Fleming, watched three World Figure Skating Championships and watched the Russians play the Czechs at the Broadmoor hockey rink."

"I get cold chills," Missy said, "every time I pass the memorial near the site of the Old World Arena and see the names of the Broadmoor skaters who were members of the United States Olympic Skating Team who were killed in that terrible airplane crash in 1961."

"Me too," Drew responded. "And I knew them all."

Paul Creaton announced that they had one more Drew Quinlin song to play called "Don't Give Me Tomorrow." Drew was pleasantly surprised when it was played to a bossa nova rhythm. He invited Rolland to go ahead and dance with Missy.

As Drew thought of the memory of the dead skaters and the dead artist and watched Rolland dance with Missy, he thought how fleeting life really was and how life went on despite the tragedies. He thought of how precious life was and how every moment counted. He wished he could turn back the clock and reverse the consequences of that disastrous cool autumn day in the Black Forest when life was full with Joy. If only he had it within his power to do so. Thinking fondly of the frivolous times with Joy was one thing, but trading them for the future with someone he loved as much as Missy was something else. The excitement of those few clandestine moments in the Black Forest was nothing compared to what he felt for Missy and the future in store with her. He had short-changed both women by his short sightedness. He regretted the affair with Joy and recognized all too well the folly of his ways. He could not undo the bad choices he had made, but he knew he had it within his power to alter his course and reverse the curse. And that he was determined to do.

Cameras in the Courtroom/Trial by Television

It wasn't a new phenomenon, but cameras in the courtroom and gavel-to-gavel coverage of sensational trials by the broadcast and electronic media was the exception rather than the rule.

On that cold crisp Monday following the start of the New Year, Drew was interrupted by Nicole, who handed him a pleading in the Dawson prosecution entitled: "Request for Expanded Media Coverage."

After reading the motion, Drew removed his reading glasses, chewed on one of the stems, and just shook his head in disbelief. *Good Lord*, Drew thought, *the media coverage in the Dawson case is headed from the ridiculous to the sublime; it has gone from interesting to sensational and will soon be elevated to the status of a spectacle.* "Lino," he yelled into the intercom, "come in here! You won't believe what I have just been handed."

Lino had the same reaction. "We knew that once our motions for change a venue and closure were denied it would be a kangaroo court. The Beas's rulings have just made the press bolder, and they consider the same to be a free pass and gateway to unrestricted access and uncontrolled media coverage. What more can I say?" Drew was too numb to respond.

As Lino read the pleading, he said, "I notice that a number of statewide television stations have joined our local television stations in the request for expanded media coverage, and that apparently they have entered into a pooling arrangement whereby they will make available their filming not only to those who have joined in the request but to network television and radio stations across the board."

"I guess that means," Drew commented, "we will only have one set of cables, cords, cameras, and lights instead of a dozen or so snaking their way through the courtroom."

"It will still create an obstacle course, you know," Lino quipped. "But it will enhance the integrity and quality of the proceedings by having the 'fourth estate' not only acting as a watch dog but making the proceedings accessible to those who can't observe in person," Drew said sarcastically.

"We need to get Bodean and Rolland in here ASAP," Lino said, looking at his watch. "I'm available if you are."

With that, Drew picked up the intercom and dialed Nicole. It was less than an hour before Rolland and the rest of the defense team was seated in their usual configuration around the large wooden table in the conference room and looking at each other with that strange look of bewilderment.

Bodean and Rolland were caught up to speed and had sitting in front of them when they arrived copies of the media request, the American Bar Association's canon 35 and revised rule 3A (7), rule 53 of the Federal Rules of Criminal Procedure and canon 3A (8) of the Colorado Code of Judicial Conduct.

After everyone had settled in, Rolland asked those assembled if they had ever faced this issue in any of the cases in which they had been involved. Drew and Lino both said they had never been involved, either as prosecutors or as defense counsel, in the trial of a case while the television cameras were rolling but that they were familiar with cases in which the request for expanded media coverage had been requested and granted.

Bodean said that in 1990 he had been involved in a case in Mesa County where he had done some investigative work in a half-ton cocaine case for a defense attorney who had been a district attorney in his old haunt, Steamboat Springs.

"Wasn't that case at the time the largest drug bust in the country where the contraband was worth something like one hundred and eighty-nine million dollars?" Lino asked.

"One and the same," Bodean responded.

"Anyway," Bodean continued, "the defense fought the request but for naught as the presiding judge granted the request. Afterwards, when I spoke with the defense attorney, he said just what he feared most would happen happened. He said that the trial turned into a circus-like or I guess he said 'carnival-like atmosphere.' The presence of the cameras was disruptive, distracting, and detrimental to a fair trial for his client and a co-defendant. He said the jury deliberated three days and the judge was on the verge of declaring a hung jury or mistrial. He said the jury ultimately returned guilty verdicts which he attributed to the pressures of knowing the trial had been viewed by thousands out in television land and the jurors were no doubt aware that the public was clamoring for convictions."

"Obviously, the jury didn't want to send a message that induction of a half ton of cocaine into the state of Colorado was okay," Drew said. "I remember reading about that case. The jury knows they are the conscience of the community, and if criminals don't want a Colorado conviction, they need to stop at the border."

"Because of the advancements in broadcast technology," Drew ventured, "the equipment today is not as intrusive or invasive as it once was. It's not what it was even in the early nineties at the time of the criminal prosecution Bodean described. We will still have to navigate our way around the courtroom and avoid tripping over cables, cords, equipment, and so on. Avoiding playing to the camera is a major concern. And, I'm not speaking just about myself, but the judge, other attorneys, court personnel, witnesses, and maybe even the jurors themselves who can be hams in their own right."

"No one wants to look bad," Rolland said. "I don't like being in the limelight and won't like being zoomed in on every time someone makes an inflammatory remark about me. I think I will be self-conscious and will not react as I naturally would but how I think the viewing audience would expect an innocent defendant to react. In other words, when this is all over I will be able to qualify for a screen-guild card or maybe an Emmy."

"I'm sure it will encourage theatrics on the part of all the participants," Lino said. "The mere presence of cameras not to mention the presence of television personalities and camera operators can't help but be a distraction. The jurors being distracted when key evidence is being presented, however, may spell the difference between a conviction and an acquittal."

Bodean wading in again said that the district attorney would be running for office again soon, and the Beas would be on the ballot in the next election cycle seeking retention. Both, he opined, appreciated that their successes would not be based on the scanty electorate in the courtroom but on the masses comprising the viewership of the various television networks covering Rolland's trial.

"Can't you just picture it now," Rolland said, "in the middle of cross-examination of a key witness, the television announcer interrupts the programming 'to bring our viewers a word from our sponsor' or 'to bring our viewers the following breaking news' or 'for the following blizzard warning.' Is a trial by televi-

DEADLY DECEPTION   199

sion important to the dispensation of justice or informative or is it mainly just to entertain?"

"Probably for all of the above reasons," Drew responded. "Or at least that is what the Beas would contend."

Nicole stuck her head into the doorway and announced that it was time for a lunch break. She then wheeled in a serving cart with an assortment of cold cuts, cheeses, fruits, breads, spreads, cold and hot drinks, vegetables, and pastries. "It's about time," Bodean chided. Nicole's only retort was "Just leave the tip on the tray."

After some rest and relaxation, the defense team settled in for some serious discussion.

They first analyzed canon 35 that the ABA originally recommended be added to each state's code of judicial conduct. It provided:

"Proceedings in court should be conducted with fitting dignity and decorum. The taking of photographs in the courtroom, during sessions of the court or recesses between sessions, and the broadcasting of court proceedings are calculated to distract from the essential dignity of the proceedings, degrade the court, and create misconceptions with respect thereto in the mind of the public and should not be permitted."

Rolland *et al.* then analyzed the latest version of rule 3A (7) which replaced canon 35. It represented a retraction of the ABA's original stance of prohibiting television coverage in the courtroom and replaced its recommendation in favor of allowing such coverage. "A complete three hundred and sixty–degree turn," Bodean observed.

Rule 53 of the Federal Rules of Criminal Procedure was analyzed in its entirety. It constituted a complete ban on cameras, and photography and recording equipment in federal courts. It appeared to be the favored position of the defense team.

Saving canon 3A (8) that was added to the Colorado Code of Judicial Conduct to last, it was dissected to its most elemental unit. However, before doing so, Lino explained that up to thirty or forty years ago, every state except Colorado and Texas had followed the federal rule in banning cameras, photography, and recording equipment from the courtroom. Although Colorado allows the use of such equipment, he said, it must be with consent of the presiding judge.

Lino then quoted from canon 3A (8). "A judge may authorize expanded media coverage of a court proceeding.... In determining whether expanded media coverage should be permitted, a judge shall consider the following factors: ...whether there is a reasonable likelihood that expanded media coverage would interfere with the rights of the parties to a fair trial,...unduly detract from the solemnity, decorum and dignity of the court... and...would create adverse effects that would be greater than those caused by traditional media coverage."

Lino then pointed out that expanded media coverage in Colorado was disallowed during jury selection, coverage of *in camera* hearings (hearings outside the presence of the jury) and close-up photography of jurors. He also reiterated that the presiding judge could restrict or limit expanded media coverage as might be necessary to preserve the dignity of the court or to protect the parties, witnesses, or jurors. He concluded by pointing out a very important restriction. Only one person at a time would be permitted to operate a videotape, television, or motion picture camera during court proceedings. "Hence, the reason for a pooling arrangement," he said.

"Otherwise," Drew volunteered, "the court would have to draw names or hold a lottery or maybe even an auction to see who the lucky television station would be."

"If the Beas grants the media's request for expanded media coverage, it's my understanding from what Lino stated," Bodean said, "that they can cover all the proceedings with the exception of *voir dire* or jury selection and *in camera* hearings."

"Am I correct?" he asked.

"Absolutely," Lino responded. "They can cover the trial from 'gavel-to-gavel' that is from the time the gavel bangs the trial to order to the time that the gavel is banged announcing its conclusion with the exception, of course, of the trial phases I just mentioned.

"They then have the right to play or replay the trial with simultaneous broadcasting or delayed broadcasting at their pleasure. They also have at their disposal the same instant replay capabilities as the sport networks. In other words, the viewers can have instant replay of the most 'probative' segments of the trial."

"You mean the most 'sensational' segments," Bodean corrected.

Rolland then asked if Judge Beasley could restrict the media from reporting on all or some of the portions of the evidence presented in their presence. "I guess my question is," Rolland continued, "can the judge selectively tell the media what they can broadcast and what they can't?"

"Not too likely," Lino responded. "What the media obtain lawfully, they are free to publish. That is their First Amendment right."

"But you remember what happened in the Kobe Bryant case," Drew said. "The Colorado Supreme Court in 2004 upheld an order by the presiding judge preventing the various news organizations from publishing information they obtained lawfully and, in fact, information that was provided to them by a court reporter."

"That involved information *inadvertently* provided to the media," Lino said. "But you make your point, 'What the judge giveth, the judge can taketh away.'"

Rolland, growing restless, asked whether the Beas was predisposed to grant the request for expanded media coverage. Pursing their lips and nodding in the affirmative, Drew and Lino answered Rolland's question.

The defense filed their objection to the broadcasters' request for expanded media coverage that same day. Hearing on the request and objection thereto was scheduled for that succeeding Monday, January 12. Dayton was out-of-town, and Terrell appeared for the prosecution. Drew was starting a trial in another district and did not accompany Lino, Bodean, and Rolland. A manager for the local television station as well as Kevin Roy, newsman for one of the Denver television stations, and the designated media representative for the proceedings, was also present along with the station's attorney, C. Milton Fullerton. Several local attorneys representing local television stations entered their appearances, but it was C. Milton Fullerton who was their collective mouthpiece.

The proceedings started promptly at 10:00 a.m., and predictably Fullerton leaned on the First Amendment for everything it was worth. Even though the present First Amendment was the third proposed amendment presented for ratification in 1791, as the first two proposed amendments were defeated, Fullerton heralded it as the foundation of America's whole form of government and the wellspring of all the rights all Americans enjoy. Actually, Lino could not argue with that and, in fact, agreed. However, as Lino would later argue, the Sixth Amendment was also a part of the Bill of Rights and needed to be balanced against the First Amendment.

Fullerton cited a number of cases generating national interest because of the celebrity status of the defendants involved wherein the courts and those various jurisdictions granted the electronic media's request for cameras in the courtroom and the gavel-to-gavel broadcast of the proceedings. Fullerton started with the rape trial of William Kennedy Smith in 1991. He said trial by television and its filming obviously was not detrimental to the defendant nor did it deprive him of a fair trial as Kennedy was acquitted of all charges.

More notable, according to Fullerton, was the O.J. Simpson murder trial in 1995. One of the largest, longest, and most extensively covered criminal trials in history, the former college and professional football star did not show the ill effects of cameras in the courtroom or the daily broadcasting of the trial, watched by millions, as he too won an acquittal on all charges.

Fullerton concluded his argument in support of the media request by saying that unless the defense could show that expanded media coverage would interfere with Dr. Dawson's right to a fair trial, or that it would unduly detract from the solemnity, decorum, and dignity of the court, or that it would create adverse effects that would be greater than those caused by media coverage, the broadcast media's request should be granted.

Judge Beasley announced that because the prosecution had not filed an objection to the pending request, it was assumed they did not oppose the granting thereof. Terrell, as anticipated, stated the prosecution had no objection to the granting of the request for expanded media coverage and because of the great public interest and concern in the case and the right by the public to know, he knew of no better way to make an accused's right to a public trial more public than by television exposure.

The defense was vehemently opposed to cameras in the courtroom. Now it was up to Lino to be persuasive in his attempt to convince the Beas to rule in defendant's favor.

"May it please the court: The defense opposes cameras in the courtroom because of the circus-like atmosphere it will create. It is critical that the jury's undivided attention be given to the proceedings and that the jury not be distracted by extraneous matters taking place in the courtroom that really don't have anything to do with the case. That's why churches have soundproof crying rooms for parents with infants. Courts should not allow the sideshow to overshadow the main event. The purpose of a criminal trial is to make sure that justice is served. It is not meant to satisfy the public's curiosity, or to serve as in instructive device or to amuse. There are enough Perry Mason–like court dramas on television to satisfy the public's appetite without having to compromise an accused's right to a fair trial.

"Your Honor, the courtroom is not a movie set where make-believe drama is meant to entertain. A trial is a real-life drama where the participants are playing to the jury and not to the public and where there are lasting consequences that can sometimes spell the difference between life and death. Characters on-screen, on the other hand, have the ability to come back and make another movie, play a whole new role, and even come back from the dead.

"The accused, if convicted, on the other hand, seldom can do a retake or change the script or be cast in an entirely new role. The whole purpose of cameras in the courtroom is to film a drama in progress and to play to the lurid curiosity of the public. It is pandering to the public, plain and simple, and serves no utilitarian purpose. Certainly it does not benefit the court process and actually poses a threat to the integrity of the criminal justice system. In a symbiotic relationship, both organisms should flourish. If the request for expanded media coverage is granted, the media is akin to a parasite benefiting at the expense of the host, here the justice system and Rolland's right to a fair trial. If expanded media coverage is so desirable, then why isn't it the rule rather than the exception. The only way for the defense to meet its impossible burden of proving that the courtroom filming will make a substantial difference in a material aspect of the trial is to wait to evaluate it with 20/20 hindsight. But, by then, Your Honor, it will be too late."

Without any hesitancy, the Beas granted the request for expanded media coverage excluding therefrom, of course, jury selection, *in camera* hearings and close-up photography of the defendant and members of the jury. In doing so, the Beas stated, "The rationale for my ruling is that that segment of the public who are not present in court should be afforded the same opportunity to observe as those who are present. The defense has offered no evidence to support their contention that expanded media coverage would interfere with the rights of Dr. Dawson or that it would detract from the solemnity or dignity of the court or would create any adverse effect."

Then directing her remarks at Fullerton, the Beas stated, "Only one person at a time will be permitted to operate a videotape, television, or motion picture camera in the courtroom and all equipment used in connection therewith will have to be positioned and operated in such a way as to minimize any distractions. If the granting of the media's request becomes disruptive or otherwise compromises Dr. Dawson's right to a fair trial, I will have to reconsider my ruling and either modify or revoke it." Fullerton said he understood.

When Rolland asked Lino what he thought about the Beas's ruling, Lino stated, "Only time will tell; only time will tell." Lino fervently hoped that Rolland's day in court would be more than hollow rhetoric and that at trial's end, the defense would have something to celebrate.

Preparing for Battle

Drew and Lino knew that they had to pass the PAP test in order to ensure success at trial. PAP was their acronym for plan, anticipate, and prepare. As experienced trial lawyers, they knew ten weeks was not a long time to train and get in fighting shape. They didn't have time to waste.

Bodean offered a perspective as a crack investigator having been a law enforcement officer for a number of years and having trained the trainers. He also had been on the defense side longer than most of his constituents. What Drew and Lino liked about him most was that he "had both feet on the ground." He was practical, intuitive, and innovative. He liked what he was doing, and he was doing what he liked. Rolland offered a different perspective. Ordinarily, the defendant was too close to the situation to see the big picture. Rolland was a *big picture* defendant. His training as a surgeon had prepared him to be dispassionate, objective, and deliberate as opposed to reactionary. His intelligence, intimate knowledge of the facts and lack of denial made his contribution to his defense all the more valuable. He was indispensible to the defense team in making his exoneration more than an impossible dream.

In the quiet of that second Saturday of the year's first month, the defense team began the first in a series of many prep sessions. They knew it would be a long, arduous journey fraught by many challenges and anxious moments, and they hoped and prayed that it would not all be in vain.

The defense team thought it would be a good idea to start by anticipating how they would proceed if they were Dayton and Terrell. "I would dismiss the case and withdraw the charges if I were the prosecutor," Drew said. "But I know they are not going to go against the grain of public opinion. It would not be politically expedient—at least not during an election year."

Lino suggested they identify the prosecution's witnesses first. Since the prosecution had to list all the names of potential witnesses and could not call any (except in rebuttal) that were not listed, the list included improbable witnesses. Sorting through the list, the defense team selected the most probable.

It was determined that the prosecution would follow the chronology of events as they unfolded. First they would call Norma Evans, the operator who took the 911 call from Rolland. She would either identify the preserved tape, which would be placed in evidence, or a transcription thereof. The defense would not object to either or both being admitted in evidence.

Next the prosecution would call the two deputy sheriffs who were dispatched to the Dawson Chalet in the Black Forest, Roger Milligan and Kevin Stanton. Their testimony for the most part would be identical. They would testify that they were dispatched to the scene shortly after 7:30 p.m. on Friday, September 12. When they arrived at approximately 8:00 p.m., they were greeted by Dr. Rolland Dawson. They would then identify

Dr. Dawson. Continuing, they would state that Dr. Dawson led them to his wife's body. She, of course, was deceased.

In plain view, they observed three blue buttons lying on the floor in various locations around the body. They saw a blue flannel shirt, again in plain view, draped across a chair in an adjacent room approximately ten feet from the body. They asked Dr. Dawson whose shirt it was, and he said it was his. When they examined the shirt, they found three buttons missing. When they compared the buttons found on the floor with those still on the shirt, they found a match. They also noticed that the pocket on the shirt had been torn. All the items recovered at the scene were turned over to Rick Tompkins, a lab technician/crime scene specialist assigned to the sheriff's office, who arrived on the scene.

When they examined the scene, they noticed hair and blood on a moss rock that protruded from the fireplace. They also observed a wound to the back of Joy's head. They were present when Henry Fisk took scrapings from the rock and also recovered fibers that were still grasped in Joy's hands. They would relate that Fisk collected those items, bagged them, and then transported them to Vincent Townsend, the evidence custodian, who transferred them to the CBI.

They were present when the county coroner/medical examiner arrived from another unattended death unconnected with this case. He examined the body and had it transported to the morgue. The names of the EMTs who transferred the body to the morgue were Taggert Williams and Cary Lamb. The name of a coroner/medical examiner was Dr. Francisco Mendoza. The body was then turned over to the pathologist, Dr. Horace Bellamy, who performed a detailed autopsy.

The deputies would also identify photographs they took of the scene upon their arrival. They would thereupon lay a sufficient foundation to justify their admission in evidence. The photographs would then, no doubt, be circulated among the jurors.

Bodean then produced the photographs that had been provided to the defense in discovery. The defense team selected the photographs they thought the prosecution would use and some they would offer in evidence in the event the prosecution didn't. Bodean also circulated some of the photographs of the scene that he had taken. However, they were taken after the body had been removed and the scene processed. For that reason, the Beas might deny their admission.

The defense team agreed that Dr. Francisco Mendoza would be the next witness called. He would testify that in his opinion the cause of death "was massive hemorrhaging of the brain due to blunt trauma." He would further testify that "it was highly unlikely that the trauma resulted from an accidental fall and the injury was more consistent with trauma caused by extreme physical force." Lino stated that the defense would be objecting to the aforesaid opinion on the ground that Dr. Mendoza was not a board-certified pathologist and did not possess the requisite qualifications to render such an opinion. Lino conceded that the Beas would, in all likelihood, overrule their objection and allow Dr. Mendoza to express his opinion.

The pathologist, Dr. Horace Bellamy, because of his qualifications and certifications, could render the opinions sought from Dr. Mendoza. So the evidence would ultimately reach the jury anyway. Because of the judge's previous ruling, however, Dr. Bellamy would not be allowed to mention his discovery of the fetus. Dr. Bellamy would place the estimated time of death at 4:30 p.m.

The defense team speculated that Henry Fisk, the sheriff's department lab technician/crime scene analyst, would be the next witness called by the prosecution. He would testify as to the collection and preservation of the evidence found at the scene, specifically the blood and hair scrapings, the blue flannel shirt, the fiber fragments, and the three buttons. He would testify that the evidence stayed in his possession until it was turned over to agent Rick Tompkins of the Colorado Bureau of Investigation for analysis and comparison.

Rick Thompkins no doubt would be the prosecution's next witness. He would confirm the accuracy of the deputy sheriffs' observations.

Lannette Castles, the receptionist/secretary/bookkeeper at Rolland's clinic, would testify that Rolland left the clinic at approximately 12:45 p.m. September 12 because he complained of being ill. From that time until she left work at 5:30 p.m., Rolland had not returned.

The prosecution would then call Rolland's neighbors, either or both Gary or Ann Anderson, who lived to the east and Dan or Lynn Staves who lived to the west. All would testify that they were home on the afternoon and the evening of September 12 and none saw Rolland or his vehicle at his home during such times.

There was no doubt in the minds of the defense team that the prosecution would end their presentation of evidence with a flurry. One of the most basic trial tenants is to start with a strong witness, finish with a strong witness, preferably your strongest. Enter Carla and Pierre Delajure. Although they weren't certain Pierre would be called because of his suspected felony conviction, Carla would most certainly be called. She would testify that she had worked for Rolland in April 2006 and that he said that he "had a foolproof way of getting rid of his wife" and that his wife's death "would be perceived by the authorities as an accident." She would also testify that Rolland had been "hitting" on her.

If Pierre testified, of course, he could be impeached by any felony there be. So far the defense team had not heard from the district attorney's office as to whether Pierre was a convicted felon. Since he was an endorsed witness, they assumed he would be called to the stand—with or without a conviction. Pierre would testify that he suspected his wife was having an affair with Rolland and he was listening in on his wife's conversations with Rolland. He would testify that he overheard Rolland's aforementioned statements. Drew reminded them, however, that Pierre would be barred from testifying if indeed he had a felony conviction because of the prosecution's failure to so notify the defense within thirty days of trial as mandated by the Beas.

Drew and Lino reiterated that the Delajures' testimony was the key that opened the door to murder in the first degree. It provided the deliberation or premeditation required as an element of the offense as well as the motive. Without the Delajures' testimony, the prosecution would not be able to sustain their burden of proof with respect to the first-degree murder charge.

All agreed that the above would constitute the prosecution's case-in-chief. Although the district attorney's investigator, William "Will" Rodgers, had been endorsed by the prosecution as a witness, they could not see anything in his reports that were not duplicitous or secondhand information. His testimony, they concluded, would be token at best.

Bodean noticed in going through the discovery, that many reports referred to where Joy's body was found as the *crime* scene. Lino assured him that he and Drew would object every time such a reference was made at trial. It was every bit an *accident* scene as a *crime* scene.

Rolland then asked if the defense would be invoking the sequestration rule with reference to not having witnesses in the courtroom while other witnesses testified—as they did during the motions hearing. Lino said that was "standard operating procedure." He stated, however, that each side could designate an "advisory witness" who would not be subject to the rule. William "Will" Rodgers would no doubt be designated as the prosecution's advisory witness and Bodean, of course, as the defense's designee. He added Rolland would be exempt from the rule as well.

The defense team broke for lunch and ate at the deli across the street.

When they returned to the offices of Quinlin, Devlin & Cummins, Bodean, every bit the philosopher, mused, "It's too bad the prosecution can't present their case in a couple hours as we did this morning."

"If that's a motion, I'll second it," Lino said sarcastically. "Keep in mind that if we push the issue, the prosecution will have to parade before the jury a litany of boring witnesses to establish what we call 'chain of custody.' To phrase it differently, technically before any physical evidence can be admitted at trial, the side offering evidence must prove that the evidence collected at the scene, for example, was the same evidence in the same condition, undefiled and not tampered with, that was turned over for testing and analysis and that is ultimately introduced into court as evidence.

"Every person into whose hands or possession every piece of evidence was placed must testify at trial. Normally, if there is a gap or break in the chain, the evidence cannot be admitted. So if it passed through the hands of A, B, C, D, and E, and C does not testify, then there is a problem. All must be able to confirm that, for example, the integrity of the evidence was preserved and remained unchanged from the time it was collected until the time it was tested or analyzed and that it is the same item being offered as evidence at trial."

"If we knew or suspected that Dayton and Terrell would have a problem or trouble establishing a chain of custody in our case," Drew said, "we would put the prosecution to the test and have them prove the chain of custody. As it is, Bodean has traced the chain and interviewed all the witnesses involved and has concluded it would be a waste of our time as well as everyone else's. We will no doubt be stipulating to the chain and will use it as a bargaining chip with the DA's office to obtain some concessions of our own."

It was now time to concentrate on the defense's case. In theory, the defendant didn't have to present evidence, and the defendant didn't have to testify. Those were Rolland's rights under the Fifth Amendment. In practice, depending on the strength of the prosecution's case, however, a defendant's silence was usually construed as an admission of guilt. This was particularly true in murder prosecutions.

"The jury wants to hear from the lips of the defendant that he didn't do it," Drew said. "We will actually be presenting our denial in the way we frame our questions during jury selection, in our outline of the defendant's case in our opening statement and in our summary in final argument. Sandwiched in between will be our cross-examination of the prosecution's witnesses and the presentation of our case-in-chief.

"At another session, we will discuss our cross-examination of the prosecution's witnesses. This afternoon, however, we'll outline our strategy as well as the evidence we intend to present. Our whole case hinges on Rolland's testimony and how he is perceived by the jury. Is he credible, caring, and concerned? Is the death of his wife more problematic than his exoneration? Is he making excuses or is he merely presenting an explanation? Will he stand up to a grueling cross-examination by a master? Will he manifest anger when he is grilled or cornered—the kind of anger that would cause him to be violent in an uncontrolled setting? Or will he be perceived as not being impetuous, impulsive, or reactionary? For those of us who know Rolland, the answers are all favorable. As for those who will be determining Rolland's fate in the courtroom, however, their judgment will be based on but a fleeting glimpse of the real Rolland."

"I only hope I'm up to the task," Rolland said. "A few months ago, I had my doubts. Today and tomorrow will be a different story. Even if you had advised against testifying, I would still insist being allowed to proclaim my innocence. The fact that you all believe in me is added incentive to testify."

"Before you take the stand in your defense," Lino said, "it will appear the Beas will be trying to talk you out of it. She will advise you that you don't have to testify, that you have a right to remain silent, the right not to incriminate yourself, and so on. She will make sure you want to testify and are making an informed and voluntary decision to testify, free from the influence of your attorneys or anyone else. Rolland, we went over this drill with you before and want to be sure you understand and are prepared."

"I am," Rolland said, "but I'm feeling the pressure. It almost appears that the deck is stacked against me. I wish I could be assured my testimony and all your hard work will not have been in vain. I hope I am not convicted because of public sentiment and law enforcement's desire for closure."

"If we think we can succeed, we can," Lino said, "and I think we think we can."

"I know we can," Bodean added emphatically.

Drew then commenced to list the defense's witnesses and summarize their testimony. He explained that the calling of defense witnesses depended on the latitude that the Beas would afford on cross-examination. If cross-examination was restricted, then the defense should consider subpoenaing some of the prosecution's witnesses and have them on call. Lannette Castles, for example, would be called to establish that on September 12, Rolland appeared to be ill and had manifested symptoms all morning and had declined lunch. She would also testify that Rolland had left work early the previous afternoon, again because of illness. The defense team was confident they could elicit all the favorable evidence on cross.

All agreed that the first witness to be called by the defense should be Dr. Homer Renning, their forensic pathologist. He was board certified and had been qualified as an expert in many high-profile cases throughout the state. He would testify that indeed the cause of Joy's death was "massive hemorrhaging of the brain due to blunt trauma," but unlike the prosecution's witnesses, he found that Joy's head injury "was consistent with trauma resulting from an accidental fall." He would be presented with the photograph of Joy's body as it was positioned when it was discovered with the hearth and the bloodstained rock of the fireplace clearly visible. He would then be asked to render an opinion as to whether tripping over the hearth and falling against the rock would have been consistent with the force required to cause the injury that resulted in Joy's death. He, of course, would be answering in the affirmative.

There were other defense witnesses endorsed, such as Rolland's neighbors, the Andersons and the Staves. However, the defense would be discrediting their observations or lack thereof and they would be of no benefit whatsoever. Just because Rolland's neighbors, who were located some distance away, didn't see him or his car on the afternoon or evening on September 12 didn't mean that he or the car were not there.

The simplicity of the defendant's case-in-chief didn't become evident until the defense team realized that the only other defense witness that would be called would be Rolland himself. Rolland's statements to Bodean on October 3 became the basis of Rolland's proposed testimony.

Rolland would testify that on Thursday, September 11, he left work early because he had flulike symptoms. Joy insisted that he come home and rest. He arrived home at approximately 4:00

p.m. and slept until approximately 8:15 p.m. Joy fed him some chicken noodle soup, saltine crackers, and hot tea, which he had a difficult time keeping down.

He felt somewhat better the next morning and kept his morning appointments and rounds at the hospital. By noon, his symptoms returned. He canceled his afternoon appointments leaving the clinic at approximately 12:45 p.m. and arrived home at approximately 1:15 p.m. He parked his car in the garage and closed the door as was his usual custom.

When Joy had called midmorning, he assured her that he was on the mend and for her to go ahead to Black Forest and finish her landscape. When he called her on her cell phone at approximately 2:30 p.m., he advised her that he was at home, but she need not return. He said he would call her if he needed her. Otherwise, it was agreed that she would be home at sometime between 6:00 p.m. and 6:30 p.m.

When Joy hadn't arrived by 6:40 p.m., Rolland tried to reach her cell phone. Unable to do so, he assumed she had stopped for grocery items at the Rustic Hills Shopping Center and had left her cell phone in the car.

At 7:00 p.m., when he couldn't reach her and she hadn't called, he became concerned. He drove out to their summer place in the Black Forest arriving at approximately 7:15 p.m. The easel with the partially painted canvas stood on the front deck where she usually painted. On a glass-top table close by was a palette with various oils and their wells, several brushes, and a white cloth. He called for her and, receiving no answer, went inside. There in front of the moss rock fireplace she lay face up with her head on the low hearth. She had no pulse, no heartbeat; her body was cold; and it was apparent she had breathed her last.

It was approximately 7:30 p.m. when he called 911 and reported Joy's death. By 8:00 p.m. two El Paso County sheriff's deputies, Roger Milligan and Kevin Stanton, arrived. Within the hour, a lab technician by the name of Henry Fisk arrived and was in the midst of "processing the scene" when the county coroner/medical examiner arrived. The county coroner confirmed their fears and called for an ambulance to transport Joy's body to the morgue.

Rolland watched as photographs were being taken and items collected from the Dawson summer place. Draped over a chair in the kitchen was a blue flannel shirt. The deputies asked if he knew who the shirt belonged to, and he said it looked like one of his. He pointed out, however, that the last time he saw it, it was hanging in a hall closet and wasn't in a damaged condition. He told them he hadn't worn it in years; that it was kept mainly for guests.

Rolland would testify that the last time he saw his wife and spoke with her, she was alive. He was not present when she died and had not been to the chalet for over a week before her body was discovered. He did not know what happened. He and his wife had not been arguing. He had absolutely nothing to do with his wife's death. He did not strike, push, or shove his wife. He would categorically and unequivocally deny the statements he allegedly made to the Delajures.

Lino explained that if the jury concluded that Rolland caused Joy's death but didn't do so deliberately as was required for first degree murder they could still find him guilty of the lesser included offense of second degree murder. If they found that he did not cause her death knowingly, that is he was not aware that his conduct was practically certain to cause the result, they could still find him guilty of manslaughter. That required that he caused Joy's death recklessly. Recklessly meant that Rolland disregarded a substantial and unjustifiable risk of some sort.

Lino then went on to explain that if the jury found that Rolland caused Joy's death but didn't do so deliberately or intentionally, knowingly or willfully, or recklessly, they could still find him

     CARROLL MULTZ

guilty of the lesser charge of criminally negligent homicide. That offense only required criminal negligence. Criminal negligence was defined by the Colorado statute as a gross deviation from the standard of care that a reasonable person would exercise. The situation would be where Rolland failed to perceive a substantial and unjustifiable risk that his actions would result in her death.

"Of course," Lino concluded, "if Rolland didn't cause Joy's death or if he did, he didn't do it, even with criminal negligence, the jury would be required to acquit or find Rolland not guilty."

"Wouldn't that be a happy ending to an unhappy story!" Bodean said.

"Ditto," Rolland said as he buried his head in his hands and sobbed.

After Rolland regained his composure somewhat, he told Lino he was confused. "Criminally negligent homicide is a lower class felony than manslaughter, yet there appears to be no difference."

"Although the difference is subtle and slight, there is a difference not to mention a distinction," Lino responded. "Manslaughter requires that a person not only disregard a substantial and unjustifiable risk but that at the time of the act such person has to be aware of the risk. Criminally negligent homicide, on the other hand, does not require awareness of the risk but only the failure unreasonably to *perceive* the risk."

"I think I understand," Rolland said, raising his eyebrows and tilting his head.

Drew then took his turn at the helm and stated that before the jury was sent to the jury room to deliberate, both sides would then give their final arguments with the prosecution going first and last and the defense being sandwiched in between.

Rolland asked who would be making the final argument for the defense. Drew announced that he would and that Lino would be making the opening statement. The remaining trial assignments were tentatively allocated as follows: starting with the cross-examination of the key prosecution witnesses. Lino would cross-examine Norma Evans, Roger Milligan, Kevin Stanton, Vincent Townsend, Henry Fisk, Taggert Williams, Cary Lamb, Lannette Castles, Gary and Ann Anderson, and Dan and Lynn Staves. Drew would cross-examine Dr. Francisco Mendoza, Dr. Horace Bellamy, Rick Tompkins, and Carla Delajure.

With respect to the defense's case-in-chief, Lino would examine the following witnesses: Dr. Homer Renning and Lannette Castles, if she was needed. Rolland would be Drew's witness.

After the lunch break, the defense team, as the last order of business for the first session, set the date for the next session. It was scheduled for Saturday, January 17 at the same time and place. In the interim each had specific assignments. Drew and Lino would schedule an appointment with opposing counsel and circumvent some of the tedium of trial by entering into mutually advantageous stipulations. Bodean would arrange to have the sheriff serve Lannette and Dr. Renning with their subpoenas. Lino would alert Dr. Renning about the anticipated service of subpoena and meet with Dr. Renning to review his testimony and review with him the accident scene photographs as well as the photographs taken at Joy's autopsy. Drew and Lino would be preparing their cross-examinations and direct-examinations. In that regard, Bodean would begin preparing Rolland's testimony by reviewing with Rolland police reports, witness statements, and other discovery documents.

So that they would know what dates to subpoena their witnesses, the defense team prepared a trial calendar, which reflected their best guesstimates. The time lines were determined on the assumption that chain of custody would be stipulated to and that jury selection would take the better part of two days.

CHART I

First Week	Monday	Tuesday	Wednesday	Thursday	Friday
MORNING	Jury Selection	Jury Selection	Opening Statements Prosecution Defense	Rick Tompkins Henry Fisk Dr. Francisco Mendoza	Lannette Castles Ann Anderson Gary Anderson Lynn Staves Dan Staves
AFTERNOON	Jury Selection	Jury Selection	Norma Evans Vincent Townsend Roger Milligan Kevin Stanton	Taggert Williams Cary Lamb Dr. Horace Bellamy	Carla Delajure Pierre Delajure Motion for Judgment of Acquittal

Second Week	Monday	Tuesday	Wednesday	Thursday	Friday
MORNING	Dr. Horace Renning Lannette Castles (if needed)	Dr. Rolland Dawson (cont'd) Prosecution Rebuttal	Instructions to Jury Final Arguments Prosecution Defense (Rebuttal)	Jury Deliberation (cont'd)	
AFTERNOON	Dr. Rolland Dawson	Judge and Attorneys Prep; Jury Instructions	Jury Deliberation		

King winter had been raising havoc all week. It appeared this Saturday, January 17 would be no different. The defense team was happy to be indoors. Only fifty-seven days until trial with plenty of lead time but no time to waste. The second session of trial prep was underway.

Drew and Lino reported they had met with the prosecuting attorneys midweek and entered into the stipulation whereby certain exhibits would be entered into evidence without objection and without the necessity of calling witnesses to establish the chain of custody. Lino said the collection and preservation of evidence was done by the book and it would be futile to require the witnesses in the chain to testify.

Lino related that Dayton had agreed that, should the defense renew their motion to have the jury view the scene that is to see firsthand the Dawson Chalet and the spot where Joy's body was discovered, the prosecution would not object. Lino also related that both sides agreed that the jury would not be sequestered or segregated or locked up during the trial but that, should their deliberations continue into a second day, they should be sequestered the night before.

"What is the purpose of sequestering the jury?" Rolland asked.

"To prevent them from being exposed to the electronic and print media and to keep them from conferring with family and friends regarding their impending verdict," Drew responded.

"Speaking of sequestration," Lino continued, "we have agreed with the prosecution to ask the court to enter a sequestration of witness order. That means that only one witness will be allowed to be present in court at a time, thus preventing one witness from hearing the testimony of another."

"Isn't that really a farce?" Rolland asked. "Don't witnesses already know what the others are going to testify to? I know I've been present when the three of you interviewed some of my witnesses."

"In a sense that's true," Drew said. "However, they haven't been present and, if sequestered, won't be present during the cross-examination of other witnesses. But you're right. Before entering the courtroom they have for the most part coordinated their proposed testimony."

"Bodean and yourself, of course, will be allowed to be in the courtroom along with the district attorney's investigator," Lino said. "The witness sequestration rule would exclude the three of you."

"We will need to inform our witnesses in advance of the order to avoid having them disqualified from testifying," Drew said. "That will be Bodean's job to make sure none surreptitiously enter the courtroom."

"Have you ever had that happen?" Rolland asked.

"It's never happened to Drew or me," Lino replied. Then turning to Drew, Lino asked, "When you were a prosecutor didn't you object to a key witness from being called in a murder case because he had been sitting listening to other witnesses testify?"

"Indeed I did," Drew responded. "It was a murder sanity trial, and it was the defendant's therapist who I kept off the stand. To this day, Milton Forrester, the opposing counsel in that case, refuses to speak to me. Somehow, I guess he thinks it was my fault he lost the case."

"Well!" Lino chided.

"Let's not go down a rabbit trail," Drew admonished. "We have a lot of ground to cover."

Drew then explained that because of the Beas's policy regarding extra-judicial statements by the attorneys or any of the participants, both sides agreed not to issue any out-of-court statements or otherwise speak to the media until after the jury verdict was returned. Drew added that the Beas at the status conference would no doubt be issuing a formal gag order to that effect anyway.

Bodean asked whether there had been any plea discussion and if so, what concessions the district attorney's office was willing to make. Drew responded that Dayton, at the outset of their meeting, made it clear that his hands were tied and that in light of the torn shirt tying Rolland to Joy's death and Rolland's statements to the Delajures he could not deviate from murder in the first degree. Even if Rolland pled guilty to the charge, he said he would not agree to probation even if he were able to do so. "So what does Rolland have to lose by going to trial?" Bodean asked, not expecting a response.

Bodean said that both Lannette and Dr. Renning had been served with subpoenas by the sheriff's department and returns of service had been filed with the court. "With all that lead time," Drew commented, "neither should be heard to complain about a scheduling conflict."

Lino said he and Bodean had met with Dr. Renning and found him to be very knowledgeable and thorough. "It helped," Bodean commented, "that Dr. Renning had visited the scene."

"As you will recall," Lino reminded, "he wouldn't issue a formal opinion until after he visited the scene and conducted what he called 'an experiment.'" Both agreed he would be impressive and persuasive at trial.

The remainder of the morning was spent analyzing the anticipated testimony of the prosecution's witnesses and formulating questions that the defense proposed to ask on cross-examination. By lunch break, they were satisfied with the progress they made and were confident that their cross-examination would create enough holes in the prosecution's case as to make it look like a piece of Swiss cheese. It was this metaphor that convinced the defense team that it was lunchtime.

For the better part of the afternoon, it was Rolland's turn in the barrel. Rolland was seated in a simulated witness chair. Drew took the podium and conducted direct examination. Rolland was every bit the witness they expected, and all were surprised at his glibness and ingratiating manner. It was obvious that Bodean had done his job in reviewing the discovery documents with Rolland and otherwise preparing Rolland for this dress rehearsal. Now, if only he could withstand the enemy fire and barrage on cross-examination that was Dayton's trademark at trial when it really counted. Rolland didn't have to wait long to be tested.

For almost two and a half hours, Rolland was subjected to the most grueling cross-examination tolerated in a civilized society. Lino, Drew, and Bodean were relentless. Yet, despite being outnumbered, bullied, and browbeaten, it was the inquisitors who ultimately waved the white flag. Rolland was imperturbable and the epitome of the ideal witness. They would not have to worry about him.

As the curtain of night began to fall, the defense team dispersed for a time only to return in the following days to sharpen their swords on a sporadic and less structured basis. Their intense training and sparring sessions would be replaced by a more civilized regimen. Besides, if justice be with them, victory could not be far behind.

Into the Fiery Pit

The ides of March drifted into the first day of trial in the case of the *People of the State of Colorado, Plaintiff v. Rolland J. Dawson, Defendant.* That dreaded day of infamy finally arrived. The once-respected local orthopedic surgeon was being prosecuted for murder in the first degree in the death of his beautiful and talented wife, a local artist of some renown. The trial was heralded by both the print and broadcast media as one of the most highly publicized criminal cases in the county's history. Hopefully, that didn't translate into "hang the wife killer now, and then determine his innocence or guilt."

The first day of trial was much like the first day of school. There was excitement in the air and frantic anticipation. There were some old faces and some new faces, some friendly and some hostile. The environment was both inviting and foreboding. For the seasoned trial lawyer inner turmoil was whether you could live up to your reputation; for the inexperienced it was whether you could be the spoiler and slay the giant. But for both, there was nervous anticipation.

Drew and Lino were no different than their contemporaries except that they had a plethora of criminal trial experience both as prosecutors and as defense counsel. In fact, their whole professional lives were spent in court or in preparation thereof. Both placed preparation above experience. Both had seen unprepared veterans lose cases to prepared neophytes. In the case now before the court both sides boasted of experience and their fair share of victories. Dayton and Terrell had the benefit of the resources, but Drew and Lino prided themselves on being more resourceful. All things being otherwise equal, even with the Beas's decisions weighted in favor of the prosecution, Drew and Lino felt they had the edge.

The spectator section of the courtroom was packed with prospective jurors. According to the jury list, there were almost two hundred of them. Bodean had picked up the jury list the previous Wednesday and had made notes beside various names. The defense team had determined who it wanted and placed a checkmark in front of their names. The ones it definitely didn't want on the jury were marked with a red X. The "don't knows" were so designated by a question mark.

When the Beas arrived, she would instruct her clerk to select fourteen names and seat them in the jury box. The two extra, jurors thirteen and fourteen, were designated the alternates. In trials expected to last longer than a week, the Beas always had two in the wings just in case one or two of the twelve became sick or incapacitated. That would mean that each side had an extra two peremptory challenges. In death penalty cases, each side had ten peremptory challenges plus the two. Since the prosecution had waived the death penalty, each side here had only five peremptory challenges plus the two for a total of seven. Each side, of course, could still exercise an unlimited number of challenges for cause if cause be shown. The peremptory challenges required no showing of cause.

Upon announcement of entry of the judge, the entire assemblage arose to their feet. It became so quiet you could hear a feather drop. The Beas called the court to order and told everyone they could be seated, she then called the case of the *People of the State of Colorado, Plaintiff v. Rolland J. Dawson, Defendant.* She inquired if Rolland was the defendant and if the attorneys were ready to proceed. Upon confirming the above, the Beas read from a canned speech outlining the nature of the case, the trial stages, the purpose of *voir dire* and some housekeeping matters. She then had her clerk swear in the whole jury panel. They swore they would make true answers to all questions propounded by Her Honor as well as the attorneys.

Before any jurors were called to the jury box, the Beas asked some generic questions. When the Beas asked if any would have a problem serving two weeks, there were a lot of hands raised. A dozen or so were released because of hardships ranging from work-related conflicts to health issues to sick relatives requiring care. Several had religious reasons why they couldn't judge others and thus could not sit on the case. After some questioning, they too were released.

When they were collectively asked if they had heard anything about the case before coming to court all raised their hands. The Beas looked a little perplexed and annoyed and informed them that that was something the attorneys would be inquiring into. The clerk, as instructed by the Beas, selected fourteen names from a box and, as their names were called, they filed into the two-row jury box starting with the back row. The first twelve filled the first six seats in each row and the last two filled the last seat in each row. The Beas referred to a chart that had been placed in front of them that was used to ask background questions followed by questions propounded by Dayton and then Drew. Because of some of their answers regarding the pretrial publicity exposure, jurors were taken back into the Beas's chambers for further examination. This was done to avoid contaminating the pool. Both attorneys were allowed to inquire.

The ones who stated they had already made up their minds and could not set aside their predispositions were released. Other prospective jurors were called to fill the void. After Dayton completed his *voir dire*, Drew followed. Only three of Drew's eight challenges for cause were granted. This meant that of the five remaining, if Dayton didn't challenge them with peremptory challenges then the defense would have to. The five were undesirables as far as the defense was concerned. By using up five of its seven peremptory challenges on them, only two peremptory challenges would remain. The risk was that two might not be enough to rid the panel of replacement jurors who might be as bad or maybe even worse.

Some of the jurors had previous jury service including criminal cases but indicated that that experience would have no effect if they were selected to serve. None indicated they knew the attorneys or had been patients of Rolland's. Depending on the nature of the relationship, having a familiarity with one or more of the witnesses or trial participants whose names the Beas read was not grounds for a challenge for cause. Later, however, when a prospective juror indicated that she had engaged the services of Quinlin, Devlin & Cummins some years before, she was excused by the Beas. The same was true when one of the prospective jurors said her sister worked for the district attorney's office.

The attorneys, starting with the district attorney, alternated the exercise of their peremptory challenges. As each prospective juror was challenged, he or she was replaced by the draw and questioned in the same manner as the first fourteen. It seemed that virtually every replacement juror had been exposed to pretrial publicity about the case and had already made up their minds. One by one they were quizzed out of the presence of the other jurors as to the nature and character of the publicity. The ones who stated they were irrevocably committed to their predispositions and could not be impartial were excused. However, the ones who admitted prejudice but said they could none-theless still be impartial, were retained. The defense challenged for cause any juror who admitted prejudice regardless of their promise of impartiality. The Beas, of course, didn't grant all such challenges because if she had, there wouldn't have been enough jurors left on the panel.

Both the prosecution and the defense used up all of their peremptory challenges. Because of the number of jurors who were examined in chambers in an effort to select fourteen fair and impartial jurors, jury selection took the better part of two days just as the defense team had estimated. Bodean calculated that of the 200 jurors in the pool, 186 had either been excused for cause or peremptorily challenged or not selected to sit. Even though the prospective jurors were not asked to reveal who they were biased for or against, at least fifty volunteered that they thought Rolland was guilty. Of the fourteen jurors selected, only five were male. The remaining jurors, including both alternates, were female. The composition of the jury, other than the gender disparity, reflected a cross-section of ages, occupations, native states, length of residency in El Paso County (EPC) and prior jury service (PJS). After the jury was selected, Bodean compiled the revised composite set forth below.

CHART 2

#	Name	Occupation	Sex	Age	State	EPC	Notes
1	Edith Corbin	Retired School Teacher	F	65	CO	65 EPC	PJS
2	Helen Shipley	Secretary RE Agency	F	61	UT	47 EPC	
3	Anthony Redland	Rancher	M	46	MT	28 EPC	PJS
4	Agnes Hill	Stock Broker	F	54	TX	32 EPC	
5	Sean Stevens	Financial Planner	M	27	NV	14 EPC	
6	Sharon Higgins	Waitress	F	49	CO	32 EPC	
7	Allen Tripp	Electrician	M	32	WY	18 EPC	
8	Tina Hart	Store Clerk	F	30	CO	30 EPC	
9	Kathy Evans	CPA	F	51	CO	27 EPC	
10	Jenny Fields	IT Specialist	F	23	CA	2 EPC	
11	Stan Petit	Banker	M	58	NM	29 EPC	
12	Henry Morton	Store Owner	M	62	MI	33 EPC	PJS
13	Megan McDonald		F	38	CO	16 EPC	
14	Joelle Craig	Computer Operator	F	24	CO	24 EPC	

Prior to their discharge for the day, the jury that would determine Rolland's fate was sworn in and given the cautionary instruction about not discussing the case with anyone and not reading, listening to, or watching anything dealing with the case and to report to the court any violations of these mandates. The jury was then escorted by the bailiff to the jury room and instructed to report back there at 8:30 a.m. on the morrow. The court was recessed until 9:00 a.m. at which time the attorneys were instructed to be prepared to make their opening statements.

On day three, with the jury duly impaneled and sworn, it was show time. Dayton delivered the prosecution's opening statement. He started out by saying that the opening statements were not evidence "but the revelation in outline fashion of the facts each side expected to prove." He then continued:

"Come back with me in point of time specifically to Friday, September 12, 2008, at 7:30 p.m., when a 911 operator, Norma Evans, received a call from someone identifying himself as Dr. Rolland Dawson. The caller said he had gone to their summer place in the Black Forest looking for his wife when she had not returned home. When he went inside, he found his wife lying face up in front of the moss rock fireplace. When he checked her, she was cold to the touch, had no pulse or heartbeat, and was not breathing. As a medical doctor, he knew she was dead. Ms. Evans advised him she would send an ambulance and notify the sheriff's department.

"Pursuant to Dr. Dawson's call, two sheriff's deputies, Roger Milligan and Kevin Stanton, were dispatched to the scene along with two EMTs, Taggert Williams and Cary Lamb. After the two deputies arrived and found the body and a torn shirt Dr. Dawson admitted was his, they summoned Henry Fisk, a lab technician/investigator/crime scene analyst who arrived and collected evidence. Henry Fisk collected three buttons found near the body and removed some fabric fragments still in one of the hands of the decedent. Then Henry Fisk made a preliminary determination that the buttons and fabric fragments came from the shirt Dr. Dawson said was his. This was later confirmed by a Colorado Bureau of Investigation lab technician by the name of Rick Tompkins.

"The body was transferred to the morgue where El Paso County Coroner/Medical Examiner, Dr. Francisco Mendoza, observed an injury to the back of the head and upon further examination concluded that the cause of death 'was massive hemorrhaging of the brain due to blunt trauma' and that it was 'highly unlikely that the trauma resulted from an accidental fall and the injury was more consistent with trauma caused by extreme physical force.'

"An autopsy was ordered and performed by a pathologist by the name of Dr. Horace Bellamy. Dr. Bellamy's conclusion was the same as Dr. Mendoza's.

"The sheriff's deputies as well as a lab technician from the El Paso County Sheriff's Department observed a moss rock jutting from the fireplace near where the body was found that appeared to have fresh blood and human hair attached that was ultimately collected from the scene. This was also turned over to Rick Tompkins of the CBI and analyzed. When it was compared to the hair and blood samples taken from Dr. Dawson's wife's body, it was determined to be an exact match. In other words, the blood and hair found on the moss rock fireplace was determined to have been that of Dr. Dawson's wife.

"A prosecution witness by the name of Carla Delajure, a former employee of Dr. Rolland Dawson, will testify that in 2006 she had a conversation with Dr. Dawson wherein he bragged that he 'had a foolproof way' of getting rid of his wife and that his wife's death 'would be perceived by the authorities as an accident.'

"The evidence will show that when the sheriff's deputies arrived at the scene, the body was positioned in such a way as to appear that Mrs. Dawson had tripped on the hearth. The investigating officers discounted the accident theory, when the buttons and fabric fragments appeared to have come from Dr. Dawson's torn shirt found on a chair only ten feet from the body. There was no one at the scene other than Dr. Dawson when the deputies arrived nor was there any indication that anyone else had been there or involved in Dr. Dawson's wife's death.

"When you've heard the testimony from the lips of the witnesses called by the prosecution, you will be convinced beyond a reasonable doubt that the death of Dr. Dawson's wife may have been made to look like an accident but was in fact not accidental in the least bit but was due to causes initiated by Dr. Dawson. And, at the conclusion of the case, we'll be asking you to return a guilty verdict. Thank you."

As Lino was positioning himself at the podium, Bodean leaned over and whispered to Drew, "Looks like the prosecution has opted not to call Pierre; he must have a felony."

"Appears that way," Drew whispered back. "However, Carla's testimony will provide all the damage the prosecution needs to get their first degree murder conviction."

Lino commenced his opening statement by pointing out the importance of the jury in the American system of justice and that there were two sides to every story and that that certainly was the case here. So far they had only heard one side; now they would hear the other. He then stated:

"I too want to take you back in time, back to 1991 when a young, promising artist by the name of Joy Armested, while attending a banquet with her father at Ohio State University, was introduced to a young, dashing medical doctor by the name of Dr. Rolland Dawson. He was thirty-two years of age at the time; she was twenty-five. To make a long story short, in less than a year she and her Prince Charming were married and rode off to Boston, where they resided for the next five years and in 1996 moved to our fair city. Here Joy and Dr. Dawson would reside together up to the time of Joy's death and where Dr. Dawson still resides and is an orthopedic surgeon.

"Dr. Dawson and his wife were inseparable and thrived on the beauty of the Colorado landscape. Joy, as a landscape artist, was in seventh heaven and spent every moment she could spare capturing the surrounding Colorado beauty on canvas.

"Shortly after the two moved to Colorado Springs, they purchased ten acres in the Black Forest not far from the United States Air Force Academy. There they erected a summer home their friends dubbed the Dawson Chalet. That became the sanctuary for both—a place for Dr. Dawson to relax after a stressful day in surgery and the home base for the artistic creations for which Joy would become known. It was at the Dawson Chalet, where Joy had been painting her last landscape and where her lifeless body was found. That was on Friday, September 12, 2008, at 7:15 p.m.

"We need, however, to go back to the preceding day, which was September 11. Dr. Dawson left work late afternoon after canceling several appointments due to experiencing flulike symptoms. He arrived home at approximately 4:00 p.m. and slept until approximately 8:15 p.m. Joy awakened him and fed him some chicken noodle soup, saltine crackers, and hot tea, which he had a difficult time keeping down.

"He felt somewhat better the next morning which was September 12. He kept his morning appointments and rounds at the hospital. By noon, however, his symptoms returned. He canceled his afternoon appointments, leaving the clinic at approximately 12:45 p.m. and arriving at home at approximately 1:15 p.m. He parked his car in the garage and closed the garage door as was his usual custom.

"When Joy had called midmorning while he was still at work, he assured her that he was on the mend and for her to go ahead to Black Forest and finish her landscape. When he called her on her cell phone at approximately 2:30 p.m., he advised her that he was at home but that it was not necessary that she return. He said he would call her if he needed her. Otherwise, it was agreed that she would be home at sometime between 6:00 p.m. and 6:30 p.m.

"September 12 was Joy's forty-second birthday. They had been planning a birthday celebration with friends at the Broadmoor, but Joy had called and rescheduled for the following evening so that Dr. Dawson could recuperate. Dr. Dawson felt bad but had a birthday cake with forty-two candles and a gift at the ready upon her return home that Friday evening. Despite his illness, they would still celebrate but not on the grand scale planned for the following evening when he would be feeling better. Joy's unopened gift still sits on the table next to her favorite recliner in the parlor at their home, in the same spot it had been placed by Dr. Dawson on that fateful day some six months ago.

"When Joy hadn't arrived by 6:40 p.m., Dr. Dawson tried to reach her cell phone. Unable to do so, he assumed she had stopped for grocery items at the Rustic Hills Shopping Center and had left her cell phone in the car. This would not have been an unusual occurrence.

"At 7:00 p.m., when he couldn't reach her and she hadn't called, he became concerned. He drove out to the Dawson Chalet arriving at approximately 7:15 p.m. The easel with the partially painted canvas stood on the front deck where she usually painted. On a glass-top table close by was a pallet with various oils in their wells, several brushes, and a white cloth. He called for her and, receiving no answer, went inside. There in the front of the moss rock fireplace she lay face up with her head on the low hearth. She had no pulse, no heartbeat, her body was cold to the touch, and it was apparent that she had breathed her last.

"It was approximately 7:30 p.m. when he called 911 and reported Joy's death. By 8:00 p.m., two sheriff's deputies arrived followed by the investigator/technician, the county coroner and two EMTs. Dr. Dawson was told his wife's body would be transported to the morgue, and since it was an unattended death, the body would be examined by the county coroner/medical examiner and perhaps an autopsy performed. He said he had no objection.

"Not knowing what caused his wife's death and having been at death scenes as a medical doctor, he was careful not to disturb anything. He was present when items were collected around his wife's body. The investigators were particularly interested in a shirt draped on a chair in the kitchen. One of the deputies asked if it was his. He examined it and said that it looked like one of his that had been hanging in the hall closet and used by guests when the weather cooled. He said he had not worn it in years and didn't remember it being in a damaged condition.

"You've probably surmised that Dr. Dawson will testify in this case. Even though he is not required by law to testify or present evidence, he nonetheless feels he owes it to you to do so. He has proclaimed his innocence from the beginning and will do so here again under oath. He was not with Joy when she died and was in no way connected to her death. The two had booked a two-week trip to Jamaica starting in mid-October and a trip to China in May of the following year. It will be obvious to you that Joy's death was not anticipated.

"The prosecution didn't mention that there were three experts who participated in various phases of the autopsy. They only mentioned Dr. Mendoza and Dr. Bellamy. They didn't mention Dr. Homer Renning, a board certified forensic pathologist. But we will in fact be calling Dr. Renning as a witness. He will testify that he examined Joy's body including her head injury and in essence performed a mini-autopsy concentrating, however, only on those parts of the body Doctors Mendoza and Bellamy attributed to cause of death.

"It will be Dr. Renning's expert opinion based on his training, knowledge, skill, and experience, after examining the body and visiting the scene where the body was found, that the cause of death was indeed 'massive hemorrhaging of the brain due to blunt trauma' just as Doctors Mendoza and Bellamy had concluded. However, unlike them, he will testify that Joy's head injury 'was consistent with trauma resulting from an accidental fall.'

"With regard to the statement allegedly made by Dr. Dawson to Carla Delajure over two years ago, Dr. Dawson will categorically and unequivocally deny making such a statement then or at any other time to Carla Delajure or any other person. He will tell you its recent fabrication and that she is not to be believed. He loved his wife and had no reason to want her dead.

"If the evidence produced at this trial, or the lack thereof, is as the defense anticipates, we will have no hesitancy at the conclusion of the case in asking you to return a not guilty verdict. Thank you."

Drew slid his notepad over to Lino as Lino resumed his seat at counsel table. On the top, Drew had scribbled "good job." Lino returned the pad to Drew after he noted: "It's a good thing I took shorthand in high school. What you heard was what the defense team composed at our first all-day trial prep session." Drew couldn't help but reply and scribbled so Lino could see "Then instead of an A+ you get an A- for content but you still an A+++ for delivery."

The Beas announced it was time for the midmorning break. Dayton was asked if he was ready to call witnesses after the break, and he indicated he had two with others scheduled for the afternoon. She advised him to be ready to call them and then advised the jurors not to discuss the case among themselves or with anyone else and not to expose themselves to any print or broadcast media concerning the case. She reminded the attorneys that they were not to speak to the media or make any public statements concerning the case.

The first witness called by the prosecution was Norma Evans, the 911 operator. Her testimony coincided with what Dayton had outlined in his opening statement. The purpose of her testimony was to lay the foundation as to why the sheriff's deputies and the EMTs were dispatched to the Dawson Chalet.

Lino operated under the theory that cross-examination always brought out something favorable for his cause. Even though it was marginal here, he proceeded as follows:

"Ms. Evans, you have every reason to believe that the person who identified himself as Dr. Rolland Dawson was in fact Dr. Rolland Dawson, don't you?"

"Yes."

"He didn't make the call anonymously or try to hide his identity, did he?"

"No."

"Did he seem concerned?"

"Yes."

"Did he answer all the questions you asked him?"

"Yes."

The second witness called by the prosecution was Vincent Townsend, the evidence custodian at the sheriff's department. He produced a large plastic bag containing a blue flannel shirt with a torn pocket and three missing buttons. He then produced three small plastic bags one containing three buttons, the second blue fibers or fragments the same color as the material of the shirt, and the third hair and blood scrapings. They were marked People's exhibits P-1, P-2, P-3, and P-4 respectively. They were identified as having been provided by Henry Fisk. The bags contained tags with the initials *R.M.*, *K.S.*, and *H.F.* with the date *9/12/08*. All four exhibits were admitted in evidence without objection. Since the defense had already stipulated as to chain of custody, the items were really offered so they could be identified by succeeding witnesses. Lino then cross-examined.

"When you took these items into the evidence, they were not in sealed bags, were they?"

"No."

"When Mr. Fisk brought them to you, both of you handled those items, didn't you?"

"Yes."

"Neither of you had rubber or plastic gloves on, did you?"

"No."

"You don't know how many others may have handled the shirt, buttons, and fragments, do you?"

"No."

"I don't imagine that you performed any type of testing such as attempting to lift fingerprints, DNA, or anything like that, did you?"

"No."

That ended Lino's cross-examination. The Beas then asked Dayton and Terrell if they were prepared to call any other witnesses. When they answered in the negative, she announced the court would break early for lunch and instructed the prosecutors to be ready to call witnesses at 1:30 p.m. The court was adjourned.

The court was called to order promptly at 1:30 p.m. The third witness called by the prosecution was Roger Milligan, one of the first deputy sheriffs to arrive at the scene. He testified that he and fellow Deputy Kevin Stanton were dispatched to the Dawson Chalet shortly after 7:30 p.m. on September 12 and arrived at approximately 8:00 p.m. They were greeted by Dr. Dawson. Terrell then had Milligan identify Dr. Dawson for the jury.

Continuing, Milligan testified that Dr. Dawson led them to the body. While viewing the body, they retrieved three blue buttons in various locations around the body and the shirt hanging on a chair in the kitchen. The buttons seemed to have come from the shirt. They asked Dr. Dawson if that was his shirt; he said it was. They noticed the shirt had been torn and missing three buttons. They also noticed cloth fragments in one of the deceased's hand. It was at this point he called his commander and a lab technician/crime scene analyst by the name of Henry Fisk was sent to the scene. Fisk collected, tagged and packaged the shirt buttons and cloth fragments. Fisk also scraped blood and hair from a moss rock on the fireplace, tagged, and packaged the same. Milligan and Stanton also initialed the tags. His initials he identified on People's exhibits P-1, P-2, P-3, and P-4.

It was time for Lino to cross-examine. "Now, Deputy Milligan, on direct examination, you didn't mention everything Dr. Dawson told you about the blue flannel shirt, did you?"

"No."

"When you asked him if the shirt was his, didn't he examine it and tell you 'it looked like one that had been hanging in the hall closet and used by guests when the weather cooled'?"

"Yes."

"Wasn't that his exact reply?"

"Yes, pretty much."

"Didn't he also tell you he hadn't worn the shirt in years and didn't remember it being in a damaged condition?"

"Something like that. Yes."

"Was it you or Deputy Stanton who first picked up the shirt and examined it?"

"Deputy Stanton."

"Would it be fair to say that you handled it, Dr. Dawson handled it, Deputy Stanton handled it, and Henry Fisk handled it?"

"Yes."

"Would it also be fair to say that everyone who handled and examined the blue flannel shirt did so with their bare hands?"

"Yes."

"Then I take it, to your knowledge at least, no one checked the shirt for DNA or performed any testing to determine who put the shirt there, is that correct?"

"Yes."

"May I ask then why no such testing was done?"

"We didn't think it was important."

"If the shirt wasn't important, Deputy Milligan, then why did you collect it and give it to the evidence custodian who brought it here to court?"

"Because buttons and fabric fragments were found at or near the body that matched the shirt."

"Exactly, Deputy Milligan. Wasn't it your conclusion then that whoever was wearing the shirt had something to do with Joy's death?"

"Of course."

"Then, wouldn't your answer to 'who killed Dr. Dawson's wife' be important in determining who last wore the shirt?"

"Yes."

"Well then why didn't someone check that out?"

"We already knew it was Dr. Dawson's shirt."

"But, Deputy Milligan, if proper tests had been conducted and someone else's hair or DNA had been found on the shirt, that would've blown your theory that Dr. Dawson was wearing the shirt at the time of Joy's death, isn't that correct?"

"I suppose so."

"Why didn't you or your fellow officers consider that?"

"We were too busy with other things. Besides, Dr. Dawson admitted it was his shirt."

"Did you find any other physical evidence that you thought tied Dr. Dawson to Joy's death?"

"Well, he was the only one at the scene when we arrived."

"Come now, Deputy Milligan, if Joy's death was not an accident and someone was responsible for it, you think that person would have stuck around waiting for the police to arrive?"

"Probably not."

"And, if Dr. Dawson was the person responsible for his wife's death, don't you think he would have boogied as well?"

"Possibly."

"Instead, he called the authorities and waited until you arrived. Didn't he?"

"Yes."

"Did you find any type of suspicious object at the scene that might have caused Joy's head injury other than a moss rock in the fireplace?"

"No."

"Did you check Dr. Dawson to see if he had any scratches on him or anything to suggest that he had been in some kind of struggle?"

"No, there were none visible."

"Did you or any other officer to your knowledge check to see if there were any tire tracks that couldn't be accounted for in the driveway or drive leading to the Dawson Chalet?"

"No."

"Now, the driveway and drive were not graveled or paved, were they?"

"No."

"And wouldn't you say the drive or lane leading to the Dawson Chalet was equivalent to one city block?"

"Yes."

"Was the reason no one bothered to check for unaccounted tire tracks because everyone was busy doing something else?"

"Probably, but a lot of people had been driving on the driveway and drive and there were a lot of tracks."

"Let's be frank, Deputy Milligan, when you discovered the blue flannel shirt, you thought the case had been solved and you didn't need to go beyond Dr. Dawson. Isn't that correct?"

"True."

"The notion of an alternate suspect never entered your mind once you focused in on Dr. Dawson. Isn't that correct?"

"Yes, that's probably true."

"Thank you for being candid."

Kevin Stanton was the fourth witness called by the prosecution. A feeble attempt was made by Terrell to anticipate and take away the sting of cross-examination. Deputy Stanton offered nothing to the case and his testimony was virtually the mirror image of Deputy Milligan's testimony. He did identify all the crime scene photographs, which were introduced, admitted in evidence, and then circulated among the jurors.

Lino asked some of the same questions directed to Deputy Milligan. Stanton confirmed that the investigators had zeroed in on Dr. Dawson and that no alternate suspect had been considered in the event Joy's death was not an accident. Deputy Stanton confirmed that there was nothing about Dr. Dawson's appearance that would suggest that there had been any kind of struggle. Other than the shirt, there was nothing to suggest Dr. Dawson was in any way connected to Joy's death. In retrospect, he admitted he and Deputy Milligan possibly should have done some things differently.

Judge Beasley recessed for the day and the jury was given their usual admonition.

When the fourth day of trial convened, there were more spectators than usual. Bodean thought the recent press coverage had been more favorable as a result of Lino's cross-examination. The investigation in the death of the doctor's wife was taking on a different hue. Even the Beas by third day's end seemed more cordial toward the defense. The defense team was pleased with how the trial was proceeding and the trial was on the pace the defense had hoped. Maybe the winds of public opinion were shifting. It certainly seemed that way.

Henry Fisk, a lab technician/crime scene analyst/specialist with the El Paso County Sheriff's Department, was the fifth prosecution witness called. He corroborated the testimony regarding the collection and preservation of evidence at the scene and in particular his scraping the blood and hair from a moss rock on the fireplace and placing the samples in an evidence bag. He identified his initials on exhibit P-4 containing the samples as well as exhibits P-1, P-2, and P-3. These were turned over to Vincent Townsend the evidence custodian at the sheriff's office. Townsend in turn delivered the exhibits to the CBI lab for analysis.

It mattered little whether Fisk was cross-examined. However, Lino felt he could make a point out of the fact that the hearth of the fireplace posed a hazard even if a person knew it was there. Also, through this witness, he could establish the height of the hair and blood splatters on the moss rock.

"Now, Mr. Fisk, as a crime scene analyst/specialist part of your training, knowledge and experience requires you to connect the dots so to speak that is to draw conclusions from the physical evidence as to what might have been the cause of say Joy's death in this case. Is that correct?"

"Yes."

"In fact, you were called to the scene to help the investigative officers, Deputies Milligan and Stanton, reconstruct what happened or appeared to happen, is that correct?"

"Yes."

"How high was the moss rock that was embedded in the fireplace that contained the blood and hair that you testified to?"

"Can I refer to my notes?"

"Yes."

"Exactly four and one-quarter feet."

"How high was the hearth?"

"Four and three-quarter inches."

"How wide was the hearth?"

"Thirty-two inches."

"And I take it you would need to know the height of the deceased to reconstruct the probable cause of death, is that true?"

"That would help."

"Did you know Joy's height?"

"I measured her body and also asked Dr. Dawson how tall she was. I was able to determine that she was five feet six inches tall."

"By the way, did you measure the distance from the floor at the base of the hearth to the spot where you found hair and blood on the moss rock?"

"I did."

"What was that measurement?"

"Five feet two inches. Remember, this was at an angle."

"Yes, and I take it that you looked at the wound on the back of Joy's head and noticed that the wound was several inches from the top of her head, correct?"

"Yes, from three to four inches from the top."

"Is it your testimony that the only wound you observed was to the back of the head?"

"Yes."

"When you arrived at the scene, was Joy's body positioned such that her head was in the direction of the fireplace and her feet toward the front of the hearth?"

"Yes."

"She was face up with her head and upper body lying on the hearth, is that correct?"

"Yes."

"So, did it appear that she had hit the back of her head on the moss rock on the fireplace where her blood and hair were recovered?"

"Correct."

"Wasn't the evidence you found at the scene consistent with her having tripped or caught the back of her heels on the lip of the hearth and, falling backwards, hit her head on the moss rock?"

"Yes, or by having been pushed."

"But you don't know whether Joy tripped or was pushed across the hearth onto the moss rock, do you?"

"No."

"You weren't there when Joy hit her head, were you?"

"No."

"So you don't know for sure what happened, do you?"

"No."

"Were you present when the county coroner, Dr. Francisco Mendoza, arrived?"

"Yes."

"Did something unusual happen to Dr. Mendoza as it involved the hearth?"

"Yes, he tripped on the hearth, skinning his hands."

"You witnessed that?"

"Yes."

"Did anyone else do the same thing?"

"Yes, I did but I didn't injure myself."

"But you didn't fall backwards, did you?"

"No."

Rick Tompkins, the agent in charge of the CBI lab, was the sixth witness to be called by the prosecution. He personally performed the analysis and comparisons on prosecution exhibits P-1, P-2, P-3, and P-4. He testified that he could state with a reasonable degree of scientific certainty that the three loose buttons (P-2) and the fabric fragment (P-3) came from the blue flannel shirt (P-1). He also opined that the hair and blood samples (P-4) were from the head of Joy Dawson.

Lino had been a terror on cross-examination and his cross-examination of this witness proved to be no different.

"Mr. Tompkins, other than to perform tests to determine whether or not exhibits P-2 and P-3 came from P-1, you performed no other tests, did you?"

"What do you mean?"

"You didn't check to see whose DNA was on exhibit P-1 for example, in an effort to determine who may have been wearing the shirt last, did you?"

"No, it wouldn't have been valid."

"Why?"

"Because any number of people handled it, and any number of people could've been wearing it."

"There was or is no forensic evidence that you are aware of that indicates that Dr. Dawson ever wore exhibit P-1, is there, Mr. Tompkins?"

"No."

"There was or is no forensic evidence that you are aware of that Dr. Dawson wore exhibit P-1 at the time of his wife's death, is there?"

"No."

After the midmorning break, the prosecution called their seventh witness, Dr. Francisco Mendoza. He had been the county coroner/medical examiner for twelve years and delighted in enumerating his credentials. He was called to the Dawson Chalet on Friday, September 12 and examined the body. He also performed a more detailed exam at the morgue and assisted Dr. Horace Bellamy at the autopsy. Over the objection of the defense, Dr. Mendoza was able to express his opinion as to cause of death. It was his opinion that Joy's death was "due to massive hemorrhaging of the brain due to blunt trauma." The most damaging testimony was his opinion that "it was highly unlikely that the trauma resulted from an accidental fall and the injury was more consistent with trauma caused by extreme physical force."

Dr. Mendoza had a pretty hefty opinion of himself. That was a polite way of saying he was arrogant. He, however, was a seasoned witness and unflappable. Drew only hoped he would be as effective cross-examining Dr. Mendoza as Lino was cross-examining the previous witnesses.

"Now, Dr. Mendoza, you are not a board certified forensic pathologist are you?"

"No."

"Are you familiar with Dr. Homer Renning?"

"Yes."

"Do you know whether or not he is a board certified forensic pathologist?"

"Yes. He is board certified."

"Is the same thing true of Dr. Horace Bellamy?"

"Yes."

"Is that why Dr. Bellamy was called in to perform the autopsy on Joy Dawson?"

"When it appears death occurred under unusual circumstances and criminal prosecution is imminent, we usually call in Dr. Bellamy."

"Have you appeared in the other cases with Dr. Bellamy?"

"I have."

"Do you know the number?"

"Perhaps fifty."

"Of those fifty cases, how many found the two of you on the same side?"

"All of them, as I recall."

"Of the approximately two hundred and forty cases in which you appeared and were qualified as an expert, as you testified on direct-examination, how many were in behalf of the prosecution and how many were in behalf of the defense?"

"I'm not sure."

"Most if not all were in behalf of the prosecution, is that not true?"

"Yes."

"When did you determine that 'it was highly unlikely that the trauma resulted from an accidental fall, and the injury was more consistent with trauma caused by extreme physical force'?"

"When I examined the body at the morgue on September 12 and later when I assisted Dr. Bellamy perform the detailed autopsy."

"Wouldn't it be fair to say that your opinion was based on the severity of the head injury?"

"Yes."

"You didn't assist the EMTs in the transport of the body to the morgue, did you?"

"No."

"You don't know whether the severity of the head injury was caused at the time of death or post-mortem, do you?"

"Usually, we can tell."

"Now, is that something that falls within the realm of a specialist, such as a pathologist, or can a physician such as yourself make that determination?"

"Ordinarily, that would be for the pathologist to determine."

"But, Dr. Mendoza, even before Dr. Bellamy was involved, you had already issued your report expressing the opinion you testified to today under oath, hadn't you?"

"I had no evidence then nor do I now that the body had been subjected to any post-mortem trauma."

When Drew returned to counsel table, Lino slipped him a note, which read: "Not bad for an amateur!" It was then time for the lunch break.

Court reconceived promptly at 1:30 p.m. Because of Drew's cross-examination of Dr. Mendoza, Terrell was forced to call Taggert Williams and Cary Lamb to the stand. They would be the eighth and ninth prosecution witnesses called. They testified as to the care they took in loading, unloading, and transporting Joy's body. On cross-examination, Lino elicited an admission that part of the road over which they traveled was in disrepair and in the midst of construction. It was obvious they had skipped lunch to prepare for cross-examination. There were really no points to be made.

The tenth witness to be called by the prosecution was Dr. Horace Bellamy. His qualifications were undeniable. He was a board-certified forensic pathologist. What Dr. Mendoza lacked in charisma, not to mention skill, training, education, and experience, Dr. Bellamy more than compensated. The jurors listened intently and from time to time were observed nodding their approval. When he said, "It was highly unlikely that the trauma resulted from an accidental fall," and "The injury was more consistent with trauma caused by extreme physical force," it was evident they believed. Dr. Bellamy also testified that the moss rock with the hair and blood splatters was compatible with the head injury Joy sustained.

It would not do Drew any good to pursue the collaboration with Dr. Mendoza angle or post-mortem exacerbation. Drew was content when Dr. Bellamy conceded that "it was *possible* the trauma resulted from an accidental fall but it was *not probable.*"

Dayton was not a cheap shot artist and none of the gruesome autopsy photographs were introduced. Photographs of the gross anatomy were confined to Joy's head and were of the type that would not tend to inflame the jury. The attorneys had stipulated to admissibility before hand, and Dayton was careful not to risk reversal of this case as was his practice in most cases.

Dr. Bellamy's testimony took to the day's end. The court recessed for the day, and the jury was given the now repetitive cautionary instruction.

Rolland had trouble sleeping that night and was puzzled by a series of questions Drew had asked Dr. Bellamy on cross-examination. In attempting to dispel any notion of an altercation or struggle to bolster the defense's accidental death theory, Drew had asked, "In your examination, other than the injury to the head, did you observe any marks on Mrs. Dawson's body that might have suggested that prior to her death she had been involved in any kind of altercation or struggle?" Dr. Bellamy had answered, "Only a mark on her right lower abdomen." Drew had then asked, "But, wasn't that mark really a scar caused by an appendectomy?"

What was puzzling was that none of the pathology or other prosecution reports mentioned the scar and none was revealed by any of the photographs. And Rolland was certain he had not mentioned the scar to Drew or anyone else. The scar had always been a well-kept secret, and Rolland was perplexed by how Drew knew of its existence.

On the fifth day of trial, the prosecution called their eleventh witness: Rolland's former receptionist/secretary/bookkeeper, Lannette Castles. She testified that Rolland, on September 12, had left the clinic at approximately 12:45 p.m. due to illness, canceling his afternoon appointments, and did not return for the remainder of the day. Direct-examination by Terrell was short and so was Lino's cross-examination.

Lino began, "Mrs. Castles, you worked with Dr. Dawson for over fifteen years and presumably saw him almost every work day during that time, am I correct?"

"Yes."

"Now your duties at the clinic involved seeing people who were ill on a regular basis?"

"Yes. Prior to being hired at the clinic, I had been a nurse for twelve and one-half years."

"Had you seen Dr. Dawson when he was both well and ill?"

"Yes."

"On September 12, were you able to tell if Dr. Dawson was feigning it or was in fact ill?"

"He definitely was ill, and in fact, it was I who encouraged him to take the afternoon off, and it was I who canceled his appointments."

"What time did he leave the clinic?"

"Approximately 12:45 p.m."

"Isn't it true that he had been ill the previous day, and you all but forced him to leave work early that day as well?"

"One of the other doctors in the clinic had the flu and several of the nurses. For Dr. Dawson's sake as well as the rest of us, including our patients, we were concerned. So, yes, I all but forced Dr. Dawson to go home."

"Did you know Dr. Dawson's wife, Joy?"

"Yes."

"Did you speak with her often enough in person and over the telephone to recognize her voice?"

"Yes, of course."

"On the morning of September 12, about midmorning, did you happen to take a call from Joy?"

"Yes, she called Dr. Dawson often."

"When you spoke with her did she appear to be friendly?"

"Yes, she was always friendly."

"She didn't appear to be frantic or distressed, did she?"

"No, she was just worried about how Dr. Dawson was feeling as she was getting ready to go to their summer home in the Black Forest."

"You remember what time she called?"

"It was about 10:30 a.m."

Lino announced he had no other questions. The rest of the morning was occupied with the testimony of Rolland's adjoining neighbors. Prosecution witnesses' numbers twelve and thirteen were Ann and Gary Anderson. Prosecution witnesses' numbers fourteen and fifteen were Lynn and Dan Staves. Terrell spent more time with the witnesses than the defense thought necessary. To call all four, the defense thought, was somewhat redundant but they didn't object. The wives were home all day and the husbands were working and traveling to and from work between 7:30 a.m. until after 6:00 p.m. on Friday, September 12.

All four were familiar with the Dawsons, having been neighbors for over a dozen years. They recognized the Dawsons on sight and were familiar with the vehicles Joy and Rolland drove. None saw the Dawsons on September 12 or their vehicles. All four were questioned by Lino and were asked virtually identical questions.

"You didn't see either Joy or Rolland leave or return to their home on September 12, did you?"

"No."

"Specifically, you didn't see Joy leave the Dawson residence at around 10:30 a.m. or Dr. Dawson arrive home at around 12:45 or 1:00 p.m. did you?"

"No."

"That doesn't mean Joy didn't leave the Dawson residence at around 10:30 a.m. or that Dr. Dawson didn't arrive home at around 12:45 or 1:00 p.m., does it?"

"No."

"Because of the positioning of your respective residences on multi-acre lots and the landscaping, to see the Dawsons coming and going would be a chance occurrence, wouldn't it?"

"Yes."

After the noon recess, Dayton announced the prosecution was calling its last witness, Carla Delajure. You could see the jury lean forward when Carla assumed the witness stand and stated her name. The courtroom was hushed in curious anticipation of Carla's testimony. All eyes were riveted on her. The jury had heard the prosecuting attorney's opening statement outlining Carla's testimony and understood only too well the implications of what she was about to reveal.

After being administered the oath to tell the truth, Carla took the stand. Her transformative appearance even stunned Rolland. She was not wearing one of her signature miniskirts or low-cut blouses but was cast as the schoolmarm in every detail including her long hair, which was rolled into a tight bun, her newly acquired wire-rimmed glasses and no makeup. *That couldn't be the woman Rolland had the affair with,* Bodean thought. By the look on Rolland's face, it was obvious Rolland was thinking the same thing.

"Would you state your full name," Dayton began.

"Carla Harriett Delajure."

"Do you know the defendant in this case, Dr. Rolland Dawson?"

"I do. I used to work in Dr. Dawson's clinic."

"Did you and Dr. Dawson have a romantic involvement while you worked there?"

"Yes."

"At the time, were you aware that he was married?"

"Yes."

"To Joy Dawson, the victim in this case?"

"Yes."

"In April of 2006 did you happen to have a conversation with Dr. Dawson concerning his wife?"

"Yes."

"Would you relate to the jury the nature of that conversation?"

"Dr. Dawson told me that he had a foolproof way of getting rid of his wife and that his wife's death would be perceived by the authorities as an accident."

Carla's testimony was short but deadly. The points the defense had built up on cross with the other witnesses were dissipated in the blink of an eye. Carla's one sentence response to Dayton's final question had the disastrous impact of an atomic bomb. Not even Drew Quinlin could pull this one out. Dr. Dawson's defense that Joy's death was "an accident" after telling Carla that he could make Joy's death look like "an accident" would make satire, parody, and rhetorical hyperbole appear awe-inspiring serious.

Drew, however, was determined to give it his best shot. It was the ninth inning of the seventh game of the World Series. He was at bat with the bases loaded, two out, two strikes, and his team behind three runs. It was now or never. He would either be the hero or the goat. All eyes were now focused on him including turquoise eyes from above which he could feel. There was nowhere to hide and only one direction to go.

"Mrs. Delajure, you realize that Dr. Dawson is on trial here for first-degree murder, do you not?"

"Yes."

"When you took the stand you were administered an oath to tell the truth, were you not?"

"Yes."

"Do you know the importance of telling the truth?"

"Yes."

"Do you realize it is perjury, a crime in this state, not to tell the truth once you've been sworn as a witness?"

"Yes, I do now."

"Mrs. Delajure, with so much riding on your testimony, it is important that you tell the truth, the complete truth, and nothing but the truth. Do you realize that?"

"Yes."

"When Mr. Dayton asked you earlier what Dr. Dawson said back in April of 2006, you responded, 'Dr. Dawson told me he had a foolproof way of getting rid of his wife and it would be perceived as an accident.' Do you remember testifying as to that?"

"Yes."

"Your answer was not truthful, was it?"

Carla did not answer and instead hung her head and began sobbing uncontrollably. She beckoned for a tissue, which the bailiff provided. The Beas advised Carla that she could take as much time she needed. It took several minutes before Carla regained her composure. She then asked Drew if he could repeat the question.

"Your answer was not truthful, was it?"

"No."

"Your husband, Pierre, conjured up the story, didn't he?"

"Yes."

"Just so the jury knows, the statements you testified Dr. Dawson made were totally fabricated. Is that your testimony?"

"Yes."

"Dr. Dawson never made the statements you testified that he made, did he?"

"No."

With that Carla broke down again. Drew announced to Judge Beasley that he had a motion to make outside the presence of the jury. The Beas said she was about to declare a recess anyway. The jury was excused, and Drew made a motion to dismiss the charge on the bases of perjured testimony or, in the alternative, to declare a mistrial. Dayton said he opposed the motion to dismiss but would leave it up to the sound discretion of the court as to whether to grant the motion for a mistrial.

The Beas said she had not encountered such a situation before and would strike Carla Delajure's testimony but was reluctant to declare a mistrial. Playing to the gallery and the media, which were unusually calm considering Carla's revelation, and, looking directly into the television camera focused on her from the back of the courtroom, stated that she would have to balance the time and expense of a retrial with the impact such testimony would have on the jury. She said she felt a cautionary instruction to the jury to disregard Carla's testimony would be just as effective as starting over with a new jury. She said she would definitely not be dismissing the charge as there was enough other evidence to sustain the charge of murder in the first degree.

When Drew requested that he be heard on the issue, the Beas said simply that she heard the testimony and was familiar with the law. His request would be denied.

The Beas, looking at her watch, asked Dayton if he had other witnesses to present in light of what just occurred. He stated "no" that he rested his case-in-chief.

The Beas then asked Drew if the defense would be making the usual motion. Drew stated the defense would be making a motion for judgment of acquittal. The Beas then stated she would have the bailiff bring the jury back in and that she would give them the cautionary instruction to disregard the testimony of Carla Delajure and not consider it for any purpose. Then the jury would be released for the week.

After the jury was brought in and given the instruction, the Beas, for the jury's benefit, asked Dayton if the prosecution had any other evidence to present. He again announced that the prosecution rested its case-in-chief. The Beas advised the jury that there were matters to be taken up outside their presence. They were then released until 8:30 a.m. the following Monday.

The Beas then decided they all needed a break, and the court took a short recess. At the break, Rolland in wide-eyed amazement asked Drew how he knew Carla would break. "I just did," Drew said with a wide smile while wiping sweat from his brow and looking heavenward. Whether the Beas would be granting their motion for judgment of acquittal was something to which they all already knew the answer.

When the court reconvened, Drew asked the court to enter an order for judgment of acquittal on the grounds that the evidence was insufficient to sustain a conviction. "The relevant admissible evidence presented in this case, when viewed in the light most favorable to the prosecution, is insufficient to support a conclusion by a reasonable mind that Dr. Dawson is guilty of the charge beyond a reasonable doubt." Drew pointed out that the record was completely devoid of any evidence showing a culpable mental state, especially deliberation, as required for murder in the first degree even if a reasonable inference could be drawn that Dr. Dawson committed the act leading to Joy's death. "If Your Honor can point to even one piece of evidence showing motive or intent, then you should deny our motion. Otherwise, at least as far as the murder in the first-degree charge is concerned, you should direct a judgment of acquittal."

Dayton opposed the motion "on the grounds that the evidence before the jury is sufficient in both quantity and quality to submit the issue of Dr. Dawson's guilt or innocence to the jury."

The Beas agreed with Dayton and, denying the motion for judgment acquittal, held that "the relevant evidence, both direct and circumstantial, when viewed as a whole and in the light most favorable to the prosecution, is substantial and sufficient to support a conclusion by a reasonable mind that Dr. Dawson is guilty of the charge beyond a reasonable doubt."

The defense team didn't even flinch. They were prepared for another adverse ruling that would be added to the list of errors in support of an appeal. Knowing what the ruling would be and preserving the record for appeal, Drew renewed the defense's motion for dismissal on the basis of the perjured testimony or, in the alternative, motion for mistrial. Both were summarily denied.

As the court was about to be adjourned until 9:00 a.m. the following Monday, Dayton stood up and stated, "I just want the court to know and the record to reflect that the district attorney's office had no prior knowledge of Carla Delajure's perjured statements. Obviously, if we had, we would not have called her to the stand."

"Understood" was all the Beas acknowledged. With the first week of the prosecution of the wife killer now history, everyone could now go about his or her business as usual. Everyone, that is, except the defense team. It was now their turn in the barrel.

The headline in the evening paper read "Prosecution Witness Admits to Perjury." The headline in the morning rag read: "Prosecution Witness Lies under Oath." The murder prosecution of the local doctor for the death of his artist wife hit the front page of both dailies for the fifth day in a row. For the most part, the articles were neutral and, if anything, were favorable to the defense. Both newspapers carried editorials questioning the witness screening process of the district attorney's office and prosecutorial discretion in general. The district attorney's office was targeted by the local television channels as well, and the channels seemed preoccupied with the induction of perjured testimony, which to the defense team was somewhat of an anomaly.

When the defense team met Saturday morning, they were still gloating over the irony of the district attorney's office switching roles with them and being the ones now on trial. Trying the district attorney's office in the press and broadcast media was not as egregious as trying Rolland in the media. Maybe, if they renewed their motion for change of venue, the district attorney's office may not now be so eager to oppose it. It was decided that the change of venue issue was probably moot anyway as Rolland undoubtedly would be acquitted of the first-degree murder charge and maybe all lesser included charges.

"Realistically," Lino said, "without Carla's testimony there is not a scintilla of evidence even hinting of premeditation or deliberation. In my mind, there is no way the jury will convict Rolland of murder in the first degree."

"I don't see how they can convict on murder two," Drew said. "Number one, I don't think the prosecution has proven that Rolland caused Joy's death, and number two, they haven't shown that if he did he did it 'knowingly.'"

"Frankly," Bodean said, "I think there is just as much an inference that Joy's death was accidental as not and that Rolland stands a decent chance of being acquitted of both manslaughter and criminally negligent homicide."

"The alleged shirt connection is what is going to hang me," Rolland said, shaking his head in apparent resignation.

"Not if they find the investigators did a sloppy job determining who last wore the blue flannel shirt and that you hadn't worn it in years," Bodean said.

"It looks pretty promising," Drew said. "But we don't want to get our hopes up too high."

"Everything hinges on whether the jury accepts our theory of the case that Joy's death was accidental," Lino said. "If it was accidental, which we all believe that it was, it won't make any difference who was wearing the shirt."

"Well," Drew said, "we will only be calling two witnesses. We don't need Lannette Castles since we've elicited everything we need to on cross-examination. Dr. Renning's testimony will be critical in establishing accidental death and Rolland's testimony will be critical in establishing that he was in no way involved in Joy's death."

"If they don't know who to believe," Bodean said, "the tie should go to Rolland since the prosecution has the burden of proving Rolland's guilt beyond a reasonable doubt."

"Well," Drew said, "Dr. Bellamy has admitted it's 'possible' Joy's death was accidental. And if Dr. Renning testifies that Joy's head injury 'was consistent with trauma resulting from an accidental fall,' aren't he and Dr. Bellamy saying basically the same thing?"

"The battle of the experts is not an impediment here," Lino commented. "Dr. Mendoza is the only odd expert out, and he's not a board certified pathologist. The other two are. And the nice thing about it is that one of the pathologists is a career prosecution witness."

Bodean said, "I've seen a lot of attorneys cross-examine witnesses. And I've seen some make adverse witnesses appear as their own. But I've never seen attorneys make every adverse witness appear as their own. And to get a witness to admit she lied on the stand is something I've never seen before."

"You two pulled the cat out of the bag time and time again," Rolland said. "By the time we reached the last witness, I had come to expect it. Both of your cross-examinations were masterful, and to you two and Bodean, I can never adequately express my admiration, respect, and appreciation regardless of the outcome."

"It's easy when you're representing an innocent client," Lino said.

"Ditto," Drew said. "But remember, we are only halfway there."

"Have we decided whether the jury should view the scene?" Bodean asked.

"I think the jury needs to see the layout of the fireplace especially the hearth," Lino said. "I don't think the photographs of the scene portray an accurate reflection of the hazard actually posed by the lip of the hearth and the proximity of the moss rock to where Joy hit her head."

"I agree," Bodean said. "The photographs distort to some extent the deceptive nature of the elevation of the hearth in relation to the knap of the plush carpet surrounding the hearth."

"Dayton said he would not oppose our motion to view the scene," Drew stated. "It is apparent that the prosecution feels the firsthand view would be probative. Whether the Beas agrees is another thing. I think viewing the scene would be appropriate at the conclusion of all the evidence."

"If we're going to renew our request," Lino said, "we should do so first thing on Monday morning so that transportation can be arranged for the jurors. The Beas doesn't like surprises, you know."

"You think we can put our case on in one day?" Bodean asked.

"We only have two witnesses, Dr. Renning and Rolland," Drew said.

"I don't think Dr. Renning even with extensive cross will take more than two hours," Lino added. "Rolland's direct and cross will probably take up the better part of the remainder of the day. However, I can't see his testimony spilling into Tuesday."

"Depending on whether the prosecution has rebuttal witnesses," Drew said, "I would think if the Beas grants our motion to view the premises that that could be done first thing Tuesday morning. The afternoon could be spent formulating the jury instructions with final arguments commencing first thing Wednesday morning. The jury would probably welcome the Tuesday afternoon hiatus."

"Will the media be allowed to accompany the jurors to the scene?" Rolland asked.

"Normally not," Drew said. "It's discretionary with the court. However, since the public is not invited, I don't think the media will be either although you don't know what the Beas will do. After all, she did allow cameras in the courtroom."

While Bodean worked with Rolland on simulated cross-examination, Drew and Lino put the finishing touches on the defense's proposed jury instructions. By noon, the defense team dispersed and went their separate ways. Rolland left for the airport to pick up his parents, who would be spending the weekend and rest of the trial with him. In the event of a conviction, Rolland's father would have to consent to a continuation of the bond. They all knew, however, that if Rolland were convicted of murder in the first degree, the Beas would be denying bail and Rolland would be headed back to the slammer.

At the first breath of dawn on that crisp spring Monday the start of the second week of Rolland's murder prosecution, Drew arose wide-eyed and eager to prove his client's innocence. Taking care not to awaken Missy and the girls, Drew took an extra long hot shower and put on his Sunday best. This was the day the residents of El Paso County had been waiting for the day they would *hear* the doctor's side of the story. This was also the day the defense had been waiting for, the day the doctor would *tell* his side of the story. If there was ever a day for Drew to be trial ready, it was this day.

When he arrived at the office at 6:35 a.m., with steamy java in one hand and his keys in the other, his eyes caught the headlines of the morning newspaper sitting in front of the door. Setting the cup and keys down he picked up the morning *Times Herald* and lip-synched "PROTECT Leader Arrested for Domestic Violence." Beneath the headline was the three-column color photograph of a man holding a placard with the following printed in bold letters thereon: "Suppress Domestic Violence." Beneath the photograph was the following: "Shown above at a protest rally at the El Paso County courthouse in September of 2008 is Pierre Delajure."

Absorbed in the front-page article, Drew was oblivious to the fact that Lino had walked up behind him. In wide-eyed amazement, the two read in unison the story of a domestic dispute gone wrong. Apparently, Pierre's argument with his wife, Carla, turned violent over the weekend, resulting in Carla's hospitalization and his arrest. Carla's injuries were listed as "critical."

"Pierre must not have been enamored over the press coverage of Carla's admitting to perjury and implicating him in the plot," Lino exclaimed.

"Obviously," Drew said, lifting his eyebrows, "it will be interesting to see which one of the Delajure's PROTECT will demonstrate against, the batterer or the battered. It puts them in a very delicate position, doesn't it?"

"I wonder," Lino said, "how Pierre feels being in the shoes of an accused."

"It's certainly poetic justice," Drew opined. "It couldn't have happened to a better man."

"And at this point in Rolland's trial," Lino added, "the timing is impeccable!"

"Looks like Dayton will be adding another felony to the subornation of perjury charge," Drew speculated. "Maybe a conviction of subornation of perjury and domestic violence will result in excoriation from his deal with the feds. Between federal prison and state prison he may be effectively removed from society permanently."

"Wouldn't that be in everyone's best interest," Lino said.

Drew and Lino were barely in the office before Bodean arrived and, in his patented bravado, said in a loud husky voice, "Well, it looks like another prosecution witness has bitten the dust. When will the Delajures of the world realize that you can fool some of the people some of the time but not all the people all the time."

"Justice ultimately prevails," Lino said just as Rolland arrived.

Hearing what Lino said, Rolland commented: "I just hope justice doesn't arrive too late to save me from *the fiery pit*."

Rolland asked if they had read the morning editorial. The three had not. Rolland said the editorial was entitled "Overzealous Prosecution" and was a scathing commentary on the district attorney's handling of his case. While Rolland spoke, the group turned to the editorial page of the *Times Herald* and read the lengthy editorial aloud. Dayton was described as "intractable" and "promoting his own political agenda." The editorial concluded by saying, "We don't know whether the elected district attorney is playing foot loose and fancy free with the justice system, but when the jury returns its verdict in the Dawson case, we will know for sure."

"Is it an aberration," Lino asked, "or is the press voicing its indignation over the lack of evidence in our case and feel they have been led down the primrose path and maybe even down a dead end?"

"Well, you know how fickle the press is," Drew said. "One minute they are polarized for you and the next minute they are polarized against you. Look out if they feel you've deceived them."

"It's obvious they feel they've been duped or played the fool," Bodean said.

"But not by us," Lino quickly added.

Back in court and before the jury was called in, Drew renewed the defense's request to view the scene. Dayton said he would join in the request. The Beas announced that the photographic evidence adequately painted the picture and weighing the time and expense factors against the marginal benefits to be derived therefrom, she felt compelled to deny the request. With that, she appeared to smile into the television camera.

"Well, that was one of the rare times the Beas has ruled against the prosecution in this case," Lino whispered to Drew.

"It may be the only time," Drew whispered back. "But just remember who has the last word and maybe even the last laugh."

When the jury returned to the courtroom, the defense was told to call their first witness.

Dr. Homer Renning was every bit as impressive as Dr. Horace Bellamy. Like Dr. Bellamy, he was a board certified forensic pathologist. It was his expert opinion that to a reasonable degree of medical certainty, Joy's death was caused by "massive hemorrhaging of the brain due to blunt trauma" and Joy's head injury "was consistent with trauma resulting from an accidental fall." Unlike the other two witnesses, Dr. Renning was asked if, other than the head injury, he detected any other areas of trauma or any indication either on the outside of her body or internally that she had been involved in a struggle. He answered no.

On cross-examination, Terrell was able to only illicit Dr. Renning's response that "yes, the injury could have been caused by a push, but it was just as likely that it could have resulted from her having tripped on the hearth and fallen backwards against the moss rock on the fireplace."

After the morning break, Dr. Rolland J. Dawson took the witness stand in his own defense. He testified just as he rehearsed. He looked the jurors in the eyes as he answered Drew's questions. He did so without any hesitancy and with the assurance of a witness who was telling the absolute truth. The jurors looked at Rolland without a hint of skepticism. The only one the defense team wondered about was juror number twelve, Henry Morton. They noticed he had his arms folded for a good part of Rolland's testimony and watched him on several occasions make eye contact with Dayton. Morton was the last juror called and, unfortunately, after the defense had exhausted their final peremptory challenge. The defense team had worried about Mr. Morton from the start but had no legal basis to challenge him for cause. Nonetheless, as far as the defense was concerned, Rolland was the poster child for a defendant witness.

The Beas had recessed for lunch, and upon returning therefrom, it was time for the cross-examination of the defendant.

Dayton did nothing to discredit Rolland. Dayton played to the television camera, the press, the spectators, and the jury for all it was worth. He no doubt was putting on a façade to mask the insecurity created by the adverse media coverage. He appeared somewhat inhibited and tentative. Some of it might have been stage fright. But it was obvious he was not his old confident and competent self. From the defense's standpoint, this was the ideal time for Dayton to disintegrate.

The defense rested. The prosecution presented no rebuttal witnesses. The defense renewed its motions for judgment of acquittal, dismissal, or mistrial. As expected, they were denied. It was now time for the attorneys together with the judge to roll up their sleeves and formulate the instructions on the law that would soon be given to the jury. The judge set aside the afternoon for the task ahead of them and discharged the jurors with instructions to report back at 8:30 a.m. the following day. In addressing the jury, the Beas emphasized the importance of not discussing the case with anyone or among themselves and to stay insulated against any publicity about the case.

Agreeing on what instructions to give the jury is often contentious particularly in a complicated case such as the one now before the court. Each side postures to have the most favorable instructions of the law and phrased coincidentally with their interpretation thereof. The trial judge has the last word but the giving of improper instructions or the not giving of a required instruction may be the basis of reversal on appeal. So, needless to say, there is pressure not only on the attorneys, but the trial judge as well.

Drew and Lino fully expected to have a battle royal with Dayton and Terrell, and maybe even the Beas, on several of the instructions particularly those dealing with lesser included offenses and defendant's theory of the case. The Beas had waiting for them the generic, canned or boilerplate instructions. There was no disagreement over them and surprisingly enough, Dayton and Terrell did not object to the defendant's theory of the case instruction. And, the ones the defense thought might cause a rift, the lesser included offense instructions, were mirrored by instructions prepared by both the prosecution and the Beas. Afterwards, Lino asked Drew how often that happens. "It was an aberration; a true aberration," Drew responded.

Later when Drew and Lino met with Rolland, Rolland had questions about the lesser included offense instructions.

"Why would the prosecution be in favor of the lesser included offense instructions? Are they that unsure of their case?"

"They have made a realistic appraisal of their case and realize that convictions on murder in the first and second degree are problematic," Lino said. "To them, any type of conviction is a win."

"What about us? Why do we want lesser included offense instructions? Aren't we just ensuring some type of conviction?"

"The defense normally doesn't want the 'all or nothing' choice for the jury," Drew responded. "In a case like this, where pretrial publicity has created a hostile jury mindset, the jury isn't about to allow the perceived killer to go free. Here, they will have the opportunity to render a compromise verdict, and hopefully if there is a guilty verdict, it will only be to the least of the least."

The eighth day of trial saw the courtroom filled to capacity. Fortunately, Rolland's parents arrived early enough to have front row seats. All were eager to hear the attorneys deliver their final arguments.

The Beas had duplicated fourteen sets of instructions for the jury. They each had their own personal copy, and each followed intently as the Beas read them aloud. The Beas concluded by telling them they could take the instructions with them to the jury room along with the exhibits that had been admitted by the court.

Dayton's walk to the podium to give the prosecution's final argument was not with the strut that marked his opening statement. He seemed more reserved and almost timid. Even his voice cracked hinting of a lack of self-assurance and confidence. He was playing before the cameras and the press for the last time in *People v. Dawson* and perhaps the beginning of the end of his political career. He knew he would be judged harshly by the media depending on the outcome of the case and his perceived handling thereof.

He started, haltingly at first, by thanking the jury.

"The role played by the jury in our American system of justice is just as important as the roles played by the witnesses, attorneys, and even the judge herself. In fact, in a few minutes when the case is turned over to you ladies and gentlemen to deliberate and return a verdict, the role you play will be the most critical of all.

"The evidence in this case is straightforward. A 911 call comes in from a person by the name of Dr. Rolland Dawson, the defendant in this case. This is on Friday, September 12, at 7:30 p.m. He reports having discovered his wife's body. The sheriff's office dispatches investigators to the scene. When they arrive, they find the body of the doctor's wife, Joy, lying on the floor near the fireplace. They observe an injury to the back of Joy's head and splattered blood and hair on a moss rock near the fireplace.

"Next to Joy's body, the investigators discover three blue buttons. Still in Joy's hand are blue cloth remnants or fragments. Next, they discover a blue flannel shirt draped over a chair in the kitchen some ten feet from where the body was located. They examine this shirt and find one of the pockets torn and three buttons missing. They compare the buttons found next to the body to the remaining buttons on the shirt. They appear to be the same.

"When the lab finishes their analysis, they determine that the buttons are identical to the shirt buttons and that the blue cloth remnants or fragments retrieved from Joy's hand came from the torn shirt pocket.

"When they asked Dr. Dawson, the only person on the scene when the investigators arrived, who the shirt belongs to, he admitted it was his.

"The county corner established the time of Joy's death as approximately 4:30 p.m. Dr. Dawson's receptionist testified that he left work at 12:45 p.m. and never returned. Dr. Dawson testified he went home arriving at approximately 1:15 p.m. and when he hadn't heard from his wife, drove out to their summer home in the Black Forest where her body was found arriving at approximately 7:15 p.m.

"However, you heard from his four neighbors that they never saw him or his vehicle at his home that afternoon. Not one saw him leave his home at 7:00 p.m. as he claims. It was only his testimony that attempts to establish his 7:15 p.m. time of arrival at Black Forest.

"When you connect the dots, you'll determine that Joy's death was not accidental; that there was some type of struggle as evidenced by the three blue buttons found near her body and the blue cloth remnants or fragments retrieved from her hand;

that the blue buttons and blue cloth remnants or fragments came from the damaged blue flannel shirt draped over the chair ten feet from the body; and that the shirt, by Dr. Dawson's own admission, was his.

"The 'smoking gun' in this case is the blue flannel shirt. Without the shirt, you would probably have reasonable doubt. With it, you have the piece of the puzzle needed for conviction.

"The only question here is whether you should return a guilty verdict for murder in the first degree, murder in the second degree, manslaughter, or criminally negligent homicide. If you find Dr. Dawson caused his wife's death after deliberation or with intent to cause her death then you should return a guilty verdict to murder in the first degree. If you don't find that death was deliberate or intentional, then you should consider murder in the second degree.

"If you find Dr. Dawson 'knowingly' caused his wife's death that is he was aware that his conduct toward Joy was practically certain to cause her death, then you should return a guilty verdict to murder in the second degree. If you don't find that Joy's death was caused either deliberately or intentionally or knowingly, then you should consider manslaughter.

"If you find that Dr. Dawson 'recklessly' caused his wife's death, that is he consciously disregarded a substantial and unjustifiable risk that his conduct toward Joy would result in her death, then you should return a guilty verdict to manslaughter. If you don't find that Joy's death was caused deliberately or intentionally, knowingly, or recklessly, then you should consider criminally negligent homicide.

"Criminally negligent homicide is an unintentional killing. So, if you find that Dr. Dawson's criminal negligence, that is his failure to perceive a substantial and unjustifiable risk that his conduct toward Joy would be certain to result in her death, then you should return a guilty verdict to criminally negligent homicide. Otherwise, you should return a not guilty verdict. However, a not guilty verdict is not warranted in this case.

"As you will note from the instructions, the law does not require that you be convinced beyond all doubt as to Dr. Dawson's guilt, only guilt beyond a reasonable doubt. Having met our burden, the prosecution asks that you return a guilty verdict to the charge that fits the evidence."

It was "do or die" time for Drew, or rather for Rolland. Drew was offended by injustice, and he was motivated and determined to see that it did not occur here. He was representing a defendant he knew to be innocent, and Rolland's fate was in his hands, and if ever he needed divine inspiration and intervention, it was now.

Drew began: "Despite the camera, cable, and cords in this court room, it is not a movie set. There is no script and there are no actors. What you have witnessed here is the real thing. What decision you render here does not end after the segment is aired, but for Dr. Dawson it defines his future.

"Mr. Dayton is asking you to convict on unwarranted assumptions. He asked you to connect the dots, but yet the dots don't lead to Dr. Dawson. They lead to a shirt draped over a chair in a room adjacent to where Dr. Dawson's wife's body was found— but not to Dr. Dawson.

"If you find that the prosecution has proven beyond a reasonable doubt that Joy's death was not accidental, that is that she did not accidentally trip or was not accidentally pushed, then it is critical that the person who caused Joy's death be brought to justice. However, it is your job to determine whether the prosecution has proven beyond any and all reasonable doubt that Dr. Dawson is that person.

"Mr. Dayton seems to think that to arrive at a guilty verdict in this case is a no-brainer. Moments ago when he held up the blue flannel shirt as I am now, he basically said it was the 'smoking gun.' He based it on Dr. Dawson's statement that that was his shirt. What Mr. Dayton didn't review with you and Deputies Milligan and Stanton forgot until cross-examination was that Dr. Dawson also stated that that 'smoking gun' was stored in a closet, hadn't been worn in years by him and was kept for guests. If you find that the prosecution has proven beyond a reasonable doubt that Dr. Dawson was wearing that 'smoking gun' at the time of Joy's death or any time that day, week, month, or year, then disregard everything I have to say.

"Remember from the instructions given you by the court, the defendant doesn't have to prove anything. The burden is always on the prosecution to prove guilt. Besides, how do you prove a negative? How do you prove you didn't do something? Such a burden would be virtually impossible to overcome. It is not incumbent upon Dr. Dawson to prove he was not the one who wore the blue flannel shirt at the time of Joy's death. It is incumbent upon the prosecution, the side represented by Mr. Dayton and Mr. Terrell, that it was Dr. Dawson who wore the 'smoking gun" at the time of Joy's death. And this, they have wholly failed to do.

"It is fundamental that one plus one does not equal three. Yet the prosecution wants you to conclude that *ownership* of a 'smoking gun' equates to *wearing* the 'smoking gun' at the time of Joy's death. They want you to make that grand but unwarranted leap. Why? Because without it, you can't convict.

"Imagine how easy your decision would be in this case, either one way or the other, if law enforcement had done their job from the beginning. The funny math, one plus one equals three, started at the investigative stage, continued through the charging stage, progressed through the prosecution's case-in-chief and was incorporated in Mr. Dayton's plea for conviction a few moments ago. Before the blue flannel shirt had been contaminated by the many hands through which it passed, including Mr. Dayton's and now mine, it could have been processed for DNA, hair samples, and other testing to see if there were identifiable or unidentifiable samples. And how about the failure to take molds and comparisons of the tire tracks or process the scene to see if there were any identifiable fingerprints that would have pointed the finger of suspicion at someone other than Dr. Dawson.

"Unfortunately, the alternate suspect theory doesn't fit into the prosecution's scheme of things. Also, law enforcement is no doubt anxious for conviction because that way the public doesn't have to be worried that there is a killer in the community on the loose assuming, of course, Joy's death was not accidental. Keep in mind, however, that there are only two board certified forensic pathologists who testified in this case, one for the prosecution and one for the defense. Neither of those two experts ruled out the possibility that Joy's head injury could have been caused by accidental means.

"I have heard all my professional life, previously as a pros-ecutor, and now as a defense attorney, that it is better to let one hundred guilty men go free, than to convict one innocent man. I don't know whether that is true or not, but I do know that to prevent an innocent man from being convicted it is critical that there be a sufficient quantity and quality of evidence to convict. And I know that funny math and unwarranted assumptions do not a conviction make.

"Defense attorneys have the onerous task of ensuring that their client, here Dr. Dawson, receives a fair and a just trial. However, Mr. Blankenship's and my duty to ensure that justice prevails in this case is complete, and now we're placing Dr. Daw-son's fate in your hands to ensure that justice is done and that in doing so you return a fair and a just verdict. On the basis of the evidence, or more precisely, the lack thereof, presented in this case and in light of the instructions given to you by the court, we're asking you to return a not guilty verdict on all charges—not just the main charge but all the lesser included as well."

Terrell's rebuttal was not really a rebuttal. He mainly went through the main charge and the lesser included offenses in descending order of severity as did his boss. He tried to distinguish and reconcile the testimony of the two pathologists but without real success. He waved the "smoking gun" in front of the jury and invited them to conduct their own comparison with the three blue buttons and the fabric fragment. Over objection, he was allowed to request that the jury draw an inference as to who was most likely wearing the "smoking gun" at the time of Joy's death "the owner thereof or a phantom intruder."

The first twelve jurors were quizzed as to their stated health and ability to undertake and complete deliberations. Finding that they were fit, the two alternate jurors were excused with the thanks of the court. Armed with the jury instructions, the jury was led by the bailiff to the jury room—a room that would soon become their exclusive domain. The court was recessed at 11:45 a.m. The attorneys were instructed to provide the clerk with telephone numbers where they could be reached if and when a verdict was returned.

Waiting in Eager Expectation

When 6:00 p.m. arrived on that windy fourth Wednesday in March and a jury verdict was not imminent, the bailiff was instructed by the Beas to keep them together and provide dinner compliments of El Paso County.

At 9:00 p.m., the bailiff was instructed by the Beas to see how close the jury was to reaching a verdict. The prognosis was not good, and the attorneys were called to the courthouse along with Rolland. The Beas asked if the attorneys wanted the jurors to be sequestered and lodged in a hotel for the night or released to spend the night at home and resume deliberations the following morning. Both the prosecution and defense moved for sequestration, and it was so ordered.

At noon on the ninth day of the scheduled two-week trial, the foreman sent a note to the judge indicating the jury was deadlocked. They had reached an impasse, and no one would budge. The jury was taken to lunch and, upon returning at 1:30 p.m., was ushered into court. With the attorneys having agreed beforehand, the jury was given what is commonly referred to as the Allen Charge, or sometimes alternatively referred to as the Alamo Instruction, Shotgun Instruction, or Dynamite Charge.

The Beas instructed the jury as follows:

"It is your duty, as jurors, to consult with one another and to deliberate with a view to reaching a verdict, if you can do so without violence and to your individual judgment. Each of you must decide the case for yourself, but do so only after an impartial consideration of the evidence with your fellow jurors. In the course of your deliberations, do not hesitate to reexamine your own views and change your opinion if convinced it is erroneous. But do not surrender your honest conviction as to the weight or effect of evidence solely because of the opinion of your fellow jurors or for the mere purpose of returning a verdict."

It was close to 5:30 p.m. when the jury announced they had reached a verdict. With the television camera rolling, press scurrying, security at the ready, diehard spectators resplendent, and the district attorney's staff, the prosecution team, the defense team, and Rolland's parents all in their places, the bailiff escorted the jury into the courtroom.

The eerie silence harkened the lull before the storm. Anticipation turned to panic when they saw the verdict forms in the hands of juror number twelve, Henry Morton, no doubt the foreman and the last person they wanted to sit on the jury. When the Beas asked if the jury had reached a verdict, Mr. Morton rose and handed it to the bailiff, who in turn handed to the Beas.

Drew had been holding his breath so long that he was turning blue. The most composed member of the defense team surprisingly was Rolland. The Beas then instructed Rolland to stand. She began reading the four verdict forms: "We the jury duly empanelled and sworn do find the defendant *not guilty* of murder in the first degree; *not guilty* of murder in the second degree; *not guilty* of manslaughter;...*guilty* of criminally negligent homicide."

There were gasps from both counsel tables and from the gallery. Soon the courtroom became frighteningly disruptive. The Beas began to bang her gavel to restore order. The force of her blows cracked the glass on the bench. After order was restored, the Beas threatened to clear the courtroom if there were any other outbursts.

The Beas asked the jury as a whole if this was their verdict. Drew requested that the jury be polled. Each individual juror was then asked if this was and is his/her verdict. Each answered yes. However, juror number one, Edith Corbin, juror number two, Helen Shipley, and juror number ten, Jenny Fields, appeared somewhat hesitant when asked the question.

The Beas then thanked the jury for their service and told them they could say as much or as little to the attorneys as they wanted and to report any abuse or criticism of their service. The jury was thereupon excused.

After the jury was excused, Drew and Lino were advised that the court would hear argument on their anticipated motion at 8:00 a.m. the next day. The Beas stated she would not enter a judgment on the conviction for criminally negligent homicide until after she ruled on their motion. Technically, she said she didn't need for Rolland's father to consent to a continuation of the bond but since she saw that his father was in court asked him if he would do so. Dr. Dawson Sr. responded "absolutely."

Rolland had been convicted of the lowest of the low. He could never be tried again on the other three counts as jeopardy had attached. This was true even if they appealed the lone conviction, and it was reversed. He could only be tried for criminally negligent homicide, and even then, it was assumed that that conviction would also be overturned.

As they walked out of the courtroom, Rolland's father asked what motion the judge had alluded to. Drew explained that the defense would be asking for a judgment notwithstanding the verdict. He explained that the judge had the power to overturn the guilty verdict. Rolland's father said he was concerned that the Colorado Board of Medical Examiners might revoke Rolland's license because a conviction was considered "unprofessional conduct" and the grounds to suspend or refuse renewal of his son's license. Drew said that a felony conviction or any conviction was not deemed final until judgment was entered thereon; if action was taken they would ask the medical board for a stay, pending appeal. "Besides," Drew said, "regardless of the outcome of the case, the board has the power to revoke a license if there is a patient safety issue involved. In other words, it can be triggered even without a conviction."

When the jurors were excused, Bodean went out into the hall to see if he could speak to some of them before they dispersed. Unfortunately, they had disappeared before he was able to do so. It was a juror's prerogative as to whether to talk or not talk to the attorneys about the case after they were discharged. Especially with the possibility of a reversal and a retrial, it was critical to ascertain what factors they considered in arriving at their verdict. Interviewing jurors, however, would have to wait for another day.

Drew seemed morose and withdrawn after the guilty verdict was announced. It was apparent that despite the odds stacked against them, Drew all along had believed they would prevail. Even though the three major offenses would no longer be an issue in the event of a retrial, most of the other issues would remain the same. Drew began to second-guess the defense strategy. Should there be a retrial he would certainly advocate that the defense hit the alternate suspect theory harder and not be so timid in attacking the sloppy police work. The authorities had zeroed in on Rolland and spent all of their time building a case against him. Consequently, they'd overlooked critical evidence.

There are a lot of "what ifs" in being an armchair quarterback. In Drew's mind, there were more obvious "what ifs," "what ifs" that would have unquestionably spelled the difference in the jury's verdict. And he was not thinking of trial strategy. He was thinking back to a cool autumn afternoon in the Black Forest. He was feeling guilty and responsible on a lot of counts.

What if he hadn't gone to the Black Forest that dreadful day? What if Joy hadn't been pregnant? Would she still have pressed the issue? What if he had just held her close and not tried to pull away? What if she had had her back away from the fireplace and fell against something other than the moss rock? What if? What if? What if?

Throughout the trial and particularly now, Drew knew it was he who had blazed the trail of guilt to Rolland. It was he who had provided the "smoking gun." What if he had been wearing the coat he had in his car when he went into the Dawson Chalet? What if he hadn't been wearing the blue flannel shirt when he went on the walk with Joy? What if he hadn't been wearing the blue flannel shirt when Joy grabbed him? What if he hadn't left the blue flannel shirt at the scene? The answers were inescapable, and it pained him to think about it all particularly at the moment. Without the shirt, there would have been no connecting dots. Without the shirt, the defense team would be celebrating total victory and shouting for joy.

Sensing Drew was distressed, Rolland tried to console him by telling him he and Lino had run the good race and fought the good fight and that he was eternally grateful for their efforts and the results. "A batting average of seven hundred and fifty is not bad; you succeeded in getting three out of the four charges dismissed," Rolland said, putting his hand on Drew's shoulder.

"We're not finished yet," Drew replied. "We still have a quarter of the way to go!"

The Friday edition in the *Times Herald* was waiting for him when he arrived at his office on that March Friday. The headlines read: "Doctor Acquitted on Murder Charge." The editorial headline read "Over Charge or Under Prosecution?" Both the article and the editorial painted the district attorney's office in a bad light. Both made the defense appear to be the victor and the prosecution the vanquished. *Amazing what a difference a trial makes,* Drew thought. *It wasn't that long ago that the doctor was the target and was being hung out to dry. Now it is the district attorney who is in the press's crosshair.*

When the defense team arrived at the courthouse at 7:55 a.m., they were greeted by the Beas's bailiff, and Drew and Lino were escorted to the Beas's chambers. Sitting on a leather sofa in the anteroom were two of the Dawson jurors, Edith Corbin and Helen Shipley. Through the open door of the Beas's chambers, Drew and Lino could see Dayton and Terrell. As Drew and Lino entered, the door was closed behind them by the bailiff.

"Come in and grab a seat," the Beas said. "I have just been made aware by the jurors you saw sitting outside the door that one of their co-jurors may have been guilty of improprieties and may be the cause for declaring a mistrial."

She then went on to relate that the two jurors were waiting for her when she arrived. They asked to speak to her. They indicated they were upset because Henry Morton, the foreman, in an effort to reach a consensus and coax a resolution speculated that the motive for the doctor having killed his wife was his being upset over her being pregnant. He said he had read that the doctor's wife was found to be with child when the autopsy was performed. They said this occurred late yesterday afternoon several hours after they received the Allen Charge and the jurors were still deadlocked nine for criminally negligent homicide and three, including them, for acquittal. They said the three holdouts argued there was no motive established and when advised of the pregnancy connection, reluctantly one by one voted with the majority. Having violated the judge's admonition and having judged the case on evidence obtained outside the courtroom, the two felt compelled to report the misconduct.

It was decided that the two jurors should be brought into chambers and on the record disclose what they had already disclosed to the judge in private and that the prosecution and defense should then be allowed to examine. This having been done and a record made, it was decided that Mr. Morton should be brought in and confronted with the allegations. Within the hour, Mr. Morton appeared and admitted to the misconduct.

The parties then, minus the jurors, met in open court. Without disclosing the misconduct or the names of the whistleblowers or the offending party, the Beas declared a mistrial. The Beas said there was no need to argue the motion for judgment of acquittal notwithstanding the verdict because a mistrial had been declared. She stated that if a mistrial had not been declared she would have denied the motion and entered a judgment of conviction. If the Beas had granted the motion, Rolland would have been home free. As it was Rolland would have to face a new trial on the criminally negligent homicide charge. The Beas stated that if the defense requested a change of venue and the prosecution didn't oppose it, she would grant it. Drew so moved, and without hesitation, Dayton announced he had no objection. The motion was granted. The case would be moved to a new county, presumably Denver County, and they would be free of a tainted jury pool and also the Beas. And, at least for the short term, Rolland wouldn't have to sweat action by the medical board, or at least so they hoped.

The Friday edition of the *Star* reported the events of the day and the headline to the front page story read: "Mistrial Declared in Prosecution of Doctor." The scathing editorial bore the following heading: "From a Death Penalty Case to Zip." Rolland had been replaced by Dayton as "Public Enemy No. 1." It would be interesting to see what the letters to the editor would be. The public was already clamoring for Dayton's ouster. "Oh revenge, sweet revenge," Bodean echoed over and over again.

To keep the pressure on, Lino wrote a letter to Dayton asking when the district attorney's office would be filing criminal charges against Pierre Delajure for subornation of perjury. Within a week Lino got his answer when he read the headline in the *Times Herald*: "PROTECT Leader Charged with Perjury."

"Guess Dayton realized he was between a rock and a hard place," Lino told Drew.

"The media's got him running scared," Drew replied. "He will always be guided by public opinion. It's in the nature of the beast."

When Rolland called to see if Drew and Lino had read the morning paper, he said one of his colleagues had informed him that Carla had filed for divorce. "Defending domestic violence and perjury charges while at the same time going through a divorce should keep Pierre busy for a long, long time and off my case," Rolland said with a grin.

The Second Time Around

The defense was overjoyed at the news that Rolland's case had been transferred to the city and county of Denver. Denver was as good as heaven as far as they were concerned. There, this would be just another homicide case and would not generate the same lurid curiosity they had just faced in their home county. "It's not going to be considered such a morbid, sordid, sensational, or tragic case that the electronic media will want to film or record it," Lino said. "Heaven knows we've already faced a court lifetime of intrusion and distraction."

"It would be nice to focus on the merits of the case for a change," Drew replied.

Wednesday, April 1, after an impromptu meeting with Dayton, Terrell, and the Beas, Rolland and his father sat in the wings as the attorneys and the judge arranged for the change in the place of trial. The judge assigned the case would be the Honorable Penelope Parker the granddaughter of Justice Conrad Ritkin Parker, who had sat on the Colorado Supreme Court for several decades.

She was referred to by the Beas as "Penney." Henceforth, out of Judge Parker's presence at least, she would be referred to by the defense team as Penney—whether a good or a bad penny they didn't yet know.

The Beas had already obtained possible trial dates. The first two-week block was during the last two weeks in May. The next earliest was late summer. If that worked, they were encouraged to reserve that time slot ASAP. And that they did. Penney's clerk also stated the judge wanted to schedule a status conference at least thirty days prior to trial. Friday, April 17, was the preferable date for all. They would meet in Denver in Penney's chambers at 10:00 a.m.

Rolland and his father were brought back into the Beas's chambers and advised of the trial date and the date of the status conference, which would be Rolland's next bond return date. The Beas called in the court reporter and they went on the record. All acknowledged their agreement to the trial date as well as the date scheduled for the status conference. Since Rolland's father was still on the bond, he was required to consent to Rolland's bond being continued to each date, which Dr. Dawson Sr. readily did.

The Beas, while still on the record, commented on the professional manner in which the attorneys on both sides had conducted themselves. She wished Rolland good luck and bid everyone a cordial farewell. With that, she rode off into the sunset and the trial participants were now under control of another power.

When the defense team, including Rolland's father, congregated in the small conference room at Quinlin, Devlin & Cummins, they speculated on why the Beas had been so anxious to accommodate them. It was actually the Beas who encouraged the defense to renew their motion for change of venue.

It was decided that the Beas washed her hands of the case for several reasons. First, she flirted with what would have been her first reversal but just through blind luck was able to avert it. Second, she was tired of the case and wanted to move on. Third, and maybe the most important, was the swing of public senti-ment regarding the case and fear that she would be the media's next whipping boy or, more appropriately, whipping girl.

"The fact that a juror—and not just any juror but the fore-man—injected evidence that had been suppressed and was not to be considered by the jury during deliberation was proof that *voir dire* was not an effective way to deal with massive and pervasive pretrial publicity," Drew commented. "The Beas knew she had made a huge mistake in not granting our motion for change of venue, and she knew she was wasting everyone's time and money."

"She also knew," Lino added, "that the public and the press would be unforgiving. She took a coward's way out."

***

It was the Friday after Easter, and precisely at 10:00 a.m., the attorneys on both sides together with Rolland were ushered into Penney's chambers and introduced to the Beas's replacement. Penney was by no means the clone of the Beas. In fact, just the opposite. The Honorable Penelope Parker was not clothed in a robe but in a stylish blue dress with white collar and cuffs. With shoulder-length auburn hair combed into a ponytail and a broad pearly white smile, she was most attractive and invit-ing. No hint of pomposity here. Professional and intelligent, she would soon gain the admiration and respect of the transplants from El Paso County.

The logistics of the trial were discussed and agreed upon. She would receive copies of the entire court file including the jury instructions. It was agreed that Dayton and/or Terrell could retrieve the exhibits from the Beas's clerk and transport them to Penney's clerk without objection as to chain of custody. The number of jurors and peremptory challenges, sequestration of witnesses, designation of advisory witnesses, and the like, were for the most part the mirror image of the first trial. Neither side would be requesting that the jury view the scene for obvious reasons.

The issue of cameras in the courtroom was raised. Penney said she doubted that the electronic media would be making such request. "This case is not of great public interest or concern in this venue," she said. "If such a motion is made, we will deal with it then." She then asked how each side felt about the issue. It was not surprising that Dayton was so vocal in opposing trial by television. The defense, of course, was opposed to the carnival-like atmosphere that would be created thereby. It appeared Penney was of the same mind.

After formal shake of the hands, the parties prepared to do battle once again. This time, however, there was much less at stake as far as the defense was concerned, and more importantly, they would be jousting on a neutral field. The worst that could happen was Rolland would be found guilty of criminally negligent homicide.

Opposing counsel met briefly in the hall of the courthouse, an elegant structure constructed in 1932 of Cotopaxi and white granite. Its low and rambling design was a deliberate attempt to prevent the obstruction of the view of the mountains from the state capitol building.

The stipulations previously entered into between the two camps would stand and govern the second time around. All agreed that the second trial would be an abbreviated version of the first. The list of prosecution witnesses, for example, would be streamlined for practical and economic reasons. That would be music to Rolland's ears since he was paying by the hour.

For whatever reasons, actual or contrived, Dayton would be unable to participate in the Dawson retrial. Terrell would be making a solo flight. The original trial judge and now the district attorney himself had fallen by the wayside. Fortunately, the attrition was on the prosecution side.

The defense's profile of the ideal defense juror had changed somewhat. The gender of a juror in the previous analysis seemed to matter little. Originally, it was thought that an older male professional or businessman might be the prototype. In a sense, they were burned by Henry Morton, a sixty-two-year-old store owner who had been selected foreman of the jury and had stumped for conviction. On the other hand, the three holdouts for acquittal were female. Bodean had learned from Mrs. Corbin that the third holdout was Jenny Fields. Two of the holdouts were in their sixties; the third was in her early twenties.

As they learned in the first trial, the makeup of the jury depended more on the luck of the draw than strategy. Nonetheless, they must hunt for the ideal juror in whatever form that may take. For now, maybe they should lean toward the female of the species. Then again, on the first jury, four of the seven women on the jury originally voted for conviction but ultimately all seven voted for conviction. On the other hand, all five of the men voted for conviction and stood their ground. The conundrum had the defense team scratching their heads.

In neutral territory and a jury pool free from outside influence, jury selection was on a fast track. By the end of the first day, the jury that would sit on the Dawson retrial was selected. Whether by design or luck of the draw, there were eight women of varying ages and occupations. The four men, who comprised the remainder of the original twelve, were in their early thirties with the exception of one who was in his fifties. The two alternates represented senior citizens of both genders. The defense liked the feel of the jury's composition and had no reservation about any of them. The prosecution had used up all of their peremptories; the defense still had two left.

Terrell's opening statement at the start of day two was long and boringly detailed. He never really outlined testimony; he in essence testified. The essence of the case was lost in rhetorical gibberish and meaningless recitation. His good points were intermingled with the weak, and it was obvious the jurors could not tell the difference.

Lino's opening statement was somewhat similar to the first. This time, however, in outlining the evidence, he placed greater emphasis on that which would establish and advance the defense's accidental death theory, the alternate suspect theory, the truncated investigation, the unwarranted assumptions drawn at the scene, the failure of law-enforcement to preserve, collect, and analyze the evidence, and the lack of evidence to prove any criminal agency or that Rolland was in any way involved in his wife's death.

After the midmorning break, Norma Evans testified as to the 911 call. Both direct and cross simulated their counterparts in the first trial.

Deputy Roger Milligan next testified as to the results of his investigation of the scene, the discovery of the buttons, cloth fragment and shirt, Rolland's admission of ownership, the location of the body, wound to the back of Joy's head, and the hair and blood splatters found on the moss rock fireplace. He identified the photographs of the scene and the various pieces of physical evidence.

Lino performed his patented surgical cross-examination on Milligan, which simulated that of the first trial. However, unlike the first, Lino went through the litany of all the things that Milligan and the other investigators failed to do. He was able to get Milligan to admit that he and Deputy Stanton drew the conclusion that Joy's death was not accidental and that her husband was involved. Therefore, only the evidence they thought pointed in Dr. Dawson's direction was collected. Milligan also admitted that in retrospect he would probably have done some things differently.

Apparently, Terrell thought Kevin Stanton's testimony was duplicitous, and he was not called. The defense speculated that maybe Terrell was saving him for rebuttal. Henry Fisk, however, was called, and the script of direct from the first trial was Terrell's guiding light. Lino had a hay day with Fisk. When Lino went through the list of investigative blunders, Fisk tried to be clever. However, Fisk ended up being backed into a corner, finally admitting his processing of the scene left a lot to be desired.

The afternoon of the second day started with the direct-examination of Dr. Francisco Mendoza. His testimony was predictable. On cross-examination, Drew first discounted his credentials and then his testimony. If Dr. Mendoza was the expert he claimed to be, then why did he call in Dr. Bellamy? Didn't his opinion differ from Dr. Bellamy's? If Dr. Bellamy's opinion was different, whom should the jury believe? Was he familiar with Dr. Homer Renning? If Dr. Renning's opinion also differed from his, who should the jury believe? Both Dr. Bellamy and Dr. Renning were board-certified forensic pathologists. He was not. And so, Dr. Mendoza was led to slaughter screaming, yelling, and protesting all the way.

After the afternoon break, Dr. Horace Bellamy was called by the prosecution. On direct-examination by Terrell, it was obvious he was changing his opinion and equivocating. His opinion was now more in step with Dr. Mendoza's than it had been at the first trial. However, with Drew chomping at the bit, Dr. Bellamy was headed down a slippery slope.

Fortunately, the defense team had Dr. Bellamy's previous testimony transcribed, and it was used to impeach the good doctor. So when Dr. Bellamy said it was "virtually impossible" that Joy's head injury was caused by an accidental fall, Drew confronted him with his prior inconsistent statement wherein he testified under oath that "it was possible" that the head injury was due to an accidental cause. Impeachment by a prior inconsistent statement is usually effective, and, after observing the jury in this instance, there was no doubt it had its predictable intended impact.

Before second day's end, CBI lab technician and analyst, Rick Tompkins, also testified. Direct examination simulated that of the first trial. However, cross-examination took on a whole new hue. What was probative was not what he did but what he didn't do. For example, he was not asked to compare fingerprints: he was not asked to analyze the blue flannel shirt to see who may have worn it; he was not asked to analyze fingernail scrapings; and he was not asked to compare footprints, shoe prints, or tire tracks. He only performed the tests he was directed to perform by the sheriff's department. The only hair and blood samples that he examined and compared were those of the decedent. He was never supplied with any item that contained any hair or blood that was attributed to Dr. Dawson.

During the forenoon of the third day, Terrell presented the two neighbors on both sides of the Dawson residence. Terrell just called Ann Anderson the neighbor to the East and Lynn Staves the neighbor to the West. He didn't call their husbands who were not home during the day as the prosecution had in the first trial. Again, both witnesses admitted on cross-examination that their view of the Dawson residence was somewhat obscured and it would be a "chance occurrence" if they got a glimpse of either Joy or Rolland and/or their vehicles—not just that day but any day.

Lannette Castles testified as before but was more of a witness for the defense than the prosecution. Direct and cross mirrored that of the first trial.

The prosecution rested their case-in-chief. The defense moved for judgment of acquittal. As anticipated, it was denied.

In the afternoon of the third day, the defense presented its case-in-chief.

Dr. Homer Renning was the first of only two that would be called. His testimony was every bit as impressive as in the first trial. Despite his efforts, Terrell succeeded only in reinforcing the possibility that Joy's death was accidental and in antagonizing the jury. Terrell's bully tactics and his misquoting Dr. Renning did not bode well with the jury.

After the mid-afternoon break, the main character in this courtroom drama was sworn in to testify in his own behalf. No one could have been better cast for the part of the perfect defendant than Dr. Rolland J. Dawson. The eyes of the jury were riveted on him during his entire testimony. Their eyes went from a reflection of skepticism to belief then to sympathy all in one rather quick swoop. He not only had to cope with the agony of his late wife's death but with the accusation of having been the cause thereof.

Surely, if he had been the cause of Joy's death, he would have eliminated all traces that would have linked her death to him and would have fled the scene. He did neither, and now he was on trial for his life. When Terrell cross-examined, he was accusatory, condescending, and demeaning. His innuendos and sarcasm evoked a series of objections from the defense, and all were sustained. On several occasions, Terrell was warned by Penney not to pursue certain lines of questioning. Disgust was written across the faces of the jurors by the time Terrell concluded. He not only failed to discredit Rolland but in the process succeeded in antagonizing the jury. The defense rested its case-in-chief.

The prosecution presented no rebuttal. The jury was excused for the day to await jury instructions and final arguments on Thursday. The attorneys met with Penney in her chambers, and in quick order, the jury instructions were formulated. They were identical for the most part to those given in the first trial minus the series of instructions dealing with lesser included offenses and disregarding certain evidence that been stricken from the record such as the testimony of Carla Delajure.

The defense had what would prove to be their last supper before returning to Colorado Springs. With all the evidence in and only final arguments left, they dined at one of their usual haunts, the Palace Arms in the Brown Palace Hotel. Rolland's parents, who attended the retrial, joined the defense team for some elegant dining. Without exception, they all felt they were on the verge of closure in this dark chapter of Rolland's life. In their hearts, they knew everything was going to be all right.

The fourth day of the retrial started with instructions to the jury followed by Terrell's final argument. This script he read from was one used by his boss, Norman Dayton. It was obvious that Terrell was not speaking from the heart but merely going through the motions. To his credit, he gave it the old college try. The jury fidgeted throughout his summation, and many folded their arms and looked down or away. It was apparent the jury was not with him.

When Drew gave the defense's final argument, all were attentive and anxious. With their eyes focused on him and his on them, Drew gave a textbook summation. It was short but deadly. He recounted the testimony with precision that established Rolland's theory of the case, the accidental death theory and the alternate suspect theory. He then put law-enforcement on trial for their sloppy investigation including, what he called their 'truncated investigation,' the unwarranted assumptions they made at the scene, and their failure to preserve, collect and analyze the evidence. He pointed out that the prosecution had wholly failed to prove beyond a reasonable doubt that Joy's death was caused by any criminal agency whatsoever, let alone that Dr. Dawson was in any way involved in his wife's death.

He concluded by saying, "On the basis of the evidence or should I say *lack of evidence*, the defense is asking you to return a fair and a just verdict. And a fair and just verdict in this case is a verdict of not guilty. Thank you."

Terrell then gave a brief rebuttal but only in name.

It was 10:30 a.m. when the jury left to deliberate. By 11:30 a.m., they had a verdict. The defense team thought the jury might wait to have lunch compliments of the city and county of Denver, but they didn't. Usually, a quick verdict in a case of this nature meant one thing. They would not have to wait long to find out.

With minutes before noon, the jury had announced its verdict: *not guilty*. Rolland had lost many battles along the way, and at times all seemed lost. But now, he would be declared the winner of the bitter war that had been raging for all too long. Judgment was entered on the not guilty verdict. Rolland's bond was exonerated, and the respective parties were free to go their separate way with the final chapter having been written on this part of the great nightmare.

While anxiously awaiting the verdict, Rolland had prayed: "Dear God, I place my trust entirely at you. Though I fear all things from my weakness, I hope all things from your goodness."

After the verdict was announced, Rolland raised his eyes heavenward and uttered this prayer: "I rejoice in you, oh Lord, for you brought me Joy and now this long-awaited joy. I praise you and give you thanks."

For Rolland to pick up the pieces and put his life back together sounded great in concept, but in reality there were pieces missing that would never be retrieved at least not in this life.

The next few weeks would see the Colorado Medical Board declining action and Rolland's clinic inviting him back and restoring the name "Dawson, Tagert & McKinnin Orthopedic Services, LLC."

Poetic Justice

He heard the deafening squeal of tires, and, as he turned around, he saw the dirty white Ford pickup bearing down on him. That was the last that Drew remembered before waking up on a hospital gurney being wheeled down a long, unfamiliar hallway.

"Where am I?" he asked the startled attendant.

"Mercy Hospital, headed for operating room 2B. That's Dr. Dawson's operating room where he is scheduled to perform emergency surgery on your damaged hip. Your wife is filling out and signing the required forms and will be joining you outside the operating room shortly."

"What date is this?"

"Thursday, July 9. The time is 7:45 a.m. You were brought in yesterday around 4:30 p.m."

"Yesterday was my birthday, and I was leaving work early to pick up my wife and daughters and go to my parents to celebrate my forty-sixth year on this earth. It looks like I almost went to another place—in which direction I'm not sure."

"Wow, you're doing pretty well for being under all that sedation and for what you've been through. But, you need to just relax, save your energy, and wait for Dr. Dawson."

With that one of the large doors of the operating room swung open, and Rolland dressed in green, looking every bit the part of the orthopedic surgeon he was, emerged.

"Good to see you're back with us," Rolland said with a relieved smile. "Our roles have switched, and now your life is in my hands."

"What happened, my friend?"

"You apparently were walking through the parking garage of your office building to pick up your car when you were struck by a truck."

"How did you know it was a truck?"

"Because, after the truck hit you, it ran into a concrete pillar, seriously injuring the driver."

"Do we know who the driver was?"

"Pierre Delajure. He apparently has blamed you for all his woes. But enough already. Unless you object, I'm going to repair your fractured right hip. The surgical team is waiting for us inside."

Just as Drew was being wheeled in, Missy arrived. Seeing Drew was alert, she broke into tears, and the two hugged and kissed until Rolland separated them.

As the anesthetic was taking effect, Drew beckoned Rolland to come near. When Rolland was close and only he could hear, Drew told him he had a confession to make. He said he was with Joy in her final moments, but that it was an accident. He had taken the coward's way out and had regretted it ever since. As he was fading into oblivion, Drew whispered he was sorry.

Rolland thought Drew was either brave or foolish to tell him what he did just before he went under the knife. The razor-sharp scalpel was not a thing to reckon with, and Rolland, more than just in the imagination of the Delajures, could make it look truly "like an accident."

"Wouldn't that be poetic justice," Rolland mused.

Rolland had suspected something from the time of his first meeting with Drew. Drew's mannerism at their first meeting, his reluctance to represent him initially, and his abrupt turnaround wanting to help—all appeared odd. The hard evidence was the turquoise necklace found at the scene and Drew's reaction to it over the telephone upon Rolland's mention of it as well as the mysterious appearance of Joy's painting of the lioness and her cub on Drew's office wall. Also suspicious was Drew's knowledge of the unique color of Joy's eyes and her appendectomy scar, and, it was curious that Rolland had received no billings after his initial retainer had been depleted.

As the surgery proceeded, it appeared that Drew's injury was more serious than first thought. The prognosis was grim. Drew, at best, would be walking with a limp the rest of his life.

Rolland was beginning to feel guilt pangs of his own. If it had not been for his run-in with the Delajures, Drew would not have sustained this life-crippling injury. If Rolland had not had the affair with Carla, there never would have been a run-in with the Delajures, and Joy would not have had the affair with Drew. If Joy had not had the affair with Drew, she would undoubtedly still be alive today.

In measuring the aforementioned indiscretions, he concluded that it was he who was the most culpable. And, during his five-hour surgery on a man who had been both his nemesis and his friend, he became very circumspect. He had asked Joy to forgive him, and now Drew was asking for his forgiveness. He remembered what his grandmother had always said: "Forgive and you will be forgiven." Now he needed to get on his knees and ask God to forgive him.

The surgery was unremarkable. There were no complications, and Drew was recovering nicely. After several days had passed and Drew was to be released, Drew, not remembering the anesthetic-induced confession, told Rolland there was something Rolland needed to know. Rolland interrupted him. "I already know, and I forgive you. Never let it cross your lips or mind again." They gave each other a manly embrace, and each bid the other a fond adieu. Truthfulness and forgiveness had set them free and each left with a heavy burden lifted, and their anguish buried in the deep recesses of their mind. The great nightmare was finally over. Drew would never forget those turquoise eyes even though the painting of the lioness and her cub had been given to Rolland. The painting would serve as a reminder to Rolland of who would be waiting for him in the hereafter along with their daughter.

As for Drew, Drew had met the enemy, and the enemy was him. To atone for his indiscretions was a cheap price to pay. He was grateful for the reprieve. The lessons he learned from the ordeal were reaping rewards in his relationship with Missy, his children, parents, and friends. He was even finding that it was making him a less judgmental and more compassionate attorney. And, as for his relationship with his God, he was still begging for understanding and forgiveness. Forever vivid in his mind would be something he heard his minister grandfather say: *Eternity is forever!*